# EMPTY NEST

BOOKS BY SUE WATSON

PSYCHOLOGICAL THRILLERS

*Our Little Lies*

*The Woman Next Door*

ROMANTIC COMEDIES

*Love, Lies and Lemon Cake*

*Snow Angels, Secrets and Christmas Cake*

*Summer Flings and Dancing Dreams*

*Fat Girls and Fairy Cakes*

*Younger Thinner Blonder*

*Bella's Christmas Bake Off*

*We'll Always have Paris*

*The Christmas Cake Café*

*Ella's Ice Cream Summer*

*Curves, Kisses and Chocolate Ice Cream*

*Snowflakes, Iced Cakes and Second Chances*

*Love, Lies and Wedding Cake*

# THE EMPTY NEST

SUE WATSON

bookouture

Published by Bookouture in 2019

An imprint of Storyfire Ltd.
Carmelite House
50 Victoria Embankment
London EC4Y 0DZ

www.bookouture.com



ISBN: 978-1-83888-042-2
eBook ISBN: 978-1-83888-041-5

*For Empty Nesters everywhere*

# CHAPTER ONE

It's no surprise that mothers find it so hard to live in their empty nests. We're with our children every day of their lives, then suddenly, whoosh, they're gone.

My daughter Amy went away to university just weeks ago – well, seven weeks and three days, to be precise. Like all parents, I knew her leaving was inevitable – they have to leave one day – but for me it was especially hard. She's my only child and we've been through a lot together and, as a result, our bond is perhaps even stronger than usual, we are so much more than mother and daughter – we're best friends. So her leaving has been a double whammy; I've lost my daughter and my best friend in one go, and it hasn't been easy. Sometimes I pretend she's still here.

Amy may be miles away, living in another town in a different home with new people, but her bubble bath sits in the bathroom, untouched. I've left the discarded lipsticks and hairbrush to wait on her dressing table, along with the summer clothes she's left hanging in the wardrobe. It's as though time's stood still in the house, everything on pause until her return, including me I suppose. Yesterday I discovered a box of her favourite peppermint tea in the kitchen cupboard and despite being a hardcore black-coffee girl, I made a cup for myself. The aroma of minty warmth revived me, and continued to permeate the kitchen long after I'd drunk it. I pretended to myself that Amy was just upstairs or on her phone in another room, and got on with my day.

I still find it hard to get my head around the fact she isn't here, because as every parent knows, once a child lands in your heart, they never leave. From the minute she turned up in my life, a wriggling screaming thing who wrecked my sleep and ruined my career, she was part of me. It's a physical thing, and even now, when my conscious mind knows she's miles away, living her life without me, my body clock is still set to coincide with hers. I wake at 7 a.m. in time to drop her off at school. Richard says I must be mad. 'I'd be staying in bed until ten at least if I were you – free at last,' he says most mornings as he rushes around the kitchen, abandoning half-eaten toast and fixing his tie, before kissing me. Each morning he heads off into a noisy, busy world of people and their problems, leaving me here in the silence, wondering what to do next. I have my work, of course, but it's hard to adjust to the fact that no one needs me anymore. For so long I've been programmed to fit my life around Amy's, everything feels so quiet and empty and I never thought I'd say this but I miss her untidiness, her teenage moods, despair dissolving into giggles or tears at a word from me, a text from a friend. Her whole life revolving around her phone and bloody Snapchat – and *my* whole life revolving around her. At times it was annoying, inconvenient and exhausting – but I miss it like hell. It's the noise and the *needing* I miss the most, those simple acts of maternal care: making meals, talking through problems, making her laugh when she was sad – and in more recent years becoming her personal round the clock Uber driver. Unpaid.

Despite being eighteen, I continued to collect her from school, even in sixth form. We live in a fairly rural area, the buses are few and far between, and our house is several miles away from her old school. And there was also the fact that I was worried she might not come home. Those old fears still lurked beneath the surface – they always will. But driving her to and fro was never a chore, it gave structure to my working day and the journey was a pleasure. The car was our little bubble, just the two of us uninterrupted – the chatter, and laughter on the way home, sometimes the tears if someone had upset her, said a mean word, or she'd failed at something. I loved that time of day, when she climbed into the car and I knew she was safe, she always chooses the CD and… Chose. She *chose*. She'd put a CD on the player for the drive and we'd sing along together, her laughing at my misheard lyrics.

Isn't it just the worst part of being a mum – that this wonderful, all-consuming job we take on ends too soon? As suddenly and shockingly as they arrive in our world, our children are ready to leave. So here I am now, at 8.30 a.m., alone in the kitchen, my reflection staring back at me from the glass doors in the early-morning darkness. Why did the music, the chatter and the laughter have to stop so abruptly? I've been left behind, a heavy blanket of silence folding around me, a slow ache of loss in the pit of my stomach.

I must shake this off, it's self-indulgent and I'm being ridiculous. What a drama queen I've become. It isn't like I have nothing to do, I have loads of work, some good friends and my own life to lead. But I also have this throb in my throat, and this weird, hollow emptiness that fills me up and grips me like grief. It walks beside me, sits next to me as I type meaningless words on the keyboard, drinks coffee with me, and lies down next to me each night.

It's like a madness over which I have no control. I can be driving along the road when I hear a song on the radio that she loves and it just grabs me and punches me in the stomach – it floors me. Like now, I'm dressed and ready for work, but as I work from home there's no escape – my office is here, and I have a whole day stretching before me, and now she's gone there's nothing to stop me working, no interruptions, no drama, no school drop off. And I miss it. I'm way overdue with my latest feature, for a parenting magazine, so much for having all this time to myself! I also have some profound wisdom to impart in an article about stepfamilies at Christmas for a website, but just can't concentrate long enough to write anything. As a journalist who specialises in family issues, and sells herself as an expert in all matters parenting, children and marriage, the irony isn't lost on me. Little do my readers know I am not the person to be advising *anyone* on how to be a successful wife and mother. My first marriage was a car crash, and, at forty-five, I'm not 'living my best life', as Oprah would ask of me. I'm not an independent woman finding herself after children, I'm an inconsolable mess mourning my eighteen-year-old daughter's departure to university. And I can't even channel my feelings to write. I think it was the writer Nora Ephron who said 'everything is copy' – and in the past I've flogged my life on a freelance basis to anyone who'd buy my features. From parenting an only child to dealing with dodgy ex-husbands, to really difficult stuff I hated sharing, I've managed to do it and make a living. But yesterday I started on a feature called 'Ten Ways to Fill Your Empty Nest' and gave up after number three.

So this morning I'm going to do what I always do when I'm unhappy. I will disregard my own advice, avoid doing the sensible thing (like working, meeting deadlines and eating healthily), defrost half a dozen Danish pastries, turn on the coffee machine and call Zoe.

'Call it avoidance, procrastination or a mild panic attack, I'm having one of those days when I feel like I'm in the wrong life,' I say when I call her. Zoe's always the one I talk to when I need someone to put things into perspective – and she always cheers me up. Zoe and I go back a long way, she only lives just down the road and recently took redundancy from her job in PR, which means she's now available on a daily basis for procrastination and pastries. I tell her it's her duty as a friend to distract me from work and assist me in carb comfort and today she is as happy as ever to fulfil her obligation.

'Put that kettle on, I'm on my way, love,' she sing-songs down the phone.

Zoe understands me like no one else. She has a daughter the same age as Amy, she knows my history, everything we've been through, and she's always around to hold my hand when I'm shaky. I do the same for her, but Zoe's a lot more resilient than me and doesn't need her hand holding quite as much, she's one of life's copers. The only real trauma Zoe has suffered was when Jodie failed to get the ridiculously high grades she needed to be accepted to do Medicine at university. Knowing Jodie's academic track record, I could have predicted there'd be trouble ahead, but Zoe has always been blindly ambitious for her only child. As much as I love my best friend, I've always felt the whole 'my daughter the doctor' thing was more about Zoe than anything Jodie's ever wanted. Anyway, at the age of eighteen, Jodie finally rebelled and when she didn't get the required grades, Zoe insisted she go to Worcester University to study Human Biology. It isn't Medicine at Durham, but Zoe doesn't give up and has a cunning plan for Jodie to transfer to the degree in Medicine further down the line.

Within half an hour of my call, Zoe's at the door, and as I open it, she's complaining about a dent in her car and the weather while telling me everything will be fine.

'Are you suffering a bit today?' she asks, shaking her umbrella on the doorstep, droplets of water landing on the wooden floor.

'Oh, I'm fine, just being silly,' I say, helping her off with her damp jacket as she checks her hair in the mirror, fluffing it with her hands. 'I should be over this moping around. I mean, Amy's perfectly happy, and missing her is just selfish. Sorry I'm being a pain.'

'No, it isn't selfish, Kat,' she says following me through the hall into the kitchen. 'I've told you before, *never* apologise for how you feel.' She's suddenly distracted by the cinnamon warmth in the air. 'Is that delicious smell what I think it is?' she asks, walking into the kitchen.

'Yes, those frozen Danish,' I smile, and for a moment I'm soothed. I have something to do, someone to look after. In the absence of Amy, I will feed Zoe, who's now sniffing the air.

'Danish? You know me so well – I'm a slut for Danish pastries.'

'I heard,' I giggle. 'And I'm happy to pay you in sweet pastries for therapy,' I laugh. 'Honestly, you're the only one who understands. Richard's very sympathetic, but he doesn't really get just how much I miss Amy,' I say, turning on the kettle. 'He has this logical approach that transforms all my agony into numbers. "She's only a hundred and twenty miles away," he says, "if you're missing her you could get in the car and be with her in two hours… if you set off back about four, you'd be home before seven." But those are just numbers, and he may as well be saying she's on the other side of the world.'

Zoe laughs. 'Yeah, and in theory it's all well and good, but you can't just turn up at her halls and say "Hi, I was just passing," she'd think you'd lost it. It would probably freak her flatmates out too.'

'Wouldn't it just? Amy would go mad. "OMG, Mum, I can't believe you'd show me up like that. I can't deal…" I say in my 'teenager' voice. 'Thing is, Richard doesn't really understand. He always points out, "I'm here for you, Kat, it isn't like you're on your own," but it's not the same, is it? That bond between mother and child – it's something he doesn't get.'

'Yeah, must be even harder for Richard to understand, being her stepdad.'

'Well, he's as good as her real dad… better actually. It's just he doesn't have that maternal thing going on,' I say.

'Well, at least you've got someone in the house with you. Count yourself lucky. I'm completely on my own now Jodie's gone. I thought it would be great, a house full of toy boys and a lot of pleasing myself – but it's so…' she starts, and then we both say in unison, 'quiet.'

'And to think we used to complain about how noisy they were and how we never had any time to do anything for us,' I add, trying to continue the jokey theme, but failing as I feel that stab of emptiness prodding me in the chest again.

'And now we've got all the time in the world,' she smiles, detecting the pain in my eyes. 'Hey, Kat, I just had the most brilliant idea to cheer us both up – let's book a spa day.'

'Great idea!' I look at her and see a look of pain shimmer across her face. My friend is so supportive that it's easy to forget that she's going through exactly the same as I am – just not whingeing as much as me. 'Zoe, I know it's not easy for you all on your own, and you're always there for me,' I say, feeling like a spoilt bitch. 'But I'm here for you too, don't forget that.' She nods and reaches for my hand and we stand by the oven, two mums who've shared so much now sharing this next stage. The older you get the more you realise how transient people are and good friends are one of the few constants in life, and have to be valued. How insensitive of me to be complaining when my friend's going through the same and she doesn't even have a partner.

'It's easier for me, Jodie's only a few minutes away.'

'I know, but you live alone now, your whole life has changed. Amy doesn't live here anymore – but Richard still does.'

'Not the same though is it?' she says.

'No.' I pause, as the feeling hits me again. It's a constant ache, I miss having her around, chatting – just being with each other, talking politics, climate change, lipstick and *Love Island*. And Zoe's right, I love Richard, but it isn't the same – he doesn't talk make-up and reality shows like my daughter. 'No. Sadly Richard is no replacement for Amy – he's quite a different housemate,' I giggle. 'You know what he's like, he rarely engages with anything less than Radio 4 or *Newsnight*. Amy's always complaining how straight he is.'

'Yeah, I remember her once saying he thought a Kardashian was a kind of car,' Zoe laughs.

I laugh along, but cringe slightly at the thought of lovely, kind Richard and his clumsy attempts at being a cool stepdad. 'He hasn't got a clue.' I sigh. 'He's this brilliant lawyer at work, fighting for justice, working on really complicated stuff, but sometimes he finds real life a bit too difficult. I tried to talk to him last night, we were in the living room, both staring at the TV, so I said, "Richard, I feel lonely sitting here," and you know what he did? He came and sat next to me. He took it literally, but I didn't mean I was lonely because no one was *sitting* with me…' I shake my head at the memory. I miss Amy all the more in moments like that – we both always seem to know what the other's thinking, what the other needs. And as for watching TV together, we didn't stare at it from different worlds like Richard and I do, an evening watching TV with Amy was a joint activity. We'd talk over it and share our thoughts about what was going on, giggle at first dates, cry over reunited families, rage over cheating lovers. How much I miss her hits me from nowhere once more, and I wonder if we'll always have the closeness we shared, and if we'll watch TV together in the same way ever again.

'If Richard happens to be in the same room when a reality show's on the TV it might as well be in a different language,' I say, frustrated. 'It just isn't the same… I love him but it isn't the same'.

'Love, I know *exactly* what you mean – you don't have to explain it to me,' she laughs. 'I once had a husband too, remember? Though I'd prefer to forget.'

'I don't blame you, he doesn't deserve to be remembered, bloody cheater,' I hiss. 'But Richard's so sweet, and he does try. I just miss having someone else around who thinks like me, who makes me laugh. Sometimes Amy and I almost don't need to say things, we know what the other one's thinking – a reflection of myself, I suppose,' then I add quickly, 'not that I'm saying Amy isn't her own person.'

'No, of course not. Amy is *definitely* her own person. I think that was made very clear when you dared to suggest she had a pink princess birthday cake at the age of seven – she put you right, didn't she?'

'Oh God, yes, she wanted a Spiderman cake, and the costume – and that's what she got,' I can't help but smile at the memory of the pretty little girl dressed as Spiderman, trying to blow out the cobweb candles while refusing to remove the mask.

'And Spiderman was a day in the park compared to her reaction when you dared to suggest she attend a university closer to home,' Zoe remembers.

'Yeah, that went down like a lead balloon, didn't it?' I sigh.

I'd always assumed Amy would want to go to a university closer to home. I felt that she wouldn't be able to cope without me – turns out I'm the one struggling to cope without her. Anyway, I was pretty horrified when she announced she was going as far away as Aberystwyth, but I gritted my teeth and smiled. She's like me, we are both quite determined and dig our heels in, so I knew this had to be her decision. And I hate myself for it but when Amy opened that envelope on results day, a little part of me deflated when I saw she had the results she needed to go there. Of course, this tiny little doubt had been almost obliterated by pride and sharing her happiness – but if I'm honest, I still struggle with her choice. Why did my daughter choose Aberystwyth, a place many miles away from home – a home she's been very happy in?

Even as we planned her move, a little part of me thought (hoped?) she might change her mind at the last minute and go to Worcester or Birmingham, both good universities offering a similar English degree – and both nearer to home. And nearer to me.

'You're so lucky that Jodie chose to stay nearby,' I say, enviously. 'I worry if Amy gets homesick or, God forbid, she's poorly, the journey will just add to the crisis,' I admit, checking my phone to see how long the pastries have been in. I'm also looking at my phone to see if Amy's been in touch. She has a couple of days study leave and she's planning to come home for an extended weekend. I'm beside myself with excitement, and as it's now Thursday, I'm waiting to hear what train she's getting so I can pick her up from the station. I don't like to hassle her, anyone with a teenager will know they rarely plan ahead, but I wish she'd let me know when I need to be at the train station to collect her and so I can get everything ready.

'I'll need to do some food shopping for the weekend,' I say, thinking out loud. 'I don't know if she's going out with her friends, or if Josh is coming over.'

'Josh... oh, so they're still together?'

'Yes, even though they're apart, they're inseparable, if you know what I mean. I thought when she went to uni it would fizzle out but... if he is coming over I'll need to plan a meal for both of them.'

'Did she say he was?'

I shake my head. 'I did ask, but she was vague, said she didn't know what his plans were.'

Predictably, I suppose along with being physically far apart, a bit of a distance has begun to emerge between us since Amy went away. It's perfectly understandable but rather discomforting as we'd always been so close.

'I can't get much out of Amy these days,' I say. 'She used to tell me everything, but it's as if eight weeks away at uni has wiped out eighteen years of being friends... she keeps everything to herself now, I feel like I'm playing twenty questions all the time with her.'

'Oh, tell me about it,' Zoe laughs. 'I'm made to feel like the bloody Spanish Inquisition just asking Jodie when she might grace me with her presence. You wouldn't think she only lives ten minutes down the road, but I never hear from her – unless she's in trouble or wants more money.'

'I wish Amy was only ten minutes down the road, but she's not even in another town, it's another country, Zoe – it's Wales, they speak Welsh!'

'It's what she wanted. And what Amy wants, Amy gets,' Zoe says, smiling as I open the oven. 'She was pretty determined to move away, wasn't she?'

'Yes, I suppose so,' I say, still a little hurt that my daughter was so adamant. 'I knew it would be harder for me to let go the further she was from here.'

'But it doesn't matter *where* they are, we have to let them go sometime, Kat, it's inevitable.' She peers in the direction of the oven and adds absently, 'But right now you've got to stop torturing yourself – and get those *damned* pastries out of the oven. What a shame I didn't start my diet today,' she winks at me.

'If you had started another of your diets I'd just have to eat all six myself,' I joke, opening the oven, 'and you know I could.'

'Oh yes, I've seen what you're capable of eating, especially when you're feeling a little low,' she says as a waft of hot, sweet air from the oven takes my breath away. I quickly pick up the hot pastries with the tips of my fingers and throw them onto a plate. 'That's why we need a spa day, a detox, a good massage…' she starts.

'Do you go into Katie's room and feel really sad she won't be sleeping there?' I interrupt, as I put the plate between us on the kitchen island.

Zoe tilts her head, breaking up one of the pastries with her fingers while considering my question. 'I do, of course I do – but I just keep reminding myself she'll be back at Christmas with loads of washing and tons of attitude.'

I'm comforted by her response, and the thought of Christmas. It's only a few weeks away and I'm looking forward to driving along the mountain road to collect Amy and all her stuff. I've promised I'll wait to decorate the tree, so we can do it together like we always have. I feel a tingle of excitement at the prospect of Christmas and Amy – everything back to normal, and Amy filling our home with chatter and laughter again.

'I'm excited about her coming home this weekend,' I say.

'I bet you are.'

'I was in her room earlier, I was going to tidy it but I want her to feel at home, so I left it as she did. I go into her room every day,' I say. 'I open her drawers and fold her clothes, even though they don't need folding, check everything's where it should be, even though no one's been in there since she left – except me.' I give a little hollow laugh. 'I pretend she's just at school and she'll be home later for tea. But when I go out in the car, I can't play her music, the old CDs we'd sing along to when we went anywhere. I can't listen to Lana Del Ray without sobbing.' I try and lighten this with a shake of my head and another little laugh, but the look of sympathy on Zoe's face almost causes me to break. 'We used to dance round the kitchen to Lana, and when Richard was away working we'd watch TV and eat chocolate flakes and she'd get chocolate bits all over the sofa… and I'd sometimes tell her off. And now I wish she was here messing up the sofa and twirling round the kitchen and…'

She's looking at me in a really odd way, like I might be going mad, so I take a sip of coffee and address the elephant in the room. 'Zoe, I know you probably think I'm crazy, I'm not handling this very well, am I? But after everything we went through when Amy was younger, I just feel so…'

'I know, I *know*, love,' Zoe says, reaching across for my hand. 'I think the kids leaving for uni… well, it's hit you more than most, and I'm not surprised.'

I nod, unable to speak, afraid my tears will start and never stop. It's a physical thing, and I know it's been coming for years, ever since she was born. Each year something lovely would come to an end – reading her bedtime stories, playing games, building sandcastles together, each activity replaced by something else, until at eighteen all she needed me for was food, the odd hug and most importantly – her Uber. But now my fridge is empty and the passenger seat in my car is also pretty empty since Amy went away. But this isn't just about my daughter leaving for university, it's about so much more. I've told lies, kept secrets from the people I love, and now I'm alone I have more time to think, and it haunts me. Ghosts wake me in the middle of the night, and I'm so scared that the past will reach into the present, and take everything I love.

# CHAPTER TWO

'What about a winter break?' Richard says that evening as we eat dinner together. 'We could get a cheap flight, a late hotel booking and get away before Christmas.'

I smile. 'I'm not sure, love, it all feels a bit… forced.' I know he's trying to think of nice things we can do together, and I really appreciate it, but I'm not ready to go off on a plane and be in a different country from Amy. Doesn't he realise the separation is bad enough without adding air miles to my agony. 'Let's do something in the spring,' I say, before adding, 'perhaps.'

It's Thursday and he's finished the week early because he's off on a golf weekend in the morning. I suspect all this talk of holidays is because he feels a little guilty at leaving me, but I don't mind. I'm excited at the prospect of a weekend with Amy, and it gives me more time to prepare for her visit. I also have plenty of overdue work to finish so can spend my alone time wisely.

'Amy mentioned coming home this weekend,' I remind Richard. 'She's got some study leave on Monday and Tuesday and I said I can drive her back to uni on Wednesday.'

'It's a long drive,' he says, looking at me. 'Wouldn't you be better just dropping her at the station and letting her take the train back?'

I look at him, and he registers his realisation with a smile; he knows that where Amy's concerned, no drive is too long.

'If she's home tomorrow you two can catch up without me in the way,' he sounds relieved, like he's just found a babysitter – for me. As lovely as it is for me to work from home, since Amy left, some days I only speak to Richard or Zoe, and I think he sometimes feels the weight of responsibility, especially on days when I don't see my friend – on those days he's usually subjected to me talking his socks off about everything and nothing as he walks through the door. After a tough day, Richard tries so hard to be engaged in my diatribes about work, global injustice and how many gentlemen callers Mrs Dorridge, our neighbour, has entertained that day. Richard, along with not being very good at celebrity gossip, also isn't interested in neighbourhood scandals, and often just sits and listens, but I know he's not really taking it in. Amy's like me, she loves the juicy gossip, which reminds me, I must tell her about Mrs Dorridge's new 'lodger', a man ten years younger.

I think for a millisecond about sharing this juicy titbit with Richard, then decide he really wouldn't be interested. So I take out a pen and start a shopping list, a slightly decadent, celebratory line-up consisting of smoked salmon, Prosecco, avocados and chocolate flakes – Amy's favourite things.

'She jokingly complains that living as a student involves too much soup and spaghetti,' I say, 'so along with the fancy stuff there'll be plenty of vegetables on my shopping list this weekend.'

He nods. 'Yes, absolutely.'

'And, as she only has a shower at uni,' I continue, 'a bath is the ultimate luxury for her at the moment. She said it's the main thing she's looking forward to when she comes home, so I'll buy her a bath bomb from her favourite shop.'

'Mmm. She's got a couple of weeks to make up for since she last came home and took over the bathroom.'

'Yeah, she could be there for days.'

'And no doubt be like a prune when she's finished,' he adds, and we both giggle at the thought of her soaking for hours, filling upstairs with the heady scent of flowery, fizzy lavender, just like when she used to live here.

Richard puts down his fork and pats my hand. 'So a holiday in December is perhaps a little ambitious, but perhaps you and I could have a weekend away before Christmas,' he says, going back to his original conversation and dragging me away from flowery bath mists.

'Yes. I have a few articles to finish, but, yes, that would be nice. We could go to Wales and call in on Amy…' I stop talking when I see the expression on his face. 'What?' I ask, knowing full well what he's about to say.

'How about we have a weekend, just us? You'll never get used to her being away if you go there every chance you get. And Amy might not want us dropping in, darling.'

'We wouldn't be *dropping in…*' I start, a flush of anger rising in my chest. 'Honestly, Richard, I feel like I'm being chastised for wanting to see my own flesh and blood.'

'No, not at all. I just think we need to let her settle. She was home only a couple of weeks ago and you *do* talk to her every day on the phone.'

'And what's wrong with that?' I say indignantly. 'I hate it when you try and make out I'm too much, like I call her every day and can't leave her alone. Amy texts me or calls me to say she's okay, because she knows I'd worry if she didn't, it's how I brought her up – to be *considerate*,' I say pointedly.

'I'm not saying—' he starts. As a lawyer he's usually better than me in an argument, but my anger is louder and I shout him down.

'*And* we don't *talk* every day – sometimes she just texts or calls to say "hello, Mum".' Having spent every day with Amy for eighteen years, I find the prospect of not even hearing 'hello' from her unbearable and just a quick call or text to say she's fine is all I ask. 'I don't think that's excessive, and I resent the implication that it is,' I snap.

'I'm not implying that at all, I'm just saying you'll get used to her being away and she'll settle if you put some space between you both,' he says, his eyebrows raised, like he knows better than me – her own mother.

'Richard, this is my daughter we're talking about, and whatever you might think, I have no intention of "putting some space between" us.'

He shrugs and goes back to his chicken. 'The truth is, you wait every day for Amy's call, and you don't even want to leave here unless it involves seeing her,' he says, before taking a mouthful.

'I do… I go out.'

'Yes, grocery shopping. That's it. Since Amy left, you haven't really done anything except work and spend hours with Zoe, even then it's always her coming here, you don't go out.'

'I don't want to… and I'm busy. I have loads of work to do for the magazine.'

'It's more than that. You don't want to go on holiday, you don't want to go out for dinner anymore, when I've suggested it recently you've said "no, let's stay home, get a take out". Kat, it's like… like you've changed since Amy left… you can't bear to leave the house. You sit in her room, fold her clothes, dust her photos. I've watched you.'

'I simply want to keep everything nice for her, for when she comes home. There's nothing wrong or weird about the way I behave, the way I feel.'

'I disagree. Your life's on hold, Kat. You refuse to go away in case Amy suddenly decides to come home at the last minute. I think you're being unfair on yourself, on us. And it's a bit weird…' He tries to make this last bit sound jokey, but I don't like how he's making me feel. I respect him, I trust his judgement, but what he's saying suggests my reaction to Amy leaving is unhealthy, but instead of telling him this, I lash out.

'Richard, you're making it sound like I'm obsessed!' I say, raising my voice in horror at his comments, at the same time asking myself if this is really who I am. 'Okay,' I admit, 'for the first few months

I want to be here for Amy, in case she suddenly gets homesick and wants to come home. And yes, I do go into her room because it makes me feel close to her.' I don't add that some days I feel like a drug addict withdrawing and in my cold-turkey state Amy's room is my only relief. 'This isn't just about me, Richard. When she first started uni she was in tears, she was homesick and asking to come home, she didn't want to stay there. I just worry she'll have another blip like that,' I add for dramatic effect, because in truth she's over the homesick stage now, and she seems very happy.

'*All* kids feel homesick when they leave home… and, yes, she will at some point probably feel like that again.'

'But she isn't "all kids". She's Amy, she's my daughter and I'm worried about her, I always will be after… everything.' I give him a meaningful look, a reminder that I have every reason to fear for my child's wellbeing.

'I understand,' he says, a look of sympathy softening his face. 'But you can't sit here waiting, you can't stop your own life. She's doing great, she's building her life, and you need to rebuild yours. Trust me, if you tell her we're going away for a weekend, she won't collapse in a heap of tears and think you're a terrible mother – and nor will anyone else.'

Okay, I have to admit that Richard's probably right. I do have this need to be here for her, just in case. And yes, I am a rather 'hands on' mum, but there's another reason I'm feeling this way. When Amy was last home she asked me about what happened with me and her father. In an attempt to hide the truth I became quite defensive, and we had a few words, and since then I've felt bruised and I want to make it up to her. It's making me even more clingy than usual, and even though we've spoken on the phone, and on the surface we're fine, I just need to see Amy. I can never tell her the truth about what really happened between me and Tony, her dad – but I'm hoping this weekend we can at least clear the air. Meanwhile, I can't tell Richard about us falling out because he'd be all over it in true criminal-lawyer fashion, asking his own bloody questions – and I don't need that.

'I'd better do some food shopping first thing,' I say, moving away from this conversation.

Richard has that look on his face, like he's going to start probing, and I don't want to slip up and say something I shouldn't. In the fifteen years since we met I've kept the truth to myself, and I'm not about to slip up now.

# CHAPTER THREE

It's Sunday and Amy still hasn't come home. I've called and texted and she isn't responding. Where the hell is she?

I phone Zoe, who, as always, has a calming effect on me.

'Oh, sweetie, I'm sure she's fine, would you like me to come over?'

'No thanks,' I say. 'I need to finish this article, and Richard's due home any minute. I just wanted to talk to someone. I'm probably being silly, I'm sure she'll call soon – or just turn up.' I glance at the kitchen clock. 'There's still time,' I add trying to convince myself as much as Zoe.

'When did you last hear from her?' Zoe asks, and I note the concern in her voice, it alarms me slightly. I want her to tell me it's all fine.

'The last time I heard from her was Friday, when she said she'd let me know her train times so I could collect her from the station.'

'Did she say anything… unusual?'

'She was just really excited to be coming home. "I've got *loads* to tell you," she said. Is that significant?' Zoe doesn't answer, so I just keep talking, like that will hurry Amy along and she'll turn up in a minute, or at least call me. 'Then, yesterday, she texted to say she'd just had breakfast with "the girls".'

'Oh well, that'll be it. She's gone off with—'

'No. She wouldn't do that without telling me. And it's odd.'

'What do you mean?'

'I'm not sure who "the girls" are. She'd normally say *who* she was having breakfast with. I know the names of Amy's friends and flatmates at uni, even though I haven't met them all. She'd name them.'

'What are you saying – do you think she was trying to hide something from you?'

'I don't know.'

After a shaky start, Zoe is gearing up for some calming talk, but it bounces off me. I'm too bothered, something's buzzing around my head. Why didn't Amy say anything in her text about coming home?

'But when I texted back to ask about collecting her from the station, she didn't respond, so I assumed she was on the train with no signal, or perhaps her phone battery had died. I called and called and then I thought about what Richard had said and wondered if I was becoming obsessive. Am I overreacting, Zoe?'

Silence.

'Am I? Please be honest.'

She sighs. 'Kat, I'm your closest friend but, love, you have to get a hold of this. You do it a lot, panicking about where she is and who she's with and you drive yourself mad. Amy's grown up now and she's gone away – you have to start making a life for yourself. I have to say I've always felt that you and Amy—'

'What?'

'Oh, just that you're so close it might be a good thing that she's moved away, she's making a life for herself, and I know you're finding that hard. But you have to do the same, love.'

I know Zoe's parenting is different from mine; she's always been less 'hands on' than me as a mother, but she's always on my side. But now I feel like she's criticising me, suggesting I'm overprotective and so involved in Amy's life I don't have my own. Perhaps she's right, but it doesn't change the fact that I'm anxious and today is not the day to stop worrying about Amy.

'She should have been home yesterday, and she still hasn't turned up, nor has she called me to say she's changed her mind about coming home. But what concerns me the most is that she isn't answering her phone. It isn't like her. And as much as I try to tell myself I'm overreacting, I don't think I am. I have this horrible feeling in the pit of my stomach that there's something wrong and this isn't about Amy being flaky and forgetting she was due home. Zoe, it's weird, it doesn't add up. Call it paranoia if you like, but I call it mother's instinct.'

'Did she definitely say she was coming home this weekend?' she asks in a voice that's meant to calm me.

'Yes, *definitely*... well, as definite as an eighteen-year-old girl is about these things.'

'Mmm. You know what they're like, Kat. She's probably got a better offer, and completely forgot to let you know. You've carried on planning and she's got other plans, you know what you're like where Amy's concerned.'

She's trying to be gentle but echoing Richard's comments suggesting my instinct can't be trusted because where Amy's concerned I'm not rational. Perhaps they're right? These two people love me, they have my best interests at heart, and they're trying to tell me something – but I'm not listening.

'I'm really worried.' Just hearing myself say this brings tears to my eyes, but I swallow the tears, I don't want Zoe to think I'm being silly.

'Oh, love, you remember what it's like to be eighteen, don't you? I never rang *my* mother! I bet Amy's drinking two-for-one cocktails in the student union bar, probably pissed. Did you ever call *your* mother when you were pissed?' She laughs.

'Do you know if Jodie's heard from her?' I ask, unable to respond to her jokey comment.

'No, I haven't heard from Jodie since... last... Wednesday? See what I mean? They're all the same – God, if I got upset every time Jodie didn't get in touch or pick up her phone I'd be in a heap.'

'They're all different, Zoe,' I say, a shimmer of anger frosting my voice. Why is she not taking this seriously?

'Sorry, Kat. I just don't want you getting yourself into a state again. I can call Jodie and ask if she's heard from her if you like.'

'No, no thanks. I'll call her later if I still haven't heard anything.'

'Good luck with that, our Jodie'll be recovering from another weekend bender. I don't know how they do it.'

'I wonder if the library's open on a Sunday?' I say, ignoring Zoe's attempts at banter for a second time. It's not funny. Amy hasn't called; why the hell does she think it's okay to treat it like a joke? 'Yes, that'll be it, she's in the library working, and she's turned off her phone,' I say, sounding relieved. Then I remember she doesn't turn her phone off when she goes to the library, she just puts it on silent, and she wouldn't have been in the library since yesterday, so why hasn't she contacted me?

Zoe doesn't answer me, she knows what I'm like when it comes to Amy; I panic sometimes and she's always been understanding. But after the incident last summer when I thought Amy had drowned at the lido, I caused a huge fuss over nothing, so who can blame her for being a little underwhelmed by my dramatics now? It was a really hot day and Amy had gone to swim at the lido with friends after school, but later when I called her to find out what time she was leaving, she didn't respond. So I drove over there, but when I arrived there was no one around and on the door was a sign saying: 'The lido has had to close early due to unforeseen circumstances, we will reopen as soon as possible.' I almost collapsed on the spot – my immediate thought being the worst – had there been some horrific accident? Was it Amy? She isn't a strong swimmer and she hadn't responded to my call and I just panicked. I called the police and asked if they'd had any accidents that day and told them I was concerned for my daughter. They asked for her details and promised to contact patrol cars and would stay in touch. Then I made Richard drive around the area one way while I drove the other, I called Jodie who was with her dad so couldn't shine any light on Amy's whereabouts, so I asked Zoe to call all their other friends for me while I drove round searching. Then eventually, about 10 p.m., when I was back at home and at my wit's end, she just wandered in. It was as if nothing had happened. She said she was fine and she'd been back to one of the girl's houses and they'd lost track of time.

'Oh My God Mum, you're too much,' was all she said. I felt so foolish. And as a result of that I'm sure the local police have me highlighted on their freak list and no one will take me seriously ever again.

'Sorry, Zoe, I know, I know, I sound bonkers, like some mad, obsessive mother who needs to know where her daughter is every minute of every day,' I say, in an attempt to address this.

Again I'm greeted by that silence at the other end of the phone, it seems that even my best friend doubts me now.

'Zoe, I don't blame you for thinking I'm mad.'

'Oh, Kat. It isn't that. It's just… well, yesterday was Saturday. Amy texted you yesterday then probably went out last night – she's probably hungover today,' she says like a teacher talking to a hysterical pupil. 'I don't hear from Jodie for days, sometimes a couple of weeks.'

'Amy would have *said* if she was going out. She'd let me know,' I say this back to her clearly and assertively. Zoe has a way of talking over you sometimes and I just don't want her to dismiss this, she has to take it on board and understand that I'm concerned. 'I know my daughter and she wouldn't just change her plans on a whim… Perhaps Jodie would, but not Amy.'

'Well, I'm sorry but I reckon she's changed her mind. People do, you need to stop thinking the worst every time she goes off radar for ten minutes,' she says.

'But even if she *did* change her mind, she would have called me,' I say for the hundredth time. 'It's what she does…'

'Love, that's what she *did*. It's what she *used to do* when she was at home, when she was a schoolgirl.'

I realise it may just be another stage in the process of 'cutting the cord'. Slowly but surely our kids take themselves out of our lives, and they do it so gently we don't even feel it. Except this feels more clinical than that. I know Amy was pissed off with me when she came home last time, but it doesn't mean she'd deliberately go AWOL and not let me know just to upset me.

Being a self-confessed, shameless, helicopter mother, I have been secure in the knowledge that I can 'track' Amy down online. Social media's like having a permanent babycam on your teenager, all you need is an Instagram account, and you don't have to be a tech genius to work out where they are and who they're with at any given time. You 'see' them, and despite the fact they're a hundred miles away, in pubs and clubs you've never been with people you've never met, you know they're still alive. One Instagram post, one comment on Facebook and you can sleep that night, knowing they're still on the planet. But along with a lack of texting, which is unusual, I haven't 'seen' Amy for twenty-four hours. No posts, no comments, no tagging me in funny cat videos on Facebook. Nothing. I feel like a junkie who hasn't had her fix.

I don't share this with Zoe, it's too complicated and I think she might judge. I put her on speaker so I can look at my phone, and there's Amy smiling into the camera, her red-check scarf wrapped loosely around her neck. I remember feeling happy, because she looked happy. There would be no more tearful phone calls, no more heart-breaking texts telling me she'd made the wrong decision about going to Aberystwyth. It was a good thing, right? But in settling in, she'd moved even further away from me, she didn't need Mum quite so much and I grieved for the minutiae, the drama, the details of her life that presumably she now shared with new friends.

'The thing is, Zoe, it isn't just that she hasn't been in touch with me, she hasn't been online,' I say. 'I'm looking at Amy's Instagram now and there's nothing since last week.'

I hear Zoe sigh. 'Oh, love, I honestly think you're overreacting. Remember last summer, and the lido…' Oh God, I knew this would happen. I just hope the police don't think the same if I have to call them. I hope it won't come to the police – I hope she calls me in the next five minutes.

Zoe continues to make soothing noises while I scroll through Amy's Instagram. For the millionth time. My beautiful child is standing on the promenade, the sea behind her, wind whipping her long blonde hair, she's throwing back her head, and laughing. Young, pretty, happy. Yes, I'm biased, but she's lovely. She's wearing a mustard jumper and a red scarf. I remember buying her that scarf, it was two years ago, she was about to start sixth form and I took her into Birmingham for a girls' day, just the two of us. We were in Selfridges and she spotted the scarf, clutching it to her like it was the most precious thing she'd ever held.

'Mum, I *have* to have it,' she'd said, as if owning it would change her life.

I wasn't so sure, it was very expensive for a scarf, but, as the saleswoman pointed out it was handknitted. 'It's unique, there is no other like it,' she'd said, and in a moment of indulgent motherly madness I bought it for her. And it was worth the money to see the delight on Amy's face. She wore it all through our lunch, refusing to take it off even to eat her soup, which made me laugh. Amy always makes me laugh.

I drag myself back from memories of our girls' day and into the present.

'I'm telling you the *fact* that she hasn't posted anything on social media since Friday afternoon; a selfie by the sea. I saw it at the time and thought, "Great, she's just headed into town and she's probably going to get her train to come home." She looks so happy Zoe – that's why nothing makes sense," I say, desperately trying to convince Zoe that I'm not mad.

'I think you've got yourself into a state,' is all she says

I don't like that she said that – but she's right – I have. I've driven myself mad all day and what started as a headache is now full blown anxiety laced with nausea. I've got that horrible, gnawing ball of worry – you know, the kind that sits in your stomach and gobbles up all rational thought.

'I keep trying to come up with a reason why she's gone completely off grid,' I say to Zoe. 'But I can't think of any.'

'There are a million reasons why she might be—'

'No, there *aren't*. She calls me all the time, about every little thing. "Mum, how do I get the margarita stains off my new white top?" or "Mum, you know that vegetable soup you make, what do I need and how do I make it?"'

'Yeah I get those calls from Jodie,' Zoe says, refusing to join in on my concern, which is really frustrating.

'But Zoe, this is *different*. She was supposed to be coming home this weekend.' As I'm talking I have Zoe on loud speaker so I can keep scrolling through my phone, checking her Instagram every few minutes. I'm desperate to see a photo of Amy with friends in the pub, or perhaps in a café eating cake… something that will tell me she's fine. But nothing – *nothing*.

'It'll be her phone,' Zoe says. 'It's been lost, stolen or the battery's died – and that's why you haven't heard from her. I have to go, love, the landline's buzzing. Let me know as soon as she gets in touch,' she says rather dismissively.

I reluctantly click the red handset sign and go back to stalking Instagram. I'm beginning to feel that Zoe's fed up of my drama and was just churning out consoling sentences to shut me up and get me off the phone. I'd be mortified if she genuinely thinks I'm wrong about this, but I can't help how I feel.

I hear Richard arriving home from his golf trip, so push away my concerns about Zoe finding me ridiculous. I was going to cook dinner, but then I was busy working, and worrying, and now I can't even think straight to chop a bloody pepper. Perhaps we'll order in

I call through to Richard, who's still in the hall. 'Had a good golfing session?'

'Yes.' He walks over to me and gives me a hug.

'I haven't had chance to make supper,' I add breezily, 'just so busy with work…'

'You okay?' he asks, dumping down his golf bag with a groan.

'Yes.' I hadn't planned to mention Amy until he'd settled down, but it seems I can't hide my anxiety.

He looks at me. 'What's the matter?'

'Oh, I'm a bit worried – can't get hold of Amy. She's gone totally AWOL since yesterday!' I try to sound like this is vaguely amusing, the student daughter doing her own thing without a thought for anyone else. But that's the stereotype – and Amy doesn't fit it, she wouldn't simply ignore my texts. She knows it would kill me. 'If she went out last night, how do I know she even got home?' I hear myself say.

Richard stands for a few seconds looking at me. 'Not this again, Kat.'

'Please don't mention the lido. This is different.'

'Is it? Is it different from any other time she's more than seven minutes late? I can hear her now when you ask her to call you when she gets back from a night out, "Oh, Mum, you're such a stressy Bessy."'

'It's our little joke, and she might *say* that, but she still messages me, and she knows I don't care what time it is,' I add, irritated by the implication that my requests to keep in touch annoy my daughter.

'Darling, you have to stop this. I worry about you; I don't want it to take over as it has in the past. It isn't good for you or Amy.'

Richard's now walked over to the freezer and is gazing in like it may contain the meaning of life. We can be having the most emotional, profound conversations, but, where Richard's concerned, everything stops for supper.

'Don't worry about dinner... or about Amy,' he says, responding to my lack of culinary effort and my only child going AWOL. 'She's fine,' he adds. 'Just enjoying her freedom, I'm sure.'

I bristle slightly. What's that supposed to mean? Is he saying that being home with me somehow curtailed her liberty and she's finally escaped? Or am I just being oversensitive?

'I know, I know she's fine...' I lie, rolling my eyes like it would be ridiculous to think anything else. 'I just wish she'd text to *say* so, or tell me her news, like where she went last night,' I say, wondering if Richard can sense the fear that tingles through my veins. I just want to read the text that tells me Amy is okay, she's just been swimming/walking/dancing – or that there's no phone signal where she is. It would make me the happiest woman alive.

A notification lights up my phone then and, like a defibrillator, gives my heart a jolt, causing it to beat faster, bringing me back to life. *Here she is.* I imagine the text, a mad jumble of words with intermittent heart emojis, assuring me I still have a daughter. That I'm still a mother. But a swift glance tells me it isn't Amy. Apparently someone has just liked my Instagram picture of Amy drinking Prosecco taken when she came home a couple of weekends ago for my birthday. Amy hates that photo, so I posted it two hours ago, hoping she'd respond, even if only in a direct message to tell me off for embarrassing her. 'Mum, I can't believe you used that photo – I look like a dog!' I half smile, seeing her there holding a flute of fizz, my little girl's smile on a young woman's face. I hold my phone up so Richard can see, but he's still distracted by the contents of the freezer. 'Here's Amy, when she was last home,' I say, like I need to bring her into the room.

'Lovely,' he responds vaguely after a quick glance, clearly hungry, and I wonder if I should offer to make something. But he's a grown-up, he can sort himself out. I have Amy to worry about. She comes first. Always has, always will.

I'm now pacing around the kitchen while Richard complains about Roger's golfing technique while trying to drag something out from the back of the freezer.

'Take your pick,' he says, finally emerging from the icy depths and brandishing two frosted boxes that look like they've been in the Antarctic for hundreds of years. I stop and look at the crusts of ice. He's holding a box of paella in one hand and what looks like spaghetti carbonara in the other. I really don't feel like eating anything but my heart melts a little, he tries so hard sometimes.

'Freshly harvested from the frozen depths,' he announces, looking from one to the other, pleased with himself. 'Will it be Spain or Italy this evening, madam?'

He wipes the front of the boxes with a tea towel, revealing vine tomatoes, drizzly olive oil and fat garlic bulbs under a setting Mediterranean sun. But we all know from experience that the inside will hold the revolting truth – black plastic trays with congealed frozen mush. It's all rather depressing, but if Amy would just text me I could embrace Italy or Spain and even laugh along with Richard. He can feel the tension, he knows what I'm like, and he's trying to be happy and jolly with his frozen Mediterranean dishes, but his tired eyes and tight jaw tell another story. I was hoping a weekend's golf would be good for him, but I'd say he looks even more tired than he did when he left on Friday morning. The last thing he needs is me going off on one about Amy, so I try to take my mind off things by attempting a normal conversation.

'Did you talk shop all weekend?' I ask.

'Yes, we did, really. I was hoping to relax, but you know what Roger's like.'

Roger is one of Richard's partners in the law firm, and very ambitious, which means he can't ever relax, even on the golf course. 'Yes, it's infectious, isn't it? You don't have to pretend, Richard.'

'Pretend what?' he looks alarmed.

'That everything's fine.'

'It is… it is,' he says, gazing at the frozen dinners, while I glance at my phone. Both our minds are on other things outside this kitchen.

'It's like a watched pot, keep looking and it won't boil,' he snaps, and I look up from my phone to see the irritation in his eyes.

My sympathy for his work stress dissipates into thin air and my defences are up, a wall around me. 'I'm just checking my phone, *that's* all,' I say, his irritation now mirrored in my voice.

'Oh, Kat, please stop this before it gets out of hand.' He sighs, placing the two boxed meals on the kitchen counter.

'It will not get out of hand, as you so sensitively put it. I know you think I'm a tiger mother – or a helicopter or whatever it is. And yes, before you say it – I know she's eighteen and an adult, but she'll always be my baby. I just want to know she's okay.'

He's looking at me and is about to say something, but pauses when I add, 'There's nothing wrong in wanting to know where my child is – she only left home eight weeks ago, after eighteen years it's been a huge wrench. I just want to stay in touch.'

He rolls his eyes. 'A bit too much in touch if you ask me,' he murmurs.

'What does that mean?' I can feel heat rising up from my chest, a flash of anger fusing with the worry in my stomach.

'Kat, darling,' he starts in a voice meant to calm, but which has the opposite effect. 'You can't always know where she is and what she's doing. All *you* need to know is that Amy's at university, she's studying and she's also having fun.' He puts his head to one side and really looks at me.

'We don't *know* she's having fun,' I say.

'Of course she is. She's away from home for the first time in her life and she's having a ball.'

'Oh, really? How would you know? It's not like you ever bother to call her.' I snap.

'No – I don't call her, but it doesn't mean I *don't* care.'

He looks hurt, and I feel bad. I shouldn't have said that – I didn't mean to hurt him, I'm just lashing out. 'Sorry,' I murmur.

That was unfair of me. Richard does his best. He took Amy on as his own when she was only four years old, and he's been there for both of us. He's not the most gregarious father, but he's solid and consistent. He makes sure she has everything she needs, and even pays the top-up part of her loan for uni without a quibble. He can sometimes be a bit embroiled in his work, and he doesn't 'see' her – he isn't the kind of dad who'd call her up just for a chat, but he's practical and supportive. She complains he's not cool, but he does his bit.

'Amy needs to find her feet,' he adds wearily, leaning against the kitchen counter. 'The thing is Kat… Amy… she's…'

Does he know something? Is she planning to surprise me and turn up later, and he's in on it?

'What?'

'Oh, I don't know,' he says, and I'm even more convinced that he does know something.

'Is this a wind up? Is Amy coming home later… tomorrow – is it a surprise?' I ask.

'No… no,' he says. But he has this strange look on his face.

'Because if she is coming home tomorrow instead of today, and it isn't a surprise – then why hasn't she let me know?'

'I'm sorry, Kat – no, this isn't a surprise.'

My stomach dips. For a few wonderful seconds I'd thought this was the answer. Richard sees the look of despair on my face and reaches out his hand as if to steady me.

'She's probably just changed her mind about coming home. Perhaps she doesn't want to tell you.'

'Why would she feel like that? I'm not some scary mother who'd refuse to speak to her if she changed her plans.'

'No – no, of course not. I mean, she's enjoying herself out with

I don't answer, I'm just so scared.

'Just wait until the end of term when she's spent her loan on booze. She'll come home then,' he says clumsily.

I can't help it, I'm annoyed at his light-hearted dismissal. And I don't like him implying my relationship with my daughter is based on money – it's too precious for that. But then, being a lawyer, Richard's always looking for motive – life is one big court case to my husband.

'Amy *wants* to come home, it isn't about being skint,' I say defensively. 'She wants to see us. You *know* that. She said she was excited about being back here – she doesn't see me as some kind of cash dispenser. Please don't insult me and push us into some stereotypical naïve, fussy mother, selfish daughter scenario. It's not who we are.'

'I didn't mean to upset you, it was a joke.' He's standing in front of me with his arms open.

'It isn't fucking funny!'

'And neither are you. Why are you so defensive, Kat?'

'I'm not… I'm, I'm – you make me angry. You trivialise my relationship with Amy, always implying I'm too clingy, and I'm a dithering mess because my child's left home. But you're wrong, and the moment she calls me I will prove to you that I'm not – until then I am allowed to be a mess because I DON'T KNOW WHERE MY DAUGHTER IS!'

'Kat, calm down. I know who you are, and what you're capable of. You're a good mother, an intelligent woman in charge of her life – but at the moment you're behaving in a really erratic way. Stop being so paranoid. I'm not criticising you, all I'm saying is that Amy lives in another city, has a different life – one you aren't part of. And where once she may have stayed in touch, told you her every movement, she's gently breaking away.'

'I find that hard to believe.'

'I know you do, that's the problem. She's not a little girl anymore.' He turns to me and gently takes both my hands in his. 'Look, it's the weekend and she probably went out, stayed with a friend, lost her phone, had a one-night stand, who knows?'

God, I feel like I've been on a bloody loop all day. First Zoe, and now Richard saying the same things, making exactly the same suggestions while I reject everything, because I'm Amy's mum, and I know. I just *know*. But no one is listening to me.

I sigh with frustration and wish he wouldn't use phrases like 'one-night stand' when referring to my daughter's list of potential 'social activities'. Amy and I might be close, but we've never discussed anything of that nature, and I'd rather Richard didn't either, I feel it's inappropriate.

'You said yourself she's started to settle in recently,' he says. 'She's already made lots of friends, goes out a lot, and… I hate to say it, Kat, but she probably doesn't *need* you quite as much as she did.'

'Girls always need their mums,' I murmur, remembering how close I was to my own mother. She died when I was twenty-four, too young to lose your mum, I remember feeling so lost without her. And it doesn't take a psychologist to work out that I probably overcompensate for my loss with Amy. I try not to think of Mum now because it always makes me so sad and I'm already worried as I scroll through my phone desperately looking for Amy's boyfriend Josh's number. I'm desperate to make contact, because he might know something, but I'm also slightly reluctant to call him because when I talked to Amy on the phone last week she said he was being – and I quote – 'a bit of a knob'. They've been together almost two years – since sixth form – and Josh is hoping to do medicine, but as it's pretty intense he decided to take a year out before starting the degree. He's working at his father's building company for a year before going to university, and I wondered if things might change between them.

'I just have this feeling, Mum…'

'What feeling?' I'd asked.

'I think he might have gone off me,' she'd said, like it had just occurred to her. But I heard something in her voice and I felt like she wasn't telling me everything, that there was a 'but' to be added.

'How do you feel about that?' I'd said.

'Okay, I guess – especially if he's being a…'

'Knob?'

We laughed and I told her she'd probably got it all wrong and next time she saw him things would be fine, it was the distance. All the time I had this irrational desire to kill him with my bare hands for daring to be a knob and making my daughter feel less than amazing.

'How could he possibly have gone off you?' I said. 'You are beautiful and perfect and he's punching above his weight.'

She laughed loudly at this. 'Yeah, but, Mum, you're a bit biased, aren't you?'

'His loss,' I said. 'And anyway, who wants to be tied down at eighteen?'

'Yeah, perhaps he isn't the one for me after all,' she'd said, and I'd wondered if she was just saying that to hide her pain.

'Whatever will be, will be,' I'd offered, selfishly hoping that if and when they did split, it would be Amy not Josh who did the dumping. I couldn't bear to see her heart broken, but there's nothing I could do. You protect your children from as much physical and emotional pain as you can, you soothe with sweets, hot chocolate and sticking plasters all through their babyhood and childhood. But then the teenage years come along and some bastard with a cute smile turns up, and wrecks their lives, hot chocolate and sweets don't work any longer. The plasters are also useless and for the first time you have to stand by and watch them fall apart, knowing that a fixed heart isn't in your gift anymore.

'Just try and build your own life while you're there,' I'd suggested. 'You need to explore new things, have fun, meet new friends.'

'Yeah, tomorrow I'm going out with some people from my course, it'll be fun.'

'Great,' I'd said, 'that's just what you need.'

Amy didn't say much else, but I wondered if she was more upset than she was letting on. We hadn't talked much about Josh recently, she seemed happier to chat about the people on her course who she started going out with after lectures.

'Perhaps Josh has turned up unexpectedly in Aberystwyth?' I say to Richard now.

'Yeah… he might.'

'I told you she said things weren't great between them, he might be there now, and they've turned their phones off so they can talk?' That would explain the lack of contact, the online absence, and the fact she hasn't turned up here, wouldn't it? A plume of relief is now blooming in my chest, and I even manage a smile at Richard, who's opening the microwave. 'You're like Gordon Ramsay, standing there with the tea towel over your arm,' I joke.

He laughs, and starts swearing profusely, which makes me giggle. Then I drift back to the comforting thought that Josh is with Amy and I poke around in that until the sliver of calm is replaced by something I suddenly remember Amy saying.

'The other night on the phone she told me he's been acting weird,' I said, almost to myself.

'Who? Josh? What did she mean he's been acting weird?'

'I don't know. When I asked her she said, "Oh, I'm probably being oversensitive." I wonder now, was she trying to tell me something?'

At the time, I'd wanted to dig deeper, to offer advice, some soothing words – metaphorically put that plaster on and soothe

I wasn't allowed back in. I asked if she was okay, I felt there was something else, but she said she was fine, and there was a hesitant 'Better than fine,' and I'd accepted this. It was what I'd wanted to hear and I didn't push it any further. Thinking about it now I wonder if there *was* something she wanted to tell me – but knew it would hurt me to know *she* was upset, and she wanted to spare me that. It isn't just parents who apply those plasters – sometimes our children do the same for us.

Harry, our fat, fluffy cat winds his way around my legs, bringing me back to the present. I'm still holding my phone to me like it's a newborn baby that can't be put down – and I check it constantly, obsessively. It's like a nagging toothache I keep prodding with my tongue; I can't let it go, can't rest until I know she's okay. I decide not to contact Josh just yet. They could well be in the middle of some lovers' tiff, or worse still some huge stand-off. If he's finished it, she'd be mortified to think I'd contacted him, like I was begging on her behalf – she'd never forgive me. I can't text him if he's with her either, finding messages from me on *both* their phones makes me look like a bloody stalker.

So instead of looking like a stalker – I become one, and go straight to Josh's account on Instagram to see if there are any photos or stories of him in Aberystwyth. Why didn't I think of this before? Yes, all I need is a snap of Josh and Amy in a café, a selfie by the sea, all blustery; Amy in her red-check scarf and one of Josh's huge jumpers with sleeves that go way beyond her hands. One photo, one comment on a post – anything to let me know he's there, she's safe and I can get on with my life.

I scroll through his latest pictures, but at each snap my heart dies like a phone battery, dropping to five per cent when I see he's not in Aberystwyth with Amy, he's here in Worcester. He's at the rugby, then a local pub, another photo of him at home with his dog. Amy always comments on his photos, but she hasn't, which

I quickly flick to Amy's photos, and Josh hasn't interacted with her either. Why? Is it over? Is she devastated? Is that why I haven't heard anything? Should I go to her? No. I'm overreacting to a few little things that are all explainable and when she calls me shortly we will laugh at how fertile my imagination is and she'll tell me I'm mad. I can hear her now, 'Mum, you weirdo, stop lurking online. I'm fine!'

Until then though, there's no harm in just seeing if I can find out what's going on. Having 'stalked' Josh's online accounts (and kicking myself for not having a Snapchat account, which may provide info about Amy's whereabouts), I scroll through my phone to see if I have any of her other friends' numbers.

I glance over at Richard, who's watching me with a concerned look on his face, but when I meet his eyes, he turns away. And I go back to my phone.

# CHAPTER FOUR

As I sit around waiting for contact, for a sign that my daughter's okay, my mind goes back and forth, round and round, just trying to think about when we last talked. Did she say anything I should have heard but didn't? Are there any clues on her social media I've missed? She knows I'll be frantic, and so will want to let me know if she's okay. But what if she isn't? *What if she isn't?*

I wonder if I should have really tried to convince her to take a year out, she's so young to be living independently. But she'd have refused to listen, she wanted this so badly no one could have talked her out of it.

Before she headed off to Freshers' Week, Amy and I shopped together for her new life. *Her* priority was to find the largest bottle of cheap gin (that she could use as an ice breaker with flatmates), while mine was to seek out the softest towels and warmest blankets to wrap her in. I was also keen to make sure she had a hundred metres of kitchen roll to clean up the vomit produced by that large bottle of cheap gin.

I saw it as my job to equip her for every eventuality in my absence: a first-aid box; rubber gloves; toilet rolls; cotton and thread; a compiled folder of favourite recipes on which I'd scrawled, 'Like Mama Makes'. I wanted her to take a little bit of home with her – I think, subconsciously, it was helping me as much as I hoped it would her. But in the weeks before she left, I'd wake in the middle of the night, horrified at the prospect of noise, the laughter, the music, the buzz of her phone. And I'd lie in the dark feeling so alone, while Richard snored quietly beside me. In those solitary hours, somewhere between midnight and dawn, I worried about everything. From her not locking the door to her room, to sharing with flatmates she didn't get on with. And whichever way I thought about it, I just wanted her to stay at home, the daughter I'd filled eighteen years of my life with. The daughter whose nappy I'd changed, whose feet I'd tickled, whose tears I'd dried. The daughter who was going away and I honestly doubted she could survive without me.

I remember telling her how I'd felt on her first day at school. 'I wanted to walk you to your classroom and loiter in the playground once you'd gone in,' I said. 'And peer through the railings and watch you at break-time to make sure you were okay, that you had friends to play with and no one was mean to you.'

'Aww, Mum, that's cute,' she'd said, giving me a hug.

What I didn't add was that now, on this big, grown-up journey, I felt exactly the same way. I wanted to hold her hand on the first day at university, protect her from the spiked drinks, the mean girls, the dark walk home with no taxi in sight.

It was clear during the supermarket shop for her new life that the gentle fraying of mother–daughter ties had already begun.

'You'll need these in case you have friends over,' I'd said, holding up a pack of drinking glasses. 'Only two pounds for six,' I'd added, standing by the supermarket shelf while pointing at the box, like a saleswoman in an advert.

'In case I have friends over? Mum, I'm not fifty,' she'd laughed affectionately, then rolled her eyes before adding, 'Anyway no one drinks out of glasses anymore.'

'Oh… so what are we drinking from if not glasses…?'

'Everyone drinks with straws from fishbowls at uni.'

'My daughter slurping vodka from a huge fishbowl? Yet another distracted by fairy lights to discreetly put the pack of glasses into the trolley.

'These fairy lights are so adorable I can't stand it,' she'd said. 'I just have to have them!'

I knew she'd silently thank me for the glassware when her and her new friends had bottles of God knows what and no receptacles. She'd think, 'Mum was right,' as she poured something akin to lighter fluid into one of those glasses from a great height. I had her back. I always will, because I'm all she has, and it's a huge responsibility. She has her best friend Jodie, Zoe's daughter, but it's not the same, especially now they are also miles apart.

I call Jodie, but there's no response. Teenagers never pick up – they seem to have their phones on permanent silence and use them for everything but phone calls. I leave her a message asking if she's heard from Amy. I know they aren't as close as they were since Amy went away, but Jodie might have *some* idea where she is. I'm praying she'll text me back to say something along the lines of: 'Hi Kat, didn't she tell you she's doing a sponsored social media silence for Battersea Dog's Home,' or 'She's off on some charity trek around Snowdonia where there's no signal'. I rack my brains to think if I've forgotten something Amy had told me she might be doing, but I can't think of anything, apart from the fact she said she was coming home.

'I can't get hold of Jodie either,' I say to Richard, who's trying to work the microwave to heat the bloody packet dinners. Like everything technical in this house, Amy is the only one who can fathom it, from Wi-Fi to TV to my laptop – she's a teenager, they know this stuff.

'Jodie's probably no wiser than you as to Amy's plans for the weekend,' he says, absently punching in numbers, hoping something might warm up.

'Maybe I could call her flat at uni?' The halls are broken up into small en suite rooms and a shared kitchen; sometimes they don't see each other for days. Her flatmates probably won't know if she's even there or not; they're all living their own lives. They won't be checking on where she's gone or what time she gets in, staying up to make sure she gets back safely or offering to pick her up.

When Amy lived at home, I was always around to collect her, even in the small hours. I couldn't sleep until she was back. I didn't relish the 3 a.m. call to pick up her and a group of friends from a local nightclub, but I lay awake anyway, waiting up for her, my phone on the bedside table, on full alert. The idea of her walking the streets would have terrified me. Having to get out of bed and drive through Worcester to be greeted by a rowdy gaggle of Amy's drunken friends wasn't my idea of a Saturday night, but I'd smile as they recounted their evening in loud, excited voices, before dropping each one off at their respective homes, waiting until they'd gone inside, creeping into the darkness so as not to wake their parents. I don't understand how anyone can sleep when their teenager is out after midnight. And I feel the same now, even though she's away – why should that change just because your child happens to live somewhere else? I'm still her mum, and she's still my little girl.

I gaze through the kitchen window, pulling my cardigan around me, wondering if Jodie's listened to my message, questioning what to do if I don't hear from Amy tonight. Is it an emergency? Should I call the police and say my teenage daughter's missing at university – when I don't even know if she is?

I comfort myself with the thought that I haven't seen her Snapchat and, for all I know, today's frothy coffees and crazy selfies with flowers in her hair are all over that. What I'd give for a silly photo of Amy with the nose of a dog or cat ears right now.

'Kat, do we have any lemons for the paella?' Richard's voice penetrates my thoughts as I stare out at the darkness. His pretension of worry dragging me under. For God's sake, it's paella in name only; I almost laugh.

'I think it'll take more than a bloody lemon to turn that mush into something edible,' I say, aware of the November chill sneaking up the lawn and under the door.

'Just pimping it up,' he murmurs, now opening cupboards, presumably seeking the redemption of herbs and spices. I'm not remotely hungry.

I check my phone for the millionth time, feeling helpless, out of control, then look up to see Richard watching me again.

'Kat, let go – she'll be *fine*,' he's saying, but I detect a sting of irritation creeping back into his voice.

'I *have* let go, she's over a hundred miles away, living with a bunch of strangers – how much more *can* I let go?' I feel sick, pinpricks of tears sting my eyes. *Where is she?* Sometimes I feel so alone when it comes to being Amy's mother.

Richard must see the fear in my eyes, the threat that I might just tip over, and he walks towards me, puts his arms around my shoulders and looks into my eyes. He knows what I've been through in the past and he tries to be there for me, he wants to be supportive, but at this point no one can do anything. I just want to know – *need* to know – Amy is okay and everything will be fine. Only Amy can make this better, and all the clichés and words of comfort Richard wants to wrap tightly around me are meaningless and won't erase any of my growing fears.

'Okay.' His brain is now working on producing yet more clichés – only these will be evidence-based and of a practical nature. 'So, she went out last night, she's been really busy today, and will call later… or tomorrow.'

Good god, does he really think it's that easy?

'Oh, thanks, Richard, that makes it all fine. I mean, why didn't you say you have a crystal ball, why am I worrying when you can

The hurt look again. But this time it doesn't appease me.

'What? Is that supposed to help? Because it doesn't.' I sigh, wishing he'd get back to pimping his sodding paella. I can't decide if it's a man thing or a Richard thing, but when I'm stressed, he often has this ability to make me even more stressed. 'How many times do I have to say this, Richard? She hasn't contacted me, or been active online since yesterday, that's *never* happened before.'

He sighs and pulls away, his boxed paella is calling. 'I understand why you're like this, but, the thing is, she's only just gone to university – you've got another three years of it – we can't go through this every time she goes offline for a few hours.'

What he's saying makes perfect sense. But he doesn't know everything, he doesn't know about me and Amy and Tony. I want to tell him about how she's recently been asking me questions – but if I do, Richard might want some answers too.

'Just stop worrying,' he's saying, but I'm thinking about the last time I talked to Amy and wondering if there's a clue.

'Kat, forget going anywhere and doing anything tonight – just relax,' he says, sprinkling dried parsley onto bright yellow rice. 'I think you need to get used to the idea that it might be tomorrow before she gets in touch.'

'And I think *you* need to get used to the idea that I will do exactly what I need to when it comes to *my* daughter,' I say.

He doesn't answer.

I sweep across the kitchen and open the fridge, where I half-heartedly gaze into the white abyss, wondering only where my little girl is. I find a couple of lemons and reach for them. I stand there for a while with my head in the fridge, feeling their cool, textured skin in both palms, grateful for a moment of peace. I'd like to climb inside and curl up, away from all the worry, the fear, the danger. Then, I hear my phone buzz, abandon all lemons, and run towards it.

# CHAPTER FIVE

'It's a text from Jodie,' I say, clicking on the screen, my mouth dry.

*Hey Kat! Soz haven't heard from Amy, she's at uni isn't she?*

Jodie's message is like a smack across the face. She was my last hope – but knows no more than I do. Less even. I was really hoping she might hold the golden key.

*Has she been on snapchat?* I start to text my response, but then realise it's silly to text when the information I need is so urgent. So I call Jodie's number to speak to her directly. But she doesn't answer.

'For fuck's sake, she just texted me, I know she's on her phone so why isn't she answering me?' I say, on the verge of tears. 'What's wrong with them all. Why doesn't anyone pick up anymore? I bet if I sent her a sodding selfie of me gazing into a mirror in my knickers she'd get back to me. That's all the Instagram generation ever seem to respond to,' I say, sounding like a grumpy old lady.

'A Pavlovian response to a photograph of one of their kind in underwear,' Richard says, and we smile at each other across the kitchen, two confused people in their forties struggling with this brave new world and making light of it. Our previous spat is now forgotten and we're back to being a team again.

I shake my head. 'Jodie hasn't heard from her.'

'Did you expect her to?'

'I don't know, I just thought she might have seen her online.'

'Of course, they're best friends.'

'Oh…'

'What?' His grasp on Amy's life is tenuous and his inability to keep up frustrating.

'I thought they'd fallen out.'

'No. I think Jodie was feeling a bit left behind and Amy said she was being a bit annoying, but they sorted it.'

'Good. But Jodie is annoying.'

I give him a look. 'That isn't worthy of you, Richard, she's a teenage girl. They are *supposed* to be annoying.'

'Fair enough, she's doing a good job then. And, Kat, just because Jodie hasn't heard from her, it doesn't mean there's a problem,' he offers. 'They're in different towns now, Amy has made new friends, they probably aren't in touch like they used to be.'

I shrug. 'Yeah, I suppose, but I don't think they've lost touch, Amy mentions her when we talk. They might be far away but they still 'talk' in their WhatsApp-Snapchat-Bluetooth-teenage way.' I smile.

'I thought Amy had finally given her the push.'

'No. I can't imagine why you'd even think that. They've grown up together; Zoe and I are so close, the girls will always be—'

'Isn't that the problem?' he asks, talking over me. 'Your friendship with Zoe's such a big part of your life, it was almost inevitable that the girls would be friends. They *had* to be. But I've always wondered how much Amy has resented babysitting her mum's friend's daughter?'

'Wow, you're suddenly all knowing about Amy's friendships,' I snap. 'And what do you mean by babysitting? They're the same age.'

'I didn't mean it literally. It just seems that Amy's the grown-up and Jodie's in her wake.'

Richard's seen what he thinks is evident, when it isn't – he's made a judgement and there's no changing him. Like I say, a lawyer

'You just don't like Zoe, so you don't like Jodie,' I say. Richard's always been a bit put out at the time Zoe and I spend together. He isn't jealous exactly, just sometimes I get the feeling he thinks I should be with him when I'm with her. It was easier before Zoe's divorce; her husband got along with Richard and the four of us were friends, so when I saw Zoe, Richard was with Pete. Now it's back to just me and Zoe, which naturally excludes Richard, especially if we're going to a girlie chick flick or on a women's march.

'Just always thought there's something sneaky about that kid,' he says, leaning on the kitchen counter.

'Don't be mean – Jodie isn't sneaky. She can be a bit shy, that's why she and Amy get along, Amy's the more confident one,' I say rather proudly. Amy used to be incredibly shy when she was younger, but in the past few years she's matured and blossomed.

'Jodie's had a tough time with her parents' divorce,' he concedes, 'but you and Amy aren't responsible for her. I doubt Amy would still be friends with her if it wasn't for the pressure from you and Zoe to "play nicely".'

'Pressure? That's absolute nonsense,' I snap. 'Amy's strong, she knows what she wants and she does what she wants – I certainly don't pressure her.'

'It isn't an *obvious* pressure,' he says this gently. 'It's just that she cares about you, she knows it makes you happy that she's friends with Jodie.'

I can see why he'd think that, but he doesn't understand the complexities of female friendship and he's wrong, but I'm not in the mood to argue. Zoe and I have a good, strong friendship, we share so much and she gets me in a way no one else ever has – even Richard. Yes, it's lovely that both mums and daughters are friends, and over the years we've had some wonderful times together, the four of us. But Zoe and I both know that if our kids stop being

'I wonder if it would be easier if we didn't have social media and mobile phones,' I say, changing the subject. 'I mean, if Amy isn't missing, and there was no way of communicating, then I'd be none the wiser.'

He smiles. 'Yes, when we left home, our parents were lucky if they got a call once a month.'

I think back to my own hurried calls to my mother from a communal phone in a communal college hallway. 'Our children live such different lives than we did. They communicate with the touch of a screen, the click of a mouse and knowledge is always at their fingertips. They'll never have to wonder about anything, it's all on Google.'

'And we've never had to order a set of *Encyclopaedia Britannica,* spending a fortune just so Amy can do her homework.' He laughs.

'When we left home and school we left people behind, but Amy and Jodie's generation take everyone with them. They're all milling about on Instagram and Snapchat, it's like a permanent high-school reunion with group chats and selfies every few seconds. They can be in different cities, different countries, and still talk every day.' I shake my forty-something head, smiling at the hugeness of their lives. 'In fact, until recently, Amy and Jodie were sending a photo to each other every single day on Snapchat. It's called streaming I think – like a chain you can't break.'

'No pressure then.' He smiles. 'I don't do that with my Snapchat – I can barely work through it.'

I'm surprised. 'I didn't know you had Snapchat?'

'I have to. Well, I got an account when I was working on that case – you remember, the two gangs, the shooting? They were all on Snapchat and WhatsApp and so I had to join to make sense of it all.'

My surprise is replaced immediately with a glimmer of hope. 'Are you friends with Amy?'

'Do you think you might be able to "see" her on there?'

He shrugs, gets out his phone and what follows is a scene from a sitcom, where two old people try and work out alien technology. He presses the screen, while I make increasingly anxious suggestions – and nothing really happens.

'I don't know,' he says, eventually putting down his phone. 'I'm not very adept at it, like I say, I only have it because I needed to know how it works for the case.'

'But you still don't.' I sigh, as this particular glimmer of hope disappears on the horizon.

'No. Nor have I ever snap-streamed… or whatever it's called.'

'I read somewhere that some kids have been doing it for years, just keeping the thing going,' I say vaguely. I don't understand it, I wish I'd listened more carefully to Amy when she explained Snapchat.

'When she's next home, I'll ask her to help me set an account up that will help me see where she is,' I say. 'I'm sure I read something about a "finding your friends" app. She can help me download that. I don't care if she thinks I'm stalking her, I can't go through this again.'

Abandoning Richard to his Mediterranean cuisine, I go back to the window, seeking guidance or inspiration. My instinct is to call the university, the police, send out some kind of flare. But what if she's just in her room asleep? I consider Amy's response to this invasion: *'The police are banging on my door because I haven't texted you since yesterday? Really, Mum, WTF?'*

Richard had a point when he said I have to get through three years of this. I must find a way of managing myself, let alone Amy. We're early on in the university term, I can't call the police every time my daughter doesn't get in touch. I'll risk embarrassing her and look like a lunatic mother. But my head and heart are at war with each other – and what if I'm right? What if she's seriously

I rack my brains trying to think of someone I can call, anyone who can give me some information. I don't know her flatmates, and stupidly didn't take any of their numbers when she moved in. Suddenly my phone bleeps, making me jump. My finger ends tingle with shock and I rush over to retrieve it from the kitchen counter, almost tripping. I pick it up to see a new message from Jodie, and can't open it quickly enough, I'm all fingers and thumbs.

*Hey Kat, I'll put a message out on Snapchat to ask if anyone's seen her, I'll say her mum's looking for her.*
*J x*

'If I'm wrong and Amy's fine, she's going to be SO pissed off with me,' I say. 'I can only imagine what she'll think seeing a message from Jodie on Snapchat to say "Amy's mum's looking for her."' I look at Richard.

'Not what Amy would call cool,' he says. I detect slight disapproval in his voice.

'I know, but there's a part of me thinks if she's pissed off enough and she's okay, she'll call me to give me a telling off for embarrassing her,' I say, returning to the kitchen stool next to him. 'Amy's uni friends and flatmates might see the message and tell Amy.'

'That's good, isn't it?' he says.

'Yeah, but you know what they're like. Jodie'll make some vague request about Amy's whereabouts, then be distracted by something and forget all about it,' I say. 'Amy's just the same – me and Zoe despair of them sometimes. Amy can't even load a dishwasher and I've sent her out into the big wide world expecting her to function. And the bloody flatmates will no doubt be just as clueless. Three of them are boys, and before you say it, I'm not being sexist, but I hate the idea of teenage boys being responsible for the location of my daughter. They could be sitting next to Amy in the kitchen,

'Sexist,' Richard confirms, turning his back to wash his hands in the sink.

I think about the boys in the flat, and remember that one of them has a bit of a thing for Amy; she mentioned it recently. She said she found him 'a bit much', but when I asked her if he made her feel uncomfortable, she laughed it off. Oh God. Should I have pursued this? My precious daughter has moved in with six strangers – three boys and two other girls – and who knows what kind of people they are? The allocations to rooms are random, decided at the click of a button once the offer of a place comes in, they had the potential to have such a huge impact on her university life and beyond. Friends for life, lovers, stalkers… the more I thought about this the more I wanted to put her in the car and take her home. And thinking about it now, on that first day, I had Tom marked down as a future serial killer.

Everyone else's parents had moved them in and gone home, but being me I'd brought a bottle of wine to break the ice and meet all the flatmates. I wanted to vet them all, I wasn't leaving my precious daughter to live with people I didn't know anything about. 'Call me Kat,' I'd said, doling out paper cups of wine, asking them about themselves in what I hoped was a subtle way. Not surprisingly after about ten minutes, when I'd wheedled out of them their parents' professions and pretty much their inside-leg measurements, everyone had disappeared to their rooms. Except Tom. He seemed happy to sit with us, while staring at Amy, and drinking wine in our awkward threesome. So I asked Amy if I could take the obligatory photo of her sitting at the desk in her tiny room and we left Tom alone in the kitchen.

The prospect of leaving her had terrified me for months, and now the moment had arrived, it was every bit as bad as I'd expected it to be. Like most mums I'd been part of everything my daughter had done in her life. From supervising, to participating, to spectating, to collecting; I always had a role, played a part, and even right up until she went away I'd pick her up after a party in 'Mum's Uber'. I'd always known how her evening ended. But not that night. For the first time in mine and Amy's life, I would drive away and leave her for longer than a sleepover or a school trip – I would leave her for weeks.

I was convinced I would never sleep peacefully again. The fear and emptiness overwhelmed me. So I took my time with the desk-photo. Deserting her in this tiny, desolate little room was against every maternal instinct in my body, especially after what she'd been through. I was trying not to cry and we sat for a few last minutes alone in her room chatting, like we always do… like we always did.

'I'm homesick already,' she'd said, and I hugged her and told her it was a lovely place and she was so lucky to live by the sea. 'You're going to have an amazing time,' I'd added.

'I know, but I'll miss Josh, and I'll miss you and I'll miss tickling Harry's fat, furry belly.' She'd looked as if she was about to cry.

'Harry's belly will always be fat and furry and available for tickling,' I joked, trying not to cry myself. 'And he can't wait for your first visit home for a tickling, but until then I'll do the honours and make sure his belly is well tickled.'

She'd smiled, and I saw the excitement and fear in her eyes; it reminded me so much of the past, I had to look away.

'You're going to be fine, you're my big, strong girl,' I'd said, repeating a sentence I'd used before in a different time and place.

She'd nodded, wiping her face with the back of her arm. At this, I almost crumpled. I wanted to say, 'Look, why don't you come back with me? We can get you a place at a university near home, you could go to Worcester Uni with Jodie and live at home?' But of course I didn't, because I knew this was the right thing to do, and was what Amy wanted. And whatever anyone may say about me now or in the future – Amy's wants and needs are, and always will be, my priority. 'So screw your courage to the sticking place,' I'd quoted *Macbeth* as I stood up, 'and do what scares you the most. What would that be?'

'Knocking on one of the others' doors?'

'Okay, then that's what you have to do,' I said, mock sternly, playing the game we'd often played when she was younger. She'd been so incredibly shy, she couldn't go to another child's birthday party unless I was with her, so I'd invented the game, because if Amy likes one thing it's a challenge.

'Okay,' she said, taking a deep breath.

'Yeah! Er, but perhaps don't knock on Tom's door, eh?' I pulled a face, which she mirrored.

'Yeah, maybe not him,' she'd laughed. 'He's a bit… scary, isn't he?'

A bit scary put it mildly, he'd freaked me out, and I was twice his age and didn't have to live with him. But I was glad to see she'd picked up on his weirdness, her radar was good. At best, he was a hanger-on who she may not be able to shake off, at worst… at worst, well I'd refused to think about that.

I remember Amy walking towards her door, ushering me gently through, and my realisation that the dynamic of our lives had suddenly, irrevocably, altered. I now had to be asked to stay, to wait to be invited – it wasn't my right as Amy's mother to just *be* here. We were beginning the delicate process of extricating ourselves from each other, two lives entwined like ivy, twisting around the other in knotty clumps grown over and around each other through the years, that had to be gradually undone. We both had to be strong, and at that point, thank God, Amy was being strong for both of us. And while I was to return home, to the past and everything we knew, in a minute we'd say goodbye and she'd knock on the door of a stranger, waiting in their own

She walked me to the outer doors linking arms, and before I left we hugged. I thought I'd never let her go and had to stop myself from breaking down by making silly jokes. 'Don't you forget your old, decrepit mother,' I said and she'd laughed along, humouring me as always. We stood with our arms around each other for a long time, and eventually it was Amy who ended the embrace. She was ready to start her new life, so I took my cue and with hollow legs and a breaking heart I walked away, turning to see her waving from the step, further and further away. I waved and waved until she went inside and I climbed into my car and honestly don't know how I drove back that night. I'd only gone a couple of miles when I stopped at a garage for petrol and it was then the tears that had been building for hours – for months, in fact – came. Here was the daughter I'd worried about for so long, and she was finally flying away, which she was meant to do, but even so, I felt like I'd left one of my limbs behind and had this compulsion to go and ask her, 'Are you sure about this?' Silly, I know, but the sense of loss was the same as leaving her on her first day at school, and I was struck once more at the shock of how quickly our children grow and leave us inch by inch. Amy's going away to university was just another part of the process, even if it was the most difficult yet, but I knew what I had to do. So I'd left her that night in her little room, with the soft towels, matching bed linen and the set of six glasses I knew she'd thank me for. Because Mum always knows best.

Richard's voice drags me back into the present, announcing that, 'Dinner will be served shortly,' and I smile as he goes off upstairs to change.

When I hear him on the phone, I guess it's work, and know he'll be a while, so I make a cup of coffee and sit in the comfy chair by the window. The hot coffee soothes my insides, jagged with worry, and I spend a long time in the dim silence, seduced into

I wait for Amy to call or text, while remembering her first steps, the little red plastic car Tony and I bought for her first birthday, the way she'd lie between us on the bed, her little baby legs kicking with sheer joy. What a wonderful time that was, just the three of us, unaware of the horror that was to come.

# CHAPTER SIX

In the few weeks since Amy started uni I've made the most of our long, late-night chats over the phone when she's described everything around her, from the lecturer known as 'Professor Perv', to the idiosyncrasies of her new flatmates. And if we haven't actually spoken, she's texted me – always in code. I know that a late-night text in capitals 'EMILY' means that the pretty little blonde biochemistry student has brought another one-night stand back from the pub. And TOM means her rather odd flatmate has knocked on her door again, for 'a chat'.

As I scroll my phone looking for clues in Amy's texts, I smile at the cryptic comments; 'The noise!' and 'OMG!' meant that Emily was having a lovely time in her bedroom with her latest beau. Even through her texts, I can catch the light and colour of Amy's life, her thoughts, new and unformed – but what a fresh take she has of this jaded old world. And the changes – she's like a flashing mood ring – intense and full on, raging against Brexit, furious with Netflix for cancelling her favourite series; loving the Labour party and wearing a badge to prove it, hating Trump and taking the train to London with me to march against him. Such passion, idealism; she wraps herself up in a wonderful sparkly hope for a better world, and I'm lucky enough that she shares it with me.

It's not just the quiet I've had to get used to since she left for uni – it's also the lack of daily drama. Living with a teenage girl is like tuning in to a soap opera, emotions run deep and the potential around the corner. One minute everything's fine and hilarious and the next someone's made a hurtful remark or Josh has said something to upset her and she's in floods. But how much my heart aches for her.

Harry climbs on my knee and I tickle his belly on Amy's behalf, praying she'll be home soon to do this herself.

Richard comes back downstairs; he seems a little tense.

'I heard you on the phone,' I say. 'Everything okay?'

'Yes. Yes of course,' he snaps.

'So it *was* work?'

'Yes, well, there's a lot going on… with the merger.'

'Still, there's not much anyone can do on a Sunday. Is anyone even there?' I'm a little puzzled by this.

'Roger… I called Roger to discuss the meeting tomorrow.'

'But you've been with Roger all weekend, surely…' I realise I'm sounding slightly paranoid, so I leave it.

'We haven't talked about work, we played golf,' he snaps.

'But you said you talked shop all weekend,' I say, confused.

He doesn't look at me, turns away and starts running the tap. Whatever the phone conversation, it seems to have caused his slightly scratchy mood to blossom into something far more tense. He isn't even making silly jokes about our food anymore. I can only guess at the stress levels of everyone at the firm, the merger's been going on a while now and it's apparently intense.

The microwave pings while Richard pours two glasses of water, both now in our own little fug of full-on stress, neither of us in the mood for Spain or Italy tonight, just going through the motions.

We sit opposite each other on stools at the kitchen counter, two plates of nothing in front of us. Richard messes around with the food on his plate, turning ribbons of pasta around his fork slowly, while I count grains of rice – our combined stress thrumming beneath the surface, like the sound of the fridge.

I check my phone several times and, unsurprisingly, it looks

I feared, Jodie hasn't even sent the message. What if Amy's in real trouble? I can't rely on other teenagers to rally, but what can I do?

'Should we call the police?' I hear my cracked voice ask. I can't bear another second of moving fake paella around my plate, I have to *do* something. He looks doubtful, but I can see by his face that Richard is beginning to show signs of concern too. He puts down his fork and stands up, moving towards me, wrapping both arms around my shoulders as I sit on the stool. I let my face fall onto his chest in an attempt to soothe myself.

'Kat?' his voice is quiet, uncertain.

'Yes?' When he doesn't answer, I pull away slightly and look up at him. 'What?'

'I'm sorry. I'm so sorry.'

For a moment I think he might burst into tears, and I'm shocked. 'What are you sorry for?'

Richard composes himself, he's still gently holding onto my upper arm, like he's tethering me to the spot and if he lets go I might just fly away.

'I'm sorry… that Amy hasn't rung, that you're worried. I hate to see you like this, I wish I could make it better.'

'There's nothing you can do, just be here for me until she calls,' I say quietly.

'I shouldn't have left you this weekend.'

I pull away to look at him. 'I was fine. I worked, and I saw Zoe for coffee.' I don't mention lying on Amy's bed, touching her clothes, smelling her perfume, and all the texts I sent asking her to call me. I have no idea how many I sent. *Too many.*

'I know, but you've been through a lot, and I worry this might… trigger something.'

'Richard, I'm fine. And I'll be even better when she calls me.'

'Yes, yes, I know, I wasn't suggesting that you—'

'Well don't, because I'm perfectly okay, and I think this is a

'I just wonder if something's… upset her,' he suggests, and I look at him, puzzled.

'I'm not aware of anything, are you?' I say, worried he might have picked up on something.

'No, no of course not.'

I lift my head and the way he's looking at me makes me think he might know something. But what could Richard possibly know about my daughter that I don't?

'So what do you want to do? About Amy?' he asks.

'*Should* we call the police?' I suggest.

'Do you think it's a bit soon? You haven't heard from her since yesterday lunchtime, is there really any cause for concern yet? I mean, we can't go bothering the police again, not after what happened at the lido last—'

'I don't care. If something's happened to her, then I *will* bother the bloody police. I'd never forgive myself if something happened to her.'

He doesn't answer me, but I can tell he's vehemently against this. Richard is still of the belief that Amy's having a wild abandoned time, but I really don't think she is. I just wish he'd believe me. I also feel like Zoe isn't fully on board with me either and I want Jodie to get back to me and let me know if anyone knows anything. But none of them are taking this seriously, because last time I made a fuss and was mistaken. But this time I really don't believe I am.

'So… should I call the police?' I say to Richard.

'I don't know, Kat. It's up to you.' He's weary, defeated, he doesn't want to be part of this. In Richard's eyes, I'm being foolish, he's already distancing himself from any call I might make to the police.

'As much as I want to call them, get help, it scares me, because she might just be fine,' I admit.

'Exactly,' he looks almost relieved. He really doesn't want me to call the police, he was so embarrassed last time. 'Give it more

'But what if she isn't fine? What if there really is a problem and we're sitting here forcing ourselves to eat a shit dinner and Amy's hurt, or upset? Richard, she might have been taken ill.'

He's slowly shaking his head. 'No. There's no reason to think that, she was fine last time we saw her.'

'That was more than two weeks ago.'

'But you speak to her every day. If she had any health issues surely she'd have said.'

'Perhaps, but I don't *know*, I can't monitor her like I used to, she doesn't even have a doctor here anymore.'

'Oh, Kat, please don't embarrass her by trying to speak with her doctor again.'

'I wouldn't,' I snap, suddenly feeling exposed, vulnerable. I just worry about her and wanted to make sure she was okay.

'She's an adult and her consultations are private, even from you, her mother.'

'I know, I know, I wasn't trying to pry. I used to make her appointments and go along with her, but when she turned eighteen she insisted on going alone. So I popped into the surgery to ask if she was okay, I mean, they knew me they know her history. But the receptionist was really quite rude. So if she is ill, I'll have no way of knowing.'

'She's not sick, Kat, she's *fine*,' he says, pointlessly. He doesn't *know*.

'But I don't *know* that. I've always been there, and now I just sometimes feel like I'm, I don't know… redundant.'

'You're not. She loves you and needs you just like she always did – just not in such practical terms. She's becoming independent and that's what we want for her. Don't we?'

'Yes, of course,' I say dismissively, while checking my watch. 'Look it's 9 p.m. I'll try her number one more time.'

Richard's shaking his head but I'm ignoring him as I press

looks back at me. Is she in trouble? Does she need me? But as I press the number I imagine Amy answering and laughing about me worrying about her when she's just been wrapped up in some social event or flat crisis and lost track of time.

I wait for the beeps, then, 'Damn, straight to voicemail.'

'Perhaps she doesn't want to talk?' Richard suggests brusquely.

'To me?' I say, shocked that he could think that. 'Why?'

'I… I don't know. I'm going there,' I say into the thick silence.

He's clearly shocked at this, but what else can I do?

'Aberystwyth? Now?'

'Yes – *now*,' I snap. Then I suddenly remember the tiny little ribbon of hope tangled up in all the darkness and uncertainty, and I pick up my phone, my lifeline. 'But first I should call Jodie again to see if she's had any kind of response to her Snapchat and she's forgotten to let me know.'

But, surprise, surprise, Jodie's phone goes straight to voicemail again. I leave a message asking her to call me straight away.

'Amy could be with her flatmates in the kitchen, her phone might be in her room,' I say, imagining her sitting around the big kitchen table drinking tea or alcohol, blissfully unaware of what she'll refer to as, 'Mum's latest drama'.

Meanwhile, as I play this drama out, Richard potters around the kitchen clearing up our barely touched meals, like nothing's wrong.

'I could kick myself for not getting her flatmates' numbers,' I mutter to myself. I rather stupidly took Amy's advice on that one. 'Oh my God, Mum, no. You can't have their numbers. If you called my flatmates, they'd think I was a freak. Just call me, or text me, and if I don't answer straight away, I'll get back to you – you know I will.' *And yes, Amy, I do know that – because you always have. But this time you haven't. Why?*

# CHAPTER SEVEN

In the end, I decide to call Josh rather than go to Aberystwyth. I need to do everything I can to find out where Amy is before I rush off in the direction of Wales. He doesn't pick up, and I wonder if I should be worried or it's just a teen thing. Perhaps it isn't 'cool' to answer your phone when it rings. All I know is that for 'old people' it's bloody frustrating. I leave a voice message asking him when he last heard from Amy, and if he can please get back to me ASAP, then I text him with the same message, which may seem obsessive, but I hope he'll see how desperate I am, take pity on me and call back. After waiting twenty long minutes for some kind of acknowledgement of my text or voice message, I have to stop checking my phone. I think I might go mad.

Then I call Zoe, who asks if I'd like her to come over.

'Do you mind?' I ask, knowing Richard isn't really engaging with this, he's just pottering around the kitchen. I know he thinks I'm being silly, but I don't care, I can feel it in my gut. 'Something's really wrong,' I hear myself say over the phone.

'I'm sure it isn't,' she says.

What has to happen for someone to believe me? I know Amy isn't at a party, or a sleepover, or on holiday. And despite saying she was coming home – she isn't here either. *So where the hell is she?*

'She may have jumped on the train last minute and she's on her way,' I suggest, more to placate myself than anything.

'Yes, she could be anywhere between here and there. I'll ask Jodie if she's heard.'

'She hadn't heard from her earlier.'

'Yes, Jodie said you'd called.'

'Is she at home with you?' I try not to sound envious.

'Yes, she came home just now, she surprised me.'

'Lovely.' I force a smile, even though she can't see it. I'm pleased Zoe's spending time with her daughter, but it's only enhancing my own fear of loss. I was hoping for the same this weekend, I'd bought all Amy's favourite food; the fridge thinks it's Christmas. 'Hey, if Amy gets back here perhaps the four of us girls could go out tomorrow? Bit of shopping, afternoon tea?' I'm trying to be positive.

'I'd love to,' Zoe says, 'but I think Jodie's back at uni tomorrow… it's Monday.'

'Oh, of course, sorry, I'm not thinking straight. Amy's got tomorrow and Tuesday free, that's why she was coming home. Could you put Jodie on the phone?' I ask, trying not to sound desperate.

'She's having a bath at the moment, I'll get her to call you the minute she's out. Okay?'

'Of course, thanks love, I'm just a bit anxious, you know?'

'I *do* know,' she says kindly. 'But I *also* know you really mustn't let it get the better of you. I understand how you feel, but there's really no need to get into a state about it, I'm sure wherever Amy is, she's fine.'

She's beginning to sound like Richard. I thank her, tell her not to come over, to stay with Jodie, and promise to stay in touch and let her know if there's any news.

Putting down my phone, I steal another glance at the screen to see if there are any messages, but there aren't.

'What did Zoe say?' Richard asks.

'Same as you. Calm down, shut up, don't be an idiot. And "*she's fine*",' I say in an annoying voice.

A half-smile crosses his face. 'Well, for once I'm with Zoe on this.' Then he looks up. 'Didn't you say Amy's got Monday and

Tuesday off uni? What if she's decided to just go away for a couple of days with some friends?'

'In November? She wouldn't. Not without telling me.'

'Kat.' He sighs. 'She's eighteen, she doesn't tell her mother *everything*.'

I don't respond. I've had enough of this not knowing, of this terrible ache in my chest that will only disappear when I know she's okay. So I pick up my phone.

'I'm calling the university,' I say, getting up from my seat and walking away from Richard, back towards the window. There's no view here now, no trees against the sky, they've been swallowed up by the blackness, that's all there is, and now the rain is pattering on the window, and I can hear wind in the distance. All I can think is, I hope to God that Amy isn't out there somewhere.

I get through to the university, who put me through to various help desks who pass me on to twenty-four-hour security.

'I haven't heard from my daughter since yesterday,' I say, aware this sounds a little weak, a touch obsessive-mother. I can almost see the guy at the other end of the phone rolling his eyes. Another doubter. 'I know, it doesn't sound like an emergency exactly – but it's not *like* her,' I go on to explain. 'This is very worrying, it's never happened before,' I add this with deliberate alarm in my voice, to get through to the man on the other end of the phone just how serious this is.

He's pleasant, calm and keen to point out that as Amy is eighteen years old 'the university is unable to confirm the student's identity or attendance at the institution'.

I, in turn, inform him this is 'absurd' and ask, 'What if she's been hurt, or she didn't come home last night, what if...?' I can't even finish the sentence; I can't *think* it, let alone say it.

'Let me assure you, your concerns will be taken seriously,' is all he says, as if he's reading from a script.

'So – what now? Do I wait for you to get back to me or should I head on over there? Will you call the police?' I turn towards

Richard, who looks up at this, he's loading the dishwasher, glasses on his head, shirtsleeves rolled up, like any other Sunday evening. Except it isn't. And every minute that goes by is turning this evening into something very different.

The voice on the other end of the phone tells me it's my call, and I must do as I see fit – or words to that effect. It's all very officious, but the man assures me that they will 'respond appropriately'.

'Whatever that means,' I say, putting down the phone and returning to the dark window, my arms folded around me. Lost.

'Let's wait,' Richard says from behind me. 'Please let's not blow this out of all proportion, Kat, until we know. Until we really know that she's missing. There may not even be a problem.'

But there *is* a problem. No one is listening.

# CHAPTER EIGHT

'I've got to go, Richard,' I say, facing him. 'I'm driving myself mad just pacing round waiting for a call.'

I see his face drop. 'No, Kat. You're not heading out to Aberystwyth now. It's a two-hour journey, along a mountain road. It's November and it's after 9 p.m. Have you seen the weather outside?'

From the pattering sound on the windows I'm aware the rain is harder now, and my heart sinks. But I feel this compulsion to go out there into the wind and the rain to find her.

'I don't know what else to do,' I say, tearful now. 'I feel so bloody helpless,' I cry, not thinking, just rushing around the kitchen, grabbing my warm jacket from the coat stand, while wrapping a thick scarf around my neck.

'No, Kat. Don't just set off like this... wait. What if she calls? What if she's on her way here?'

'And what if she isn't? What if something's happened? I'll sit up all night anyway. I know you think I'm mad, but I have to do something.'

'Yes, but this isn't the answer. You're doing that Kat thing of responding only with your emotions and tearing around here like a headless chicken. You can't just head off into the night, you're likely to have an accident – or cause one.' He's following me from the kitchen through to the living room as I search for my handbag. 'And if she is on her way home, what then? She turns up here and you're in Wales and... Kat, it's madness. It's bloody madness. Why are you so hell-bent on making something *of* this?' he asks, and I stop.

'And why are you so hell-bent on making *nothing* of this?'

For a moment we just stare at each other.

'I… I feel so helpless, Richard.' I'm angry with him, but I say this in a calm voice so he doesn't think I'm losing it and try to stop me. Right now, I'm finding calm hard to do, but I pull my jacket around me and face him.

'Okay, okay, call the police.' He holds up both his hands in a surrendering gesture. 'Do *that* before you set off. I still think it's too soon to register her as a missing person, but you can at least take the police's advice – because, let's face it, you'll never take mine.'

I ignore his petty little remark, there are far bigger things going on than his hurt face because I refuse to do as he suggests. He still seems to think I'm overreacting, but he knows me well, and he knows I won't rest until I know Amy's safe. Our relationship was forged in pain, and Richard is only too aware I still live with the threat of losing my daughter every day.

Eventually I find my handbag in the living room, check my car keys are inside and, against Richard's advice, I leave the house. I should probably call the police, what I'm doing doesn't make sense, but instinct is driving me forward, and I have this compulsion, this need to search for her, like I have a sixth sense and only I can find her. It's pitch-black, blowing a gale, and rain is slashing diagonally across the darkness. I run to the car and jump in, relieved to be dry, but unable to see through the windscreen for the splashing of wind-lashed rain hitting the glass. But I don't care that I can't see in front of me, I'm going to Aberystwyth to find Amy, and if she's having a lovely time and simply forgot to let me know, then that's fine – it's better than waiting, and waiting.

I'm about to start the car, when Richard makes me jump, appearing at the driver's window, carrying a large blanket. 'I can't let you go alone,' he's saying, as I wind down the window. 'I'll come too,' he offers, still in his slippers, rain smacking his face.

I know it's the last thing he wants to do, and I honestly don't want to drag him on a journey that might be fruitless. 'Look, Richard,' I start, but he runs round to the other side of the car. He opens the passenger door and sits in the seat, leaving the door slightly open, a sign he isn't really committed to coming along.

'Call the police first, get them to check the flat,' he says.

'I'm not sure I want to do that yet, because she might have just lost her phone or it's damaged and she's fine… or, as you said earlier, she might just be out.'

'Exactly!' he snaps, irritated. 'She might just be out, and what will you do then?'

'Nothing, I won't need to do anything, but at least when she turns up at her room this torment will end.'

'But you can't drive all the way there and all the way back tonight.'

'No, I'll sleep on Amy's floor and take her out for a full Welsh breakfast in the morning. I'll be back by lunchtime,' I say with fake brightness.

I reach for his hand, wipe the speckles of rainwater from it and calmly try and convince him I'll be okay, but just at that point, the wind whips up even more. It's battering the trees, it's thundering past, making the car shudder. Am I being foolish?

Richard must see the glint of doubt in my eye and he pounces. 'Let's give it until morning, sleep on it, and if we still haven't heard from her, we'll call the police.'

Another blast of wind whips along, my little car is fragile against the elements, and so am I. My resolve begins to crumple, and like a paper bag it's carried away on the wind, disappearing into the darkness, and I just break down in tears. I'm petrified, I want to run and find her, but run where? What should I do? I have no plan, no map. I'd just be setting off into bad weather on a blind mission that might achieve nothing.

Richard walks round to my door, opens it and leans in, putting both his arms around me. They're strong and warm and I melt into them. I'm sobbing as he helps me from the car and walks me back to the house, quickly taking off his jacket and holding it over my head as he opens the door, his shirt now wet through, his hair stuck to his head with rainwater, while, thanks to him, I'm still dry.

We walk back into the hall, and silently I head up the stairs, leaving Richard at the foot of them, watching me. I walk along the landing, drawn back to the place where I know I'll find her in my mind. Opening the door to Amy's bedroom, with stars on the ceiling and a once loved soft toy abandoned on the bed, I lie down.

I've been here before. The not knowing, the not listening, my loved ones not believing me, my instinct raging, pushing me forward, making me fight for what I knew to be the truth. That was fifteen years ago, I was right to trust my instinct then. And I am now. I lie on Amy's bed, in the room where I feel closest to her, gazing up at the starry ceiling, the waft of vanilla lip balm and lavender-scented bath bombs permeating the air, bringing her into the room. And as sweet as that feels, I'm frightened I might never see her again, and I'm thrust back to a past where I felt this fear and didn't know where we were heading. Like now.

On the second of June 2004, in what seems like a different life, my first husband Tony and I took Amy on her first holiday abroad. She was just two years old and though she didn't really understand what was happening, our excitement was catching, and she ran around in circles at the airport, to the amusement of onlookers and her proud parents. I was totally smitten with her and every day was special, every milestone a treasure to be locked away in my memory collection, and as we'd never taken Amy on holiday before, this was going to be a fortnight of firsts. We were flying to Menorca, where we'd booked a family-friendly hotel, complete with pool, and a playground – all just a few steps from the beach. Amy had been tired and grizzly on the flight – but on arrival could barely contain herself with pleasure at the sight of the brightly coloured children's playground and the brilliant-blue pool. She began to disrobe the minute she spotted the little toddler swimming pool, and, petrified she'd fall in, I had to catch her to put on her water wings. I took so many photos of her splashing Daddy in the water, squealing with delight, my bright, funny, happy little girl. It's probably the last time I ever felt really happy, with no shadows on the horizon, just a golden sun suspended in a big, blue sky, the future as wide and open and promising as that wonderful view.

When, on the second day, Amy fell off the swing and cried for a long time, there was nothing to suggest it was anything more than exhaustion and too much excitement. 'She's overwhelmed,' I'd said to Tony, 'let's have a couple of calm days.'

So we did. For the next two days we just played with her on the beach, all very gentle and easy, under that persistently blue sky. But on the fourth day we returned from the sea and I was bathing her when I noticed several bruises. Tony appeared as confused as me, but I suspected his confusion was caused by the sneaky drinks he'd been having in the hotel bar. Over the next couple of days, Amy seemed to be constantly tired, and though I couldn't pin down what it was, I just knew it wasn't right.

Like now, as I lie in her bedroom fully clothed on top of her navy-blue duvet, I *know* something isn't right. What seems perfectly normal and explainable to everyone else is a mystery to me.

I turn on the lamp by her bed and am greeted by a poster of Ed Sheeran looking down on me while holding a cat. 'Where are you Amy?' I murmur into the gloom.

I check my phone again, nothing. We didn't have phones with internet in Menorca, so I'd headed for the hotel computer room. I spent too long in that hot little space where the signal came and went, as I conjured many scenarios in what became my own private hell. Whatever ingredients I put into Google, the same alarming diagnoses results kept recurring and, desperate for peace of mind, I insisted to Tony that we call a doctor.

He wasn't happy. Just like Richard now, Tony doubted me, thought I was just 'fretting' and 'making a fuss'. He'd virtually accused me of pretending Amy had had pneumonia a few months before. 'I think you like the attention,' he'd announced, as we left the hospital with a healthy baby. 'From now on, no more calling the ambulance just because the baby's teething.'

As a new mother I had been naturally anxious and had taken Amy to the hospital several times, worried about various different childhood illnesses, including that visit for suspected pneumonia. She'd had a stuffy nose and, as I'd sat with her throughout the night – Tony having gone to bed telling me it was just a cold – I'd watched her little chest rise and fall ever quicker, and I knew from checking online that these were both classic symptoms of pneumonia. I wasn't prepared to leave it any longer, and made a disgruntled Tony get up and take us to the local A & E. After testing and an overnight stay, I was told there was nothing wrong with her, and Tony looked at me as if I was mad.

Consequently, when I wanted to call a doctor on our first foreign holiday as a family, Tony at first refused, telling me I was the one who needed to see a doctor. But I didn't listen to him, I listened to my instinct, which told me my daughter needed medical attention.

The resort doctor was rather monosyllabic but said he doubted Amy had anything serious, just some bad bruising from a fall. I didn't like his laid-back approach, and I tried to make him see that this might be potentially serious.

'But she's tired,' I insisted, 'and this bruising isn't normal, it's everywhere.'

To Tony's I-told-you-so joy, the doctor said Amy was fine, and looked at me suspiciously as I described her symptoms in more detail. But I wasn't giving up, and demanded he take me seriously. He reluctantly referred her for blood tests at the regional hospital, probably just to get me out of his face. But I didn't care, Amy was my priority, and just like now, it seemed like no one but me believed anything was wrong.

The following day, amid much complaining from Tony about me ruining the holiday, we ordered a taxi and set off for the hospital.

'Who goes for blood tests on holiday?' he'd snapped as we drove away, Amy subdued and whimpering in my arms.

The blood tests made her cry again, and at the end of a long day we were told we had to go back to the hotel and wait forty-eight hours for the results.

On our return to the room Tony held her protectively in his arms, as if I'd physically hurt her. 'You're obsessed, Kat,' he said. 'I can't believe what you put her through today.'

I was so upset by what I feared was wrong with her, and by the distress I'd caused her, I couldn't retaliate – but still I believed I'd done the right thing. And for the next forty-eight hours I checked her temperature, gave her cool baths and kept her in the quiet of our room out of the heat, while Tony stayed mostly in the hotel bar.

'You won't be happy until she's genuinely ill,' Tony had said as we climbed into the hire car two days later to get the results of the blood tests. 'You're like one of those Munchausen people who keep taking their kids to the hospital even though there's nothing wrong with them.'

For him to say that was unforgivable, and something even he regretted later, because the outcome of my 'obsession', my supposed Munchausen behaviour, was the diagnosis I'd feared.

'Your daughter has leukaemia,' the doctor told us in a soft Spanish accent that made it sound like an exotic dance rather than a deadly illness.

The word hit me in the chest with such impact I thought I might faint, the only thing that kept me conscious was the fact I was holding Amy, and my need to know what the outcome might be. But of course the doctor couldn't commit to anything, wasn't prepared to lay any bets on whether she'd survive this terrible thing or not. I wept, while smiling at little Amy so she didn't pick up on my anguish. I wished that Tony had been right and that I was just an obsessive mother, how I wished I'd been wrong, how I hope I'm wrong now and she's fine. But I have a mother's instinct, and I had known my daughter was dangerously ill.

The following day we took emergency flights home. In my hand luggage I'd carried a hypodermic needle, an adrenaline shot and an oxygen-mask kit given to me in case Amy showed any reaction to the platelet transfusion she'd been given that morning to be 'fit to fly'. I remember taking off, my stomach hitting the floor, as Amy slept in my arms, and later glancing over at Tony, his head slumped against the window, a handful of mini whisky bottles, all empty on his tray. I knew then that we were returning to the UK as different people. And I had to be so much stronger, for Amy. If anything happened to her, I knew I wouldn't survive.

Sometimes the pain of that time fills me up. And now she's missing, it's flooding back, like a tide sweeping over me, taking me away from reason, and pushing me towards a horrible and too familiar madness.

# CHAPTER NINE

I wake up on Amy's bed. Still fully clothed. My phone still missing her text. Her Instagram still empty of anything new. It's now early morning, and nothing has changed since last night. I am petrified. I'm also horrified that I fell asleep when my daughter is missing, what a terrible mother I am to let that happen. I may have missed Amy's call or a message from Jodie or Josh, and I scroll through my phone desperately searching for something. But there's nothing.

I rush into our bedroom, where Richard's still sleeping. It's 6.30 on Monday morning, and she hasn't called or come home. Surely now he'll agree that it's right to turn this niggling fear, this horrible nothing, into something tangible. Something terrifying.

I call his name, and he murmurs from the bed, so I go over and turn on the lamp. He sits up startled and looks at me. 'Has she called?'

I shake my head. 'Now we really have to do something.'

He nods and gets out of bed. We both get dressed quickly, silently, and while he finishes putting on his jumper, I go downstairs and stand in the kitchen, my whole body frozen in fear. I catch my reflection in the blackness of the kitchen window, my hair's a mess, I look old, tired, not me. If I don't calm down, I'll make myself ill again.

I can't wait for the coffee machine, so turn on the kettle, the sound as it reaches boiling races along with my heart. I pour the steaming water onto instant coffee and while it cools I call Zoe, who after only a couple of rings answers immediately.

'Sorry, did I wake you?' I ask. It's only just occurred to me how inappropriate it is to call someone before 7 a.m., even if she is my best friend.

'It's fine, has she... have you heard anything?' she asks tentatively.

'No. Nothing,' I say.

'I'm coming over.'

A surge of relief floods through me, perhaps she's finally realising that this is serious. She's a mum and she knows just how I feel, in fact, Zoe's probably the only one who does.

'Thanks,' is all I say. She knows I need her and we don't even discuss it, she'll drop everything and just be here, because that's the kind of friend she is.

I drink my coffee in silence and wait. I wait for Zoe to arrive, and for Richard to come downstairs. It seems like forever. I hear him messing about in his office and my worry and fear blooms into anger at his total lack of engagement. Eventually he's padding downstairs, calling my name. He appears in the kitchen doorway, his hair ruffled, bags under his eyes.

'So what do you want to do? Shall we call the university again first, just to check she's definitely not there?'

As pleased as I am that he's finally starting to get on board with this, it's a stupid suggestion. 'No, the university made it quite clear on the phone that they can't tell us anything.'

He nods slowly, just as the front doorbell rings.

'That'll be Zoe,' I say and he rolls his eyes, which is what he always does when her name is mentioned.

'Richard, I need some support,' I snap, walking from the kitchen.

'You've got me, I'm here.'

'I know,' I say more gently. 'I just need all the support I can get.'

'I know, I know,' he says, disappearing into the living room. 'Just give me half an hour to sort out work stuff – I need to hand over the information for tomorrow's court case as I won't be there.'

I quickly open the front door and there, in the darkness of a cold winter morning, stand Zoe and Jodie. My friend's daughter looks small and vulnerable, and any resentment I may have had about her not picking up yesterday disappears when I see she's been crying.

'Oh, Jodie, it's so good to see you, darling,' I say, ushering them both in, hugging Zoe and bundling Jodie into my arms. I hug her for too long and then, when I finally release her, I look into her face. 'Jodie, have you heard *anything*?' I say, my arm still around her as we walk into the kitchen, leaving Zoe to hang up their jackets on the hooks in the hall.

'No, Kat. I'm sorry. I… I…' and she bursts into tears, which makes me feel even more wobbly.

'Jodie, pull yourself together,' Zoe barks from the hall. 'Kat doesn't need you weeping and wailing all over her, she needs us to be here to help her.' Then she comes into the kitchen and addresses me, more gently. 'Jodie's going to take a couple of days off uni – just to be around and help and—'

'I hope she doesn't need to take a couple of days off, I hope we find Amy today,' I say, trying to be positive even though I don't believe it myself.

Zoe nods. 'It's best to try to stay optimistic. Amy will call soon I'm sure.'

Easy for Zoe to say, it isn't *her* daughter who's missing, I think. Then hate myself for thinking it. This is my friend who's here for me.

'Yes, yes of course,' I say, extremely grateful that Zoe has come straight round but concerned for Jodie who is clearly distressed.

Zoe makes tea and coffee while I quiz Jodie on Snapchat and she confirms my worst fear that Amy hasn't posted anything for two days. 'It might not mean anything though,' she adds. 'Sometimes we all get fed up of social media and we just detox.'

I think she's trying to placate me, and I don't contradict this but doubt very much that Amy would just stop all communication with everyone.

'I wonder if Josh might know something,' I say.

'I called Josh, but he hasn't heard from her at all,' Jodie replies.

'That's even more worrying,' I say, 'and it might have been nice if he'd actually contacted me to tell me that. I left him several messages yesterday.'

'Oh… He said he'd come over and see you. Today, I think he said.'

'Good!' Zoe says, handing Jodie a mug of peppermint tea. The strong aroma catches my throat, reminding me once more of Amy, and I have to stop myself taking the cup from her and immersing my face in the perfumed steam. Then Zoe hands me a strong, black coffee, and I take it gratefully. As Richard enters the kitchen she hands him a cup of white coffee, one sugar – his drink of choice. He mutters his thanks and nods at Jodie, who shrugs back. She's always been quite shy of adults and even now, at eighteen, she doesn't have the easy confidence that Amy's managed to attain.

'Thanks for coming over,' I say to them both. 'Richard and I decided last night that if we hadn't heard from Amy by this morning, we'd call the police. We're about to do it now.'

'We can call them, but it's only been forty-eight hours,' Richard adds. 'I'm still not sure I'm convinced she's missing.' I feel the sting of betrayal. Last night he'd agreed if we hadn't heard from Amy we'd act this morning, in fact, he's the one who suggested it. So why is he back-pedalling now?

'I'm calling them,' I say assertively, then I lose it slightly. 'Richard – she's missing, she's missing, she's MISSING!'

'Love, don't, you'll upset yourself and that won't help.' Zoe's shaking her head. I see a look of concern pass between her and

Richard, and I almost laugh at the irony – they're finally agreeing with each other in some weird way. They think I'm mad. Jodie looks from one to the next, wide eyes, tear-stained cheeks, she's scared like me, because calling the police makes this even more serious.

'I just want to make sure we've asked everyone and checked everywhere before we involve the police,' Richard's saying in his lawyer's voice.

'There's no one else to contact, and nothing else we can do,' I say, trying not to snap. 'And I'm damned if I'm going to sit here for another day and be told by everyone that she's fine and she'll call and she's just having fun. She's *not* having fun!'

'Okay, okay. I'll call them,' Richard says. He can see how stressed I am and he knows if he doesn't make the call I will, and I'll probably end up shouting down the phone in tears.

Zoe shrugs. 'I suppose there's nothing else for it.'

Jodie looks upset, like she might cry again, and I put my arm around her. It seems crazy for me to be comforting Jodie at a time like this, but it's a natural instinct. I've known her since she was little and she's like a second daughter to me. She's Amy's best friend, and at that age, for your friend to be missing must be almost as scary as your daughter being missing. So I stand with her, my arm around her shoulders, hers around my waist, with Zoe standing close by as Richard picks up his phone and calls the Aberystwyth Police.

Hearing him say that Amy, his stepdaughter, is missing is like a knife to my chest. This makes it real – no more placating talk, no more assumptions that she's fine. This is it.

Richard gives the police all Amy's details and looks at me to check when I last heard from her and her vague plans for the weekend. I think they're asking us to go down to Aberystwyth, and Richard makes the point that there's a chance Amy may be on her way home, this is followed by 'yes' and 'okay' and another few minutes of him just listening.

I'm irritated, frustrated, I want to grab the phone from him and talk to them myself, but I don't because, in truth, I can't trust myself. It's all becoming real. We're opening something up that could lead us to a place we really don't want to go, and as much as we need the police's help, I know that in calling them we've started something that we can't stop.

# CHAPTER TEN

After Richard has spoken to the police, he puts down the phone and Zoe, Jodie and I look at him.

'So are we going to Aberystwyth?' I ask.

'Yes. I've officially reported her missing. The police will now be in touch with the university and, with any luck, by the time we get there they may have some information,' he says. I still get the impression that Richard's doubtful, but at least he's doing something now, if only to appease me.

'They might have even *found* her,' I say, as Zoe and Jodie nod eagerly.

'No one's actually been in her flat or her room, right? She could be there. Or have left a note, or something?' Zoe suggests, but I'm not buying that. The only notes people ever leave are suicide notes, so what's Zoe suggesting?

'What do you mean a note? Has Amy said anything to you?' I say sharply to Jodie, who shakes her head and seems to shrivel under my gaze. So I continue in a softer tone. 'No, she wouldn't leave any notes. She'd call me. I'm always the first person Amy calls if she's worried, or if something happens,' I add. I must be sounding a little too desperate, because I'm sure I see a knowing glance pass between Zoe and Jodie. Do they think I'm crazy? Am I wrong? Am I always the first person Amy calls, or has that changed?

I don't have the time or the inclination to even work it out, but I'm beginning to wonder if there's more going on in my daughter's life than I know. Why hasn't she told me if there is? We always tell each other everything, don't we?

'So, let's go now,' I say to Richard, who nods reluctantly.

He says, 'I'm a little concerned about us both going seeing as Amy was planning to come home. She may still turn up.'

'Yes of course,' I say. 'Something might have happened to delay her, and she might just appear and if no one's here…' I feel another layer of confusion and panic piling on top of me. I'm finding it hard to breathe.

'Look, until we know where she is and what's happened, *someone* needs to be here,' Zoe says. 'So why don't you two go to Aberystwyth, see the police and I'll stay here until you come back. And the minute she walks through that door, I'll call you. After that, I'll give her a good telling-off.' She smiles.

I'm so grateful for my friend. I thank her, hug both her and Jodie, and within minutes Richard and I are heading out through Worcester towards the Cambrian Mountains.

While Richard drives, I text Amy to tell her we're on our way, but there's no response. I knew there wouldn't be, but I'm not giving up hope that this is all a big mistake and there's a logical reason why she hasn't been in touch. I just can't think of one.

There's no direct motorway from Worcester to Aberystwyth, and by the time we reach the mountain road, the now freezing rain is being whipped along by a wild untethered wind lashing the car. I'm reminded of the much milder day I drove Amy here at the start of term, I'd been anxious then, but nothing compared to now. I suppose I wasn't the first mum to worry about something happening to her daughter at uni, and though I know something's horribly wrong I can't bear to think that the worst might have happened.

Twisting through the Cambrians, the car wipers are moving comically fast, and as much as I want Richard to join them in their speed and put his foot down, he drives carefully, taking the bends at less than twenty miles an hour in places.

Richard changes gear, slowing right down around the curving mountain road, making me anxious in my desperation to be there. I just want to get to the uni and find her, but we continue slowly through the barren 'wilderness', often referred to as the Desert of Wales, as if we're tourists on a leisurely road trip. Any other time, I guess, I'd appreciate the scenery more, this wild winter wonderland, in such stark contrast to Worcester, our bustling Cathedral city, chocolate box perfect with beautiful historic buildings and a picturesque cricket ground. Out here it's wild, and right now it feels like a forbidding and sinister landscape, another obstacle between me and Amy.

Zoe said she once went to Aberystwyth with Pete, her ex, and what they'd hoped would be a romantic weekend turned into a horrible two days of rows and nastiness. She said they argued all the way home.

'Honestly, Kat, as we drove along, I seriously considered opening the bloody passenger door and kicking him out,' she'd said. 'Better still, I could have murdered him and no one would ever have found his body out there.'

I shiver at the memory, and distract myself from horrible thoughts by texting Zoe to ask if she's heard anything. I know it's only half an hour since we left, and I know she'd have called me if she had, but the signal around here's intermittent, so I do it anyway.

I try not to stress over the phone and the lack of signal. There's nothing I can check until the internet's back so I gaze out onto the bleak, windswept vista. This journey is one we've taken many times before, but today it's so different. The drive here has always been a lovely one, leading to a weekend retreat for the three of us when Amy was younger. And, more recently, though it was daunting taking her to university for the first time, it was also filled with promise, a positive step into the future. But now I don't know what we're driving into and I'm so scared.

I try to take myself back to when the purpose of this drive was happy, and we'd take the long road through the Elan valley, where freshwater streams, reservoirs and lakes live within the valleys. Today the water's grey, the sky's cloudy and the mountains are imposing, shadowy. But back then, the vibrant green against the blue of the lake and mountain was stunning as we drove along, the sun was in the sky and everyone was safe and happy. Much to Amy's great delight, we'd slow down the car and sheep and young lambs would waddle over, looking for snacks. My heart hurts to think of my little one laughing at 'the sheeps' and yelling at Richard to slow down as we approached. I suddenly think the unthinkable. What if I never see her again?

I have to keep my mind away from horrible, hopeless thoughts. I have to be strong, and in order to do that I mustn't allow my head to drift to thoughts that aren't helpful, that will just grind me down and leave me with no hope. I concentrate on the road, and keep checking my phone for the return of the signal, as Richard and I say little on the two-hour drive, both of us tense, both in our own worried worlds. I'm playing back conversations, still trying to work out what's happened and thinking of her last visit home.

I feel so bad about the way things were when she came home for my birthday. Her visit was great in so many ways, but, for some reason, she chose that weekend to ask some difficult questions about Tony. She knew the basics, that he now has another family and lives in a different country. But she doesn't know what *really* happened. And she's always been so accepting, but suddenly out of the blue she starts asking me these probing questions. We broke up for lots of reasons, but what hurt me more than anything else was that he wasn't there when we needed him. He couldn't cope with life and he took comfort in the bottle – then, when things went horribly wrong for us, he lashed out at me and I had to fight back the only way I could. Amy doesn't know about this, I never wanted her to feel the hurt I felt because of the way he behaved. Then again, my own behaviour wasn't exactly the stuff of role models, and that's why I find it hard to talk to her about the way her father and I split.

Until that weekend, Amy's never really asked about her father. As a child, she accepted Richard immediately, as he did her, but I was always honest with her and told her that Tony was her biological father. I didn't want him turning up in the future and surprising Amy, catching her off guard, so I was keen she knew he existed, but I had no intention of letting him into her life. She'd sometimes ask vague questions about him. I remember once when she was little she asked if he was Spiderman or a prince. I tried not to laugh, and assured her he wasn't either of those things, but I imagined she saw him in quite heroic terms, which bothered me. After that I tried to change the subject gently if she asked about him, but still I made no secret of Tony, because secrets are exciting, and our instinct is always to unravel them. But there are secrets about me and him that must never come to light.

Just talking about him made me feel uneasy, scared, and I never wanted that for Amy – and though sometimes I question the lies I've told, I know it's best for her that she doesn't know what went on when Tony and I parted. So when she was home on my birthday and started asking questions about why we divorced I was unnerved. I'd hoped I'd erased him from our lives, but, of course, I hadn't. I realised then that I'd been stupid to think she'd always passively accept my explanations; my daughter is bright and inquisitive, of course she wants to know about her biological father, he's part of who she is, where she came from. I realise it's about her identity, but I don't know what prompted this fresh interest. She wanted the anecdotes, to know about the father-daughter fun, the few years of family bonding we'd all shared. I wasn't prepared to romanticise a time that was so painful for me and nor did I want to intrigue her enough to look for him. So, I'm ashamed to say, I edited out the rare occasions we were happy, and said, 'He left us and didn't look back, love.'

I could have said so much worse, but I couldn't tell Amy how her dad had stayed out drinking rather than be with his only child on her third birthday. A birthday spent in a hospital bed with tubes in her arm and an exhausted mother who hadn't been able to leave her side to buy the gifts she would have loved to buy for her.

I'd always put the break-up down to Tony moving away and having another family, and Amy had always accepted this. But that weekend she'd wanted to analyse what had happened, questioning me quite harshly, and not simply listening to what I said and accepting my version of events, which panicked me.

'Did you leave my dad for Richard?' she'd asked.

'No, your dad left me. I met Richard later, he was my divorce lawyer, you know that,' I'd replied, trying to stay calm and unflustered.

But she pursued her questions in a very single-minded way, almost as if she was trying to catch me out. 'Do you know where my dad is now?'

What I wanted to say was, 'Yes, your dad is the one in the garden cutting the lawn now, the man who's fed and clothed you for the past fourteen years.' But I didn't. I'd hoped she'd see Richard as her father – after all he'd been the father Tony never could be – and Amy had always seemed happy and comfortable with him. But that weekend Amy was different with Richard. Gone was the easy friendship, her teasing about his bald spot, him teasing her about the state of her bedroom. She'd closed in, become stand-offish and rolled her eyes at everything he'd said, even contradicting him, laughing at him. I know Richard felt this, and I hurt for him, but a part of me didn't want to ruin the weekend, it was her first time home after starting uni and I wanted to make sure she enjoyed herself. I figured it was just Amy readjusting after tasting a few weeks of independence and nothing significant, but all the same I asked her if she was okay, and if Richard had perhaps annoyed her in some way.

'*Annoyed* me? He's always *annoyed* me,' she'd spat.

I was taken aback by the venom in her and the fact she said he'd *always* annoyed her really struck home. I'd never been aware of any animosity between them, Amy was never like this and it unsettled me.

'I don't understand,' I'd said. 'You and Richard have always got along, it upsets me to see you being so cold towards him. What's changed?'

'Nothing's *changed*, he just thinks he can tell me what to do – and he isn't even my real dad.'

'That's not fair,' I'd said. 'Richard's always been kind to you, Amy, and in my opinion has rarely told you what to do.'

'God, why is it always about bloody Richard? Why do you care so much about his feelings but not about mine, or my real dad's?'

After everything Tony had failed to do as a father, to have Amy saying this now lighted a spark in me.

'Richard isn't your biological father, and never will be. But he's been a damn sight better than that… that…'

'What? Why are you being so mean about him?'

'I'm not, I'm being honest.'

'Honest? No you're not – he's my father and you've kept him away from me all this time.'

'He isn't someone you want in your life, Amy,' I said, trying to be calm, even though inside I was shaking. 'He wasn't a good father, he… he used to go out with other women, he'd leave us on our own to go to the pub and sometimes he didn't come home and—'

'You're just saying that so I won't see him, you're telling me all this… shit so I forget about him. Well I won't because he's my dad and I want to see him. I have a right to see him!' She was so angry, so bloody angry. This was my worst fear, I couldn't let it happen.

'I'm sorry, Amy, but he's no knight in shining armour. He will ruin your life.'

'No, Mum. YOU'VE already done that!'

She'd yelled this in my face, causing tears to spring into my eyes.

'Amy, Richard and I have always tried to—'

'Richard. It's always about Richard – he always came first, you picked him to be the father in your perfect family. But it doesn't exist!'

This took my breath away. I was so hurt that she could even think of me like that, let alone say it. We don't argue like that, we're friends, we've always talked everything through, respected each other, but she was different – angry, hurt – and when I tried to reach out to her, she pulled away and ran up the stairs in tears.

I was also angry at the way she'd spoken to me, but my prevailing feeling was complete shock. I just didn't understand, we never fall out, and as a family we'd been a pretty solid unit – Amy had accepted Richard into our lives so readily, and I had thought they were like father and daughter in everything but blood. She was almost four when I married him. I'd felt very lucky. I'd heard so many awful stories through friends whose children had never accepted their new husbands. But had I been too smug, and while I continued to think we were a happy family, Amy's resentment had been building up over the years? Despite me attempting to balance the tightrope of dad and stepfather, writing endless articles on how to do this, applauding my little family and using personal anecdotes, perhaps I'd failed? By pushing Richard into the role as the only father she should love I'd made Tony seem more exciting. Had I really been trying to create and present the perfect family so much that I hadn't seen the cracks forming?

My stomach lurches now at the thought of Tony, why I never told Amy the truth, and how hurt she'd be if she discovered what I did. And that weekend, I knew even as I'd cut my birthday cake, that Tony must never cast a shadow over our lives again. I'd worked so hard to keep him away, I would not, after all this time, let him ruin Amy's life like he'd almost ruined mine.

I've always had this fear that one day Amy would meet Tony and be enchanted by him, as I had been. I was in my twenties, and I'd gone along to a gig with a girlfriend and Tony was in the band. He was the singer, and the best-looking – well, the singers usually are. I just watched him all night on stage. He was the most handsome man I'd ever seen, and not only was he of Italian descent, with dark hair, brooding Latin looks and a sexy accent, he drove a sports car. He was also amazing in bed, and our relationship was all about fire and passion. I was young and impressionable and adored him.

Thinking about him, as we drive along the treacherous, icy roads, twisting round the mountains, plunging through the valleys, I feel the tears running down my cheeks. I have a good life now, a kind and loving husband and a trusting daughter, and I've betrayed them – I'm not the perfect wife and mother I make out to be.

And then it occurs to me. What if, after all these years, Amy's somehow discovered what I did? And what if she's punishing me?

I glance quickly at the console between the front seats, where my phone sits untroubled beside me, a constant reminder that Amy is still silent.

Richard glances over. 'Nothing?' He's referring to my phone.

I'm scrolling now, back on Instagram. 'No, nothing,' I say, tearing myself away from the human traffic online and staring ahead at the empty, open road. I hear myself say, 'Until now I haven't even contemplated the idea, but what if Amy's run away?'

'But why?' he asks.

'I don't know,' I say, holding back from telling him my suspicions. Has Amy found out about me and her father somehow? Everything is online these days, and who knows what she may have stumbled across. Has Tony said something in a post, on a forum about what I did to him? I don't mention this to Richard, he doesn't know, he must never know.

'Well, if she has run away there would be a reason wouldn't there? Someone who has upset her,' he suggests.

'Yes, but *who*? And what has she run *from*?'

He sighs. 'I don't know.'

'You don't think she's run away from *me* do you?'

His silence speaks volumes.

# CHAPTER ELEVEN

Pulling into the car park at Aberystwyth University, I'm relieved to be here. It's been a tiring journey, and the only thing that's kept me awake and alert is anxiety – and blind hope.

When I brought Amy here in late September, I was immediately reminded how, at nine, she went to her first sleepover. I didn't sleep a wink, I can only describe it as an emptiness, an almost-grief; it made my legs feel hollow and gnawed at my insides. And it came again when I left her here, in one of these concrete blocks – great waves of emptiness filled me up until I thought I might choke. And just like all the other times, I was leaving another little piece of me with her, another fragment of my heart for her to carry with her always. She'd held it in her blazer pocket on that first day of school, her rucksack when she went on a geography field trip to Betws-y-Coed, and when she turned fifteen in her first handbag containing a pack of tissues and a pot of vanilla lip balm. And now it nestled among her new books on a shelf in a tiny room with its little desk and the wall filled with heart-breaking photos. I just hope Amy knows that wherever she is, she has my heart there with her.

We sit in the car, the rain battering the windows. Richard seems reluctant to leave its sanctuary, scared to go out into the cold and rain and whatever it is that may be waiting for us. I'm thinking about the last time I was here, which was also the first time. Amy and I were about to say our goodbyes, but I just needed a few more precious minutes. I folded her soft new towels too much, smoothed her duvet one last time, then did it again, and again. Then finally I took that photo of her sitting at her little desk. I look at the photo now on my phone, she looks so proud, she's smiling, excited, but I see in her eyes she was just a little bit scared. My Amy in Wonderland. I wonder if this will be the photo the police use, the one in the newspapers, on news feeds everywhere, 'Missing Student Amy Russo'.

'So… Mum, you'd better get off, it's almost dark,' she'd said that night, stretching, a fake yawn emerging – always a sign that Amy was feeling awkward. She wanted me to go, yet she didn't. I know her like I know myself. I was feeling exactly the same, but I had to be the grown-up, the one to cut the string for both of us, because despite her still being a huge part of *my* world – I didn't belong in Amy's anymore.

'If you're sure you're okay?' I'd said, aware that it was actually me who wasn't okay.

I call Zoe to tell her we've arrived safely and she asks me if we've heard anything.

'No, nothing. You?' I say, a faint glimmer in my voice.

'No, sorry, love,' she says, like it's her fault she has no good news. Zoe would have so loved to call me up to say, 'She's here.' I know she would, because if it were me and Jodie was missing, I'd have loved to tell my friend she was okay. As mums we have this kind of telepathy, both completely across the other's feelings when it comes to our children.

'Thanks, Zoe, for staying at the house… in case.'

'You never know, she could walk through this door any minute,' she's saying. 'And she'll be so pissed off with you for showing her up.' She laughs.

This makes me smile. 'How wonderful would that be? Funny how a telling-off from Amy would make me so happy right now.'

'You go and find her and give her a big hug,' she says, and for a few seconds I allow a little hope to seep in.

But when I put down the phone, I'm faced with the reality of the situation – what if Amy isn't here? What if she really is missing?

Richard, as always, is there for me, leaning awkwardly over the gearstick, both his arms around me.

'I don't know where my little girl is. I feel like wherever she might be, she isn't safe, and I haven't felt like this since she was three years old. I hoped I'd never have to endure this horrible pain again, this fear of losing her,' I sob.

And after a long time in the warmth of Richard's arms as he strokes my back, I pull away, and we look at each other, both knowing what we have to do.

'Are you ready?' he asks, and I nod, reluctantly, take a deep breath and brace myself for what's to come.

It's after 10 a.m. when we walk up to the halls of residence. I press the door buzzer and wait in the dark, rain lashing down, my feet and heart frozen. It's Monday morning and there's a buzz of activity as students start their week, dashing through the rain to their lectures in little huddles. Some are just splashing wildly through puddles and laughing – no mothers around to spoil the fun and nag them to take a brolly.

'God, wouldn't it be wonderful if she was here?' I say, and Richard nods, giving me a reassuring pat on the back.

'And she may well be,' he says as we stand in the freezing cold, waiting to be let in.

The door is eventually opened by a security guy, who, when we explain who we are and why we're there, nods and ushers us quickly into a small office.

'The police are on their way,' he says, a look of sympathy on his face as he gestures towards a row of plastic chairs by the wall for us to sit on, and offers us coffee, which we both politely refuse. Neither of us can stomach anything. It feels like a waiting room, but what are we waiting for? What happens here will either confirm or dispel my fears – this is where she should be, it's the final sliver of hope that she will be here. I am terrified.

We sit side by side, Richard and I. We're waiting, but for what we're not sure. I just desperately hope there's a happy ending.

When I'd come round to the idea of Aberystwyth being Amy's first choice, and abandoned my hopes that she'd stay closer to home, I'd been relieved to discover when I researched the university online, not only that it had a good reputation and it's by the sea – but the accommodation seemed secure. I liked the fact that it was a student village with security, someone always on site watching, keeping danger out.

*But what if the danger is already in?*

Finally the guy in the uniform says the police are almost here and they'll meet us at Amy's room. At this moment Richard's phone goes off.

'Sorry, it's the office,' he says, looking at me. 'I should be in court, someone's standing in for me, I'll need to brief her. Do you mind if I join you as soon as I've spoken to her?'

'No, of course not,' I say and he leaves to take his call in the car, and the security guard and I make our way to Amy's room.

'Even if she isn't here, one of her flatmates might be… they might know something,' I say to this stranger, who's now knocking on the flat door.

He shrugs mid-knock. 'Hope so.'

Eventually there's the sound of a key scratching on the inside.

The door opens and I recognise the boy from when Amy moved in, the one who seemed instantly fixated by her.

'Tom?' I say, and he looks back at me, vague, confused. He doesn't remember me, I'm not part of his tribe, I'm just a stranger standing on his doorstep, wet through and windswept.

'I'm Amy's mum,' I explain.

He's wearing a towelling dressing gown and a slightly bemused look.

'I'm sorry, I hope we haven't woken you up.'

'Haven't been to bed yet,' he says proudly.

'Oh. It's just… it's Amy… we can't seem to get hold of her… I think the police are on their way.'

He raises his eyebrows and I suddenly feel rather foolish, and for the first time ever I wonder if Amy has said something about me. I can't imagine it, but even a passing 'my mother the stalker' joke might carry quite some weight here amongst these flatmates who don't know me, or mine and Amy's relationship.

'Do you have any idea where she might be?' I ask, and it seems to dawn on him that it might be an idea to invite me in.

He beckons me inside. The security guard says to call if we need him, he has to get back on duty.

'I haven't seen her. She might be in her room? I'll check,' Tom says as he leads the way down the hall towards the communal kitchen.

*He hasn't seen her.*

'Since when?' I ask, and he turns to look at me blankly. 'When was the last time you saw her?' I'm trying not to raise my voice, but he seems really slow on the uptake, even unconcerned. Does he really not know anything? Or is it just that he doesn't care?

'Last week… Thursday, Friday? Not sure.'

My stomach feels like lead as I follow him down the narrow hall. The smell of frying food goes straight to my stomach and I think I might be sick. He gestures for me to go into the kitchen, while he wanders off – presumably to check Amy's room, but without a key I doubt he'll discover anything.

The kitchen is a fug of chatter and laughter, four students sitting round the table, another at the oven. I scan the room, desperately hoping to see Amy, part of this merry little band, laughing, eating pancakes, none of them look like they've been to bed yet. But that's what being a student is about – being away from home and allowed to do anything, anytime.

I stand in the doorway viewing this scene of domesticity, feeling like an intruder, wondering momentarily if they should be in lectures, but realising I don't care. Then within seconds Tom's by my side.

'I just knocked on Amy's door, no answer,' he says with a shrug, like he can't find a pencil or something equally insignificant. I want to shake him, to shout in his face, 'This is my daughter, she's my life and if she isn't in there I am lost.'

At uni you can't choose your flatmates, in the same way you can't choose your family, you have no way of knowing *who* you're going to live with. So having nurtured and protected our children all their lives, at the tender age of eighteen we drive them to another city, move them into a house full of strangers, and leave them there. Are we mad?

It's so random and computerised, six strangers thrown together in a new town. Yet watching this little group of people thrown together by fate, I can only marvel at the harmony as they sit eating pancakes. How like a family they've become. Humans need homes and family units and when they don't have them, they improvise. We find each other, make a home wherever we are – even if it's a rather dysfunctional situation.

'This is Amy's mum,' Tom adds, as an afterthought, as he takes a seat at the table.

They all stop what they're doing and stare at me. A couple nod and murmur a kind of greeting and I feel like a teacher who's just walked into a rowdy classroom and by my very status has everyone's attention.

I feel awkward, but introduce myself. 'I'm Kat, you might remember me moving Amy in?'

One of the girls, Becky – who's standing at the oven, nods vaguely, no smile – but her eyes follow me as I enter their space.

'I know it might seem mad,' I say, immediately on the defensive. It's only a little over forty-eight hours since I last heard from her and to them that may seem over the top. I'm trying not to sound dramatic or overanxious – which right now is near impossible – as I hear myself say, 'I haven't heard from Amy since Saturday, and I can't get hold of her. She hasn't returned any of my calls, or texts, and… we've called the police.'

They all look up from their pancakes, like meerkats, weighing me up and down. I'm bringing danger into their midst, they are now on full alert. I'm sure all they can think about are the spliffs stuffed in drawers and where they can hide them if the police search their rooms. I wish that was all we had to worry about.

'I don't know if you've noticed, but Amy hasn't been online since Friday,' I say, still trying to justify what might be perceived as a rather dramatic reaction to Amy not texting her mum for two days. 'Have any of you seen her…? Did she say *anything* about going anywhere…? Can you think back? Her friend Jodie put a message on Snapchat about it.'

This is met with a shrug and a sympathetic smile from the other girl I recognise as Emily of the noisy one-night-stand fame), and what can only be described as an 'I dunno' look from the two boys sitting at the table. I think they are the other two flatmates – Ahmed and Jack.

Awkward silence envelopes us as I stand there helpless in front of them, begging for their help, and they stare down, unable to look at me. I'm sure this is uncomfortable for them, for their flatmate's mother to be in the middle of their den on the verge of tears, but for several seconds they sit and I stand, like we're all made of stone.

Finally Emily is the first to remember her manners and gets up, saying, 'Has anyone actually checked if she's in there?'

Tom mumbles that he just knocked.

'I meant actually opened the door and gone in to check?' she says.

'Not appropriate, mate.' He shakes his head, making a sad face.

'Okay,' she says, getting up from her chair, 'I'll look. I haven't seen her since last Tuesday.'

'Last *Tuesday*? That can't be right,' I say, a further rush of fear filling my chest.

'Oh… sorry, no, I've been home, I only came back last night,' she says walking to the kitchen door. 'She's definitely been here since Tuesday, I think?' She gazes around the room for confirmation, Becky nods, the boys shrug. She passes me to go to Amy's room, but before I follow her, I ask if anyone's seen Amy today. They all slowly shake their heads, and I'm about to follow Emily to Amy's room when Ahmed says something that makes the hairs on the back of my neck prickle.

'Last time I saw her she was with a guy, an old guy…' he says.

'Who, when?' I manage to say.

'Can't remember when, but he's been here before.' He speaks slowly and throws his head back in what I see as a rather affected effort to remember. I have this irrational desire to shake him.

'When was he last here? Can you remember?'

'Yeah… er I think it was Friday, or was it…?'

I'm a mess and don't have the time or patience to stand around and wait for him to work out the bloody calendar in his head, I just want to know who this man is. 'What did he look like?'

'He was… an old man, grey hair, I think.' He looks confused and wishy washy and I don't think he gets how important this might be. I need him to be definite and descriptive and clear.

'Where did you see them?' I'm still trying to sound calm, like I'm not about to run over and scream, 'Think, think!' into his face.

'He was here, he came for her. I answered the door, then he was in her room for a bit – and they went out.'

*In her room?* What the hell does this mean? I want to know more, but at the same time I'm not sure I can take it.

'And when you say "old", how old?'

He looks at me, then runs his fingers through his hair and doesn't immediately answer, he knows he has the floor and he isn't going to give it up, he's probably the kind who no one listens to and he's just eating this up as everyone looks at him, waiting for what he's about to say.

'About as old as my dad, and he's *old*.' He stresses this and someone sniggers but it barely registers. 'I only saw him walk through the hall, I didn't really look properly.'

'And he definitely went in her room?'

Ahmed nods, like it's something he sees all the time.

*What on earth is an old man doing in my daughter's bedroom?* I can only think of one person, and I turn so cold, I start shivering.

'When was the last time *anyone* saw her?' I want to find out as much as I can before the police arrive, because once they take over, I'll be on the outside.

I look around the room to be greeted by shrugs and blank faces, but before I can push this further, Emily's at my side.

'Amy isn't in her room,' she says, slightly breathless.

'I knocked earlier to see if she wanted any pancakes, but she didn't answer – I thought she was out,' Becky says, going back to the business of cooking breakfast.

These kids are like everyone else – they don't seem to be taking it seriously. One of them might be missing! What's wrong with them? How can they all be so blasé about this?

'So does anyone know if…? Did she come back after she left with this… this old man?' I say, hoping to God it wasn't him.

# CHAPTER TWELVE

The continuous stare of blank faces is frustrating, and the smell of pancakes is making me nauseous. No one has any more to offer on what happened to Amy that night, the man she was seen with or where she might now be. I can't stand around here, watching these kids acting as if everything's fine, as if I'm the problem here.

I ask Emily if I can go into Amy's room. I know once the police arrive I may not get a chance.

'I just want to see if there's anything in there that will give me a clue where she is.'

'Of course,' she says, 'it's unlocked, just go in.'

'Has she left it unlocked?' I ask, slightly alarmed at this.

Emily looks around at the others uncertainly. 'It's always unlocked. Amy lost her key so she can't lock her door… it's not like she needs to, sometimes I don't lock mine,' she adds, like she doesn't want Amy to get into trouble.

Amy never mentioned that she'd lost her key, and the fact her flat has been left unlocked concerns me. Apart from this 'old guy' there are also three young, hormonal men in this flat – and any one of them could walk in on her asleep, or undressed.

I try to put this from my mind as I leave the kitchen and go down the little hallway, my legs shaking, my heart breaking remembering the last time I was here, when I moved her in. Back then I was more worried about her health, too much drinking. And though, of course being the mother I am, I'd worried about her personal safety, I'd never thought this could happen to us. We had our share of terror when she was ill, how much do I have to take in one lifetime?

I open her door, and the first thing I do is look for signs of a struggle. I walk around the little postage-stamp room alone, but it looks pretty neat, and her bed's made. *Anyone could have tidied it after they'd hurt her.* I immediately make a frantic search for the small, yellow rucksack she carries everywhere and her phone – and can't find either, which is as I'd thought. She left the flat with both. I wander around in a daze, unsure of what I'm looking for. *I'm looking for Amy, but she isn't here.*

The lovely lavender bed linen we bought together is on her bed, the soft blue towels in the bathroom, the fairy lights sit around her bed unlit. And I think of all the hope, all the planning we did for this brand-new life – and now she isn't here living in it.

I open her drawers, and the door creaks; I'm suddenly aware I'm not alone.

'Hello? Hello?' I say, walking towards the door, thinking it might be the police, who are due any moment.

'Kat, you made me jump!' It's Richard, standing in the doorway, fiddling with his phone.

'Why are you standing there?' I snap.

'Because they told me you were in here.' He looks a little surprised.

'Sorry, I'm a little on edge,' I say, feeling bad that I snapped at him.

'It's perfectly understandable. No sign of the police yet?'

'No. But I've talked to the flatmates, they haven't seen her since Friday – but one of them said he saw her with an old man.'

The colour drains from his face, he's as protective of Amy as I am, and I can see this horrifies him.

'What… what? Did they describe him?'

'No, just said it was an 'old guy' with grey hair coming out of her room.'

'Oh, it could be a caretaker or some handy man perhaps?'

'Perhaps,' I said, hopefully, the idea of an old man hanging around Amy's room gives me the creeps. But I try to put this aside and continue to go through her stuff, knowing it's a matter of minutes before the police turn up, they might not even let me stay in the room if they need access to it.

'I can't say what clothes are missing. Her purple padded jacket isn't here with the other coats hanging on her door,' I say, going through them.

'Presumably she's wearing that,' Richard says as he looks along her bookshelves. 'Kat…' he starts…

'What? Have you found something?' I say and hold my breath.

'No…'

I'm relieved and irritated. 'Thank God for that, I think. Oh, Richard, I don't know what to do.' I start to cry and he comes over and puts his arms around me.

'Kat, I… I…'

My head's buried in his chest when I suddenly remember the photo on Instagram and realise her red-checked scarf isn't anywhere in the room.

'I can't find her red scarf or rucksack,' I say. 'You must remember it, canary yellow?'

He nods. 'Yes, didn't she put a big rainbow sticker on it?'

'Yes, you can't miss it.' I try to smile. I bought it for her and half-jokingly commented that she wouldn't get run over if she had that on her back.

*Always keeping her safe from harm.*

'Amy posted the photo of herself wearing this outfit – on Instagram,' I say, holding my phone up for Richard to see. 'A mustard jumper, the red scarf – and I haven't come across either of them, which means she might still be wearing them. But as any parent of any eighteen-year-old girl knows, they don't wear anything more than once.'

'Yes.' He smiles. 'The washing basket when she's home is testament to Amy wearing an item of clothing once, sometimes for a matter of hours – and then hurling it in the washing.' I know he's trying to keep the mood light but right now I can't smile or joke along.

I check her washing bag now hanging on the door, no sign of the jumper or the scarf. 'Okay, so wherever she is, she's wearing the mustard jumper, the red-checked scarf – and she's carrying the yellow rucksack. Which means she probably hasn't come back here since Friday – even for a change of clothes…' I feel sick. I just keep wondering who is the man Ahmed saw Amy with – and is she with him now, against her will?

'It's okay, we're going to find her, just keep telling yourself that. We have to be positive, Kat. Now, is there anything else here that will help work out where she might be… is her passport here?'

'No, her passport's at home, I checked this morning – so she hasn't left the country – or been forced to.' I look at him and something passes across his face. 'She can't have, can she? Passports can be made, bought if you know the right people can't they?' I say, wanting him to tell me I'm stupid, but he doesn't really answer me. 'Do you think… Tony might…?'

'He lives in Italy now doesn't he?'

I nod.

'He hasn't been in touch for years has he?'

'No,' I lie.

'He's moved on, mark my words. He paid his dues and got out of the country, though God knows how he managed to get residency in Italy after being in prison.'

'He knew people,' I say. 'That's what I mean – could he have arranged to get a passport for Amy, to smuggle her out of the country?'

'If he was going to do that he'd have done it years ago. But probably worth mentioning to the police – you never know.'

Ironically, I wish Richard would dismiss this out of hand, tell me I'm being dramatic, that my imagination is running away with me, but he doesn't. As much as his earlier cynicism around Amy's disappearance annoyed me, it also grounded me and prevented my mind from taking me to places it mustn't go. But now it seems he's bought into this and is finally showing some concern over what may have happened.

'I don't know what Tony's capable of. But at this stage we just need to tell the police what we know, and not what we think might have happened,' he says in his lawyer's voice.

'I don't know what to do, Richard,' I say. 'Student life seems so transient, no one's looking out for anyone else, they're all just trying to survive in these first few weeks and I think she's just gone off radar and no one has spotted it. Everyone thinks I'm too much, that I was always keeping track of her at home – damn right I was, because now look what's happened.'

He says a few soothing words and strokes my arm but I can't hear or feel him.

'Amy's flatmates live with her and even *they* don't know when they last saw her. I remember a few first names of students on her course, but I have no idea who they are, so if she has gone away with someone, an old man, we can't know. There's a big sea out there, the last Instagram she posted was by the sea… it's stormy and rough and she isn't a strong swimmer. Oh God, Richard, what if—'

'Stop. You're torturing yourself and all this conjecture is pointless.'

'But I don't know where to start to look for her, don't have a clue as to how to find whoever took her. If they did. Richard… why would an old man be anywhere near Amy's room?'

'That's enough, Kat,' he says assertively. 'There's nothing we can do or should do until the police get here,' he says.

And after gazing out of the window at the other concrete blocks I sit next to him on the lavender patterned bed linen and wait.

*More waiting.* More time to think, but I don't *want* to think. I can feel it in my throat, the pain from the past that's never far away, it adheres itself to the anxiety already settled, nudging me hard every time I swallow.

I look around the few feet of Amy's life, and, agitated, I get up. I pick up trinkets from her desk, look through her clothes, feeling all the time like she might walk in any minute. But I know she won't.

Photos of friends and family smile from the door of her wardrobe, but I don't see any of an old or older man I don't know. Nor do I see any of Josh, and I'm sure there were quite a few of him when she first moved in. So what's the story there, and why hasn't she told me?

'Should we be worried about Josh?' I ask Richard, who can't give me an answer.

He's about to say something, when his phone rings again. He apologises profusely, but apparently there's a problem with the court case, and he leaves again. Anger now permeates my fear, I'm hurt and upset at his inability to be completely present, to give everything to finding Amy. I sit down on Amy's bed, exhausted already and it isn't yet noon. I know Richard's her stepfather, but she's a daughter to him, and I would have expected more.

A few minutes later, the police arrive. Just hearing the knock on the door and Emily bringing them to Amy's room is an ordeal. I can't actually stand up to greet them, they feel big and noisy with their wet overcoats and buzzing radios. Their masculine presence overwhelms Amy's little lavender bedroom. I'm uncomfortable, I don't want them in here leaning against the wall, looking around the room, surveying her personal space. It feels too intimate, too intrusive.

They close the door, which makes me feel immediately claustrophobic, but I presume they want to make this as private as possible. They introduce themselves as Sergeant Mather – a tall, rugged man in his fifties with a weather-beaten face – and Sergeant Kraft – a younger man in his thirties, almost as tall as Mather.

Mather leads the conversation, asking obvious questions in a lilting Welsh voice, and I answer while trying not to notice they're dripping dirty rainwater on Amy's cream rug. It feels like a violation, and I want to push them out into the hall, but thankfully Emily distracts me by popping her head round the door and asking if anyone would like a cup of tea. I'm touched, and we all say yes as the two policemen begin to make small talk. I'm almost grateful when Kraft asks banal questions like, how long has it taken us to get here? And how well do I know Aberystwyth? I tell him we've been on several holidays here over the years and to get through it I pretend nothing's wrong, we're here to visit, just shooting the breeze. If the officers aren't worried, then why should I be? Except I am, because during this 'casual' chat they're probably trying to get a feel for the situation, to work out what's going on and where everyone fits into Amy's life. I can feel them sizing me up, trying to work out just who and what I am – good mother, bad mother, overprotective mother… obsessive mother?

After a little while, Emily returns with the tea and they tell her they'll probably need to speak to the other flatmates after they've taken some details from me. She nods, turning to give me a small smile. I watch her move around the room placing mugs down for the officers, thinking if things were different that Amy would make tea for Emily's mum.

'So, let's just get this straight,' Mather starts when Emily has left and closed the door behind her, and I repeat myself for the millionth time about how Amy and I communicate daily, how there's been no sign of her online and I haven't been able to reach her.

'It's now been forty-eight hours since anyone heard from her,' I say, hearing the panic in my voice. 'Her flatmates haven't seen or heard from her either – and I'm worried because Ahmed said she'd been here on Friday, with a man – an older man.'

'Okay,' Mather says calmly, making a note. 'Any idea who that might be?'

'Not sure. I wonder if it might be her father,' I say, keen to press home the significance of this person. 'But he's in Italy, so I doubt it's him… and he isn't exactly *old*. Then again I suppose anyone over forty is old when you're eighteen.'

'Yeah.' He looks up from his notes. 'So what makes you think it's him?'

'I don't know, he… once threatened to take her from me. We're divorced. He isn't in our lives.'

'Oh. And this man, who might be your ex-husband – he was seen – yesterday?'

'No. It was Friday.'

'So Amy's been seen since then?'

'She texted me on Saturday to say she was having breakfast with the girls. She was due home this weekend you see… but she never came, and she put a picture on Instagram on Saturday. Ahmed thinks he saw the man coming out of her room on Friday – but apparently that wasn't the first time.'

'So, do you have a contact for Amy's biological father?' Mather asks.

I shake my head. 'He lives abroad, in Italy. He has a new family, we aren't in touch. He wasn't the world's best father.' I pause. 'He wasn't the world's best husband either,' I add, almost under my breath. 'He remarried, has kids – I hope he's doing a better job with them. You'd think he'd let go of the old, broken family, but even though he didn't want Amy, he refused to allow Richard to adopt her.' I realise I'm rambling and in my anxiety I'm saying far too much.

'His name?' He stands with pen poised over his notebook.

'Tony… Tony Russo.'

'Thanks.' He smiles.

'Amy doesn't have a relationship with him,' I add, making it clear by my expression that I'm not a fan of my ex.

I'm trying to be clear and concise, but I'm shaking, and I can't stop. And in my head I'm building up so many scenarios they're becoming entangled in each other. All the people, the circumstances, and the possible explanations and conclusions are twisted around my brain like pulsing arteries and I can't disentangle them. I think I might cry.

'I'm sorry…' My voice falters.

'Don't worry, Mrs Ellis, it's understandable,' Kraft says gently, spotting the sheer terror in my eyes. 'We're often called out by worried mums and the fact is most young people reported missing usually return within a couple of days.'

I know he is only trying to be nice, but I'm not 'a worried mum', I'm *Amy's* mum. And I have good reason to be worried, in spite of the bloody statistics. 'Yes, but I'm worried because it really isn't like her. I really don't believe she's run away,' I say. 'And if her phone died she'd use someone else's or message me on Facebook from her laptop.'

'Doesn't mean she hasn't decided to take off for a few days of her own accord,' he says, glancing over at his colleague.

'I can assure you that isn't the case,' I say, rummaging for a tissue in my bag and wiping my eyes. I can't seem to staunch the tears.

'Might she have had a few drinks Friday or Saturday night and stayed over at one of her pals'?' Mather suggests, as Kraft nods vigorously.

If I wasn't so distressed I'd be laughing at their double act. I imagine Amy seeing this, she'd be in hysterics, but in truth there's nothing funny about the situation. Despite me telling them everything I think might be useful, they don't seem to be hearing me and they've clearly formed ideas of their own.

'Look. She posted this photo on Friday afternoon,' I say, thrusting my phone at them. 'And the clothes she was wearing in the photo are missing,' I add. 'So if she'd gone out Friday in these things, she wouldn't still be wearing them now.'

'Are other clothes missing?'

'It's hard to tell,' I concede.

'Okay,' he says, in a way that suggests he's thinking 'so she might have taken some spare clothes.'

'Why am I having to convince everyone my daughter's missing?' I say. 'I thought you, the police, would get it – would see what I see, that something isn't right.'

'You don't have to convince us of anything. We just have to look at all the angles and make sure everything's been covered before an investigation can go ahead. And, with respect, it's always tricky with students. You know what it's like, you're eighteen, away from home and...' Kraft's eyes alight on a selfie of Amy in a bikini that she's stuck on the wall.

*I know what you're thinking, but that isn't who she is. And stop looking at my daughter in her bikini.*

I don't know how many more times I can stress that every teenager is different, and we can't assume that forty-eight hours missing means a night on the tiles.

'Everyone but me is convinced Amy's out having a wonderful time and hasn't told me because I'm her mother,' I say, throwing my hands in the air. 'But that's exactly *why* she would tell me – *because* I'm her mother, *because* we have a bond. We care and don't want to cause stress or worry to each other. And, contrary to popular belief, some teenage girls actually *like* their mothers, some even *talk* to them,' I end with a flourish.

'Mrs Ellis, I can't tell you how many times I've heard that. We think we know our kids, but they can be little sods sometimes,' Mather says, like he's imparting great parental wisdom that hadn't occurred to me. 'We think we know what they're up to, but they don't always tell us everything.'

I just shrug, I'm exhausted; there's no point in arguing, I'm just repeating myself again and again and nobody's listening, the whole fucking world seems to be turning against me. What I want to say is, 'Actually, I *do* know who my daughter is and I don't need *you* to tell me, so please fuck off and let's get on with finding her.' But instead I just look at Mather, waiting for him to do something – anything.

He puts his notebook in his pocket and turns his radio back on, I hope this is an indication that he's going to stop spouting his sermon on the psychology of missing teens and do some bloody policing.

'Could you send me that photo she took on Friday, Mrs Ellis?' Mrs Ellis?' he asks, giving me his number so I can send them.

I screenshot the one from her Instagram taken Friday on the beach, I can see the pebbles and the pale-grey sea behind her and linger over it a moment before sending it to him. Then I find the one where she's sitting at her desk in her little room, at the beginning of what she hoped would be this great adventure, and send that.

The door creaks open and I'm relieved to see Richard standing there.

Mather looks from me to Richard. 'Your husband?'

'Yes, Richard… this is Richard. He's Amy's stepfather.'

They say their hellos and Mather assures Richard they will do their best to get her home and Richard steps forward and sits on the bed next to me. It's such a tiny room and now, with four of us inside, I feel claustrophobic again.

'We've just talked to your wife, but if you have any more information about your stepdaughter, however insignificant, just let us know. Even the slightest thing can make a difference in a missing-person's case, sir,' Mather says.

Before he can speak, I butt in. I need them to see that Amy isn't just another student statistic. She isn't an eighteen-year-old out on a bender, she's my wonderful, kind, talented daughter who was once four years old in pink tulle with a tiny tiara – she's my Amy.

As Mather continues to scribble more notes, I start to feel fidgety.

'Finally, Mrs Ellis, would you consider your daughter to be at risk, vulnerable, unsafe?'

For a moment I don't answer. My silence causes him to look up from his notes. 'Yes, of *course* she is – she's all of those things. I haven't heard from her, she hasn't been online – she said she was coming home and never turned up, it's now Monday morning, she's eighteen and she isn't in her bloody flat,' I snap. 'How at risk does she have to be for you to take this seriously?'

'I can assure you we are taking this *very* seriously, Mrs Ellis, but in order that we can move forward, we need to establish the facts.'

I've just spent at least ten precious minutes 'establishing the facts' and answering what I see as their insignificant questions.

'Look, I've watched enough crime dramas to know that we have to go through this torturous process in order to start the ball rolling. But while two police officers are standing around asking me if I think my daughter's vulnerable, nothing is being done to find her,' I say.

They look at each other and words aren't needed, I almost see the eye roll. Meanwhile, Richard is patting my knee in a very annoying way, the equivalent of shushing me. I pull away and give him a look that tells him to stop.

'Mrs Ellis, I can see you're upset, and perhaps I wasn't clear,' Mather says, in a patronising tone. What with Richard's knee patting and this double act, I feel like banging their man heads together and taking over the bloody investigation myself. But I bite my lip and metaphorically sit on my hands so I don't physically attack anyone. Mather's still blabbering on. 'I meant *specifically* vulnerable or at risk.'

His question makes me think, *Aren't all teenagers vulnerable when away from home for the first time?* But we let them go, don't we? We encourage them to spread their wings and fly, despite the fact that they're quite helpless – hell, they can't even stack a dishwasher or vacuum a carpet. But us parents just throw them up in the air and pray their wings work. *But what if they don't?*

'Does Amy have mental-health problems? Has she ever tried to take her own life?' he's asking now.

I'm ashamed to say for a millisecond I almost say yes to both. If it means shooting her to the top of their list of priorities, I'll say anything. Do anything. But I know Amy has never had any problems, nothing that would take her to such a dark place, that she'd consider that. *That hasn't changed since she left home, has it?*

'No. No, she hasn't, but that doesn't mean she isn't vulnerable or at risk – she's an eighteen-year-old *girl*, for God's sake… where the hell is she? I keep on saying it, and at the risk of being boring, I repeat – she's *never* done anything like this before.'

At this my phone goes and there's an audible sigh in the room. I pick up my phone, which I've laid on the bed next to me. I see the name lit on the screen and my heart bounces off the bed. Josh.

'Hey, Kat, sorry I'm late, but I just got home, I saw your message asking about Amy.'

'Yes, yes – have you heard from her? Do you have any idea where she is?' I say, without a 'hi' or a 'how are you'. I need him to know this isn't just a social call.

'No… no I haven't. So you still haven't found her?'

'No. I'm at the university now, she isn't in her flat. The police are here,' I add, again stressing the seriousness of this.

I almost hear him gulp on the other end. 'Wha— The police? Do you think something's *happened* to her?' People ask the most annoying questions at the most stressful times – of course I think something's bloody happened to her, I'm not doing this for a laugh.

'Thing is, Josh, no one's actually seen her since Friday – I had a text on Saturday – but she was supposed to be coming home this weekend.'

'Oh… I didn't know.'

'She didn't tell you?' That's odd. I'd have assumed she'd want to see Josh while she was home, even if they were having a few issues. 'Do you have any idea at all where she might be – who she might be with? I'd be really grateful, Josh. I know how close you two are and she may have told you something she hasn't told me… do you know if she's worried about anything?'

There's a moment's silence as he takes all this in.

'No… no she hasn't said anything. Thing is, Kat…'

'Yes?'

'I'm sorry. I'm probably not much help – I haven't spoken to her for over a week.'

My stomach drops. 'But I thought you spoke every day, or texted, messaged – whatever.'

'We did.' He doesn't speak for a few seconds and I wonder if we've lost the signal, I'm just about to say his name when he says, 'Didn't she tell you? We broke up.'

'No. She said things weren't great, but she didn't actually say you'd broken up.'

'Yeah. About two weeks ago.'

'Oh.' I'm shocked. I don't know what to say. I can't believe she didn't tell me something so important. I guessed there was more to this than she'd told me. He's bloody dumped her – just eight weeks into her first term at uni. Josh was her first real boyfriend, and even if she'd guessed he was cooling off, for him to break up with her must have been such a shock. I suppose she had her reasons for not telling me, I'm sure she would have done so when she was ready, but I can't believe Josh did this to her.

Josh doesn't volunteer anything more, so I ask him straight, 'Why?' I want him to feel a sense of responsibility for his actions, it must have hurt her so much. 'Is it because she's in Aberystwyth and you're in Worcester?'

'Yeah… yeah, I guess it was about the distance,' he says vaguely. But I'm not convinced.

I'm aware of shuffling police feet and I don't want to hold them up while I interrogate Josh. There are bigger things to deal with right now, and I'm sure it will all come out at some stage.

'Look, Josh, can you keep your phone on?' I say. 'The police'll probably call and ask you stuff too.' I'm hoping this won't happen because Amy will be found soon.

Mather nods, asks me for Josh's number and I relay it, then put down the phone.

'So. Boyfriend trouble?' Mather says, rolling his eyes like that explains Amy not coming home.

'Not really. They've been together for ages, they sometimes have little spats – I'm sure they'll sort it out.' I really hope he doesn't assume she's run away because of a break-up and send any investigation in the wrong direction. At the same time I wonder why they've broken up – and what it was *really* about.

When the police have everything they need, I ask what we should do now.

'I think the best thing would be for you both to head back,' Mather says. 'Given that Amy may have been on her way home to Worcester, we'll now start checking CCTV to confirm whether she took the train.'

Kraft looks at him then explains in a gentle voice. 'Either way we'll be able to work out whether she set off for home, or elsewhere – or stayed here. We'll pass any information on to Worcester police, liaise with them, and vice versa.' I see the empathy, the concern as he tries to reassure me that they will do their best to find my child.

'But, Mrs Ellis,' he adds, 'there's just one thing, and I do have to tell you this, though it may not be easy to hear.'

'What?' I say, holding my breath.

'Sometimes people don't *want* to be found.'

# CHAPTER THIRTEEN

Walking away from Amy's room is painful. Part of me is desperate to stay, to just sit there and wait for her, but as Kraft gently points out as we leave, 'It might be wise for us to close the door on her room now, to be on the safe side.' I don't ask what he means, I *know*. My head is filled with visions of stripy police tape over Amy's lavender duvet, a DO NOT ENTER, CRIME SCENE notice on the door to my teenage daughter's fairy-lit room.

Before I go, I walk into the communal kitchen for a few minutes, just trying to work out what's happening, and to think about what to do now. Richard holds my hand as we walk down the narrow hallway into the kitchen, where the group have congregated to talk to the officers.

The police want to talk to her flatmates, but before they do, I want to say goodbye. We must have really unsettled them all today, turning up on the doorstep asking questions, bringing the police with their walkie-talkies and rain-drenched boots into their warm, pancake-scented nest.

'I'm sorry for the intrusion,' I feel like one of those mothers at a press conference who tearfully begs everyone to remember if they've seen their child. 'Just try and tell the police everything… anything you can think of. Even something small, that you might think isn't significant, might just help us find Amy and bring her home.'

There are a couple of murmurs, and Emily nods. 'Of course,' she says.

Richard also adds his thanks and says he hopes Amy will be back soon. Then we leave, with me in floods of tears and Richard holding me up.

'Before we go back, I need to go to the beach,' I say to Richard as we climb in the car. He nods, and we are soon driving towards the blustery seafront where the charcoal sea rages against an unhappy sky.

We pull up near the pier, the wind is whipping rain across the windows, it's freezing, and I feel only guilt that I'm in the car, warm and protected from the elements, when my daughter might be out there. We get out and the wind and stinging rain smack me in the face, but I keep walking towards the edge of the sea. Richard talks, but I don't hear him. My mind is tethered to wild, imagined horrors, tangled around a hoped-for miraculous return, only to be caught by a stray terror and plunged back down into darkness again.

I think about the last time I lived with such unpredictable fear, not knowing if my daughter would live or die – Amy was in a hospital bed, and Tony and I were sitting at her bedside in shock. Our lives had changed from that moment, and everything stopped. I took immediate leave from my job so I could be with her, but after a couple of weeks Tony had to go back to work. Back then we lived just outside London and he was working in a mobile-phone shop to tide us over until he made the big time with his band. Tony hated his job, but I think he welcomed going back there, leaving behind the bald children and grey-faced mothers for the optimism and fresh-faced youth of the Carphone Warehouse. When, just a couple of weeks later I found a letter in his overcoat pocket from someone called Lexi, telling him she had 'the best night of my life last night', I guessed she may not have been referring to one of his handsets. But given the situation with Amy, I had neither the time nor the inclination to deal with it. So I hung the coat back over the hospital chair and continued to worry about my little girl.

Over the next six months, she went through three rounds of chemotherapy and a stem-cell transplant. During that time, she suffered sepsis and anaphylactic shock and, while I spent many nights on a camp bed in the hospital, I almost never knew where Tony was. I didn't care, because my priority was Amy, but I'd have welcomed the emotional support from her father. On her third birthday, our little girl was so poorly she was still in hospital, and I spent the whole day singing happy birthday while trying not to cry. The nurses brought her a Teletubby cake with three candles, and just before she blew out the candles, she turned to everyone and said, 'Let's wait for Daddy.' Tony eventually turned up, a day later, reeking of whisky and cheap perfume that I later discovered belonged to someone called Anna. I couldn't believe it – and from that moment, I've never hated anyone more than I did Tony. I was used to him letting me down, flirting with girls at his gigs and drinking the money we didn't have. But after everything she'd been through, this might have been our daughter's last birthday and I wanted to make it as special as possible, even though she was in a hospital bed, wired up to various machines. And I will never forgive him for not being there to see her blow out her candles on her birthday cake. *You might let me down, but not my child.* And when I eventually went home from the hospital with Amy, I slept in the spare room. I couldn't look at him, our marriage was over.

For a while I lived in a horrible stalemate, I was a prisoner in my own life – I didn't want to be married to him, I didn't want to live in the same house, but financially I couldn't survive alone. The very thought of leaving Amy to go out to work appalled me, so the only alternative was to stay with Tony in our hopeless life.

Then, one day, during a particularly difficult month of chemo for Amy, Tony took me out for lunch. I thought he was giving me a break, a sort of treat in the middle of all the horror – but over the ricotta gnocchi with spinach and gorgonzola, he said he didn't love me anymore. I suppose I didn't love him either, but quite honestly I'd been so busy trying to keep our child alive I hadn't had the chance to ruminate on our relationship, I was just trying to get from one day to the next. I don't know why, but I was shocked that he'd do this now. Not to me, but to Amy in her hour of need. In my mind I often hear her little baby voice from the propped-up pillows in hospital, 'Where's my daddy, Mummy?' and my heart still breaks.

Within weeks, Tony moved out to live in a rented cottage with his latest conquest, a student called Sophie who was soon pregnant with his child. So while our sick child struggled to cling on to life, he'd been out making a new one. I knew there and then I could never – would never – forgive him, but I didn't have the energy then to react, I had to save all my emotional energy for Amy. He made some attempts to see Amy, some vague threats about taking me to court for custody, but I didn't think he'd see it through – apart from anything he didn't have the money. In truth, I didn't care about Tony anymore, I just wanted my daughter well again – and to have him popping in and out of her life would not be good for her. I decided that for Amy's sake I had to do whatever it took to cut him out of our lives. Forever.

Richard's now speaking to me, dragging me back into this unwelcome turmoil, but I can't hear him due to the roar of the sea and the noise in my head. Giant waves are lashing over the pebbles, and I stand on the promenade, leaning out, trying to look through the greyness at what might be out there. I'm drawn to the sea, I half-think I hear Amy's voice in the swell of the ocean as it rises, angrily. Its power scares me – it could sweep us out there any second if we stepped just inches forward. Between life and death. I feel like I'm standing on the edge of the world. I came here for answers, but there are none, just a growing confirmation that my instinct was right – and Amy's gone.

I go back again to that other time, Amy a fragile, pale little set of bones, tubes in her arms, just waiting for someone to tell me what happened next. A nurse came into the room and I asked what

I could do now. She replied, 'When you're walking through hell, love, the only thing you *can* do is keep walking.' Well, I've walked this way before, and I'm not religious, but back then I promised whoever or whatever has the power, that if Amy survived the terrible disease that was taking her from me, I'd keep her safe forever. But standing here, at the mercy of the elements, the sea banging the wall and spitting into my face – I realise I've failed to keep that promise.

I look at Richard, facing out to sea, the same pain on his face as must be on mine. Amy had a point when she said I tried to create the perfect family – I knew that Richard would be perfect. He's kind and gentle and he wanted a family too – he told me he'd always wanted a daughter, and I know he loves her like a father. He's here for us again now in a way that Tony never was, never could be – and I just want Amy back to complete us. But I feel so lost, I don't know what to do, who to call – I just keep going over the conversations I had with Amy over the phone recently and wonder if I missed something.

'Perhaps I should have listened to what Amy was saying – I mean *really* listened,' I say to Richard as we walk back to the car. 'She said things weren't great between her and Josh – but should I have asked more? Were things happening with him that she wanted to tell me but couldn't because she knew I would worry?' I think about what Sergeant Mather had said about how our kids don't always tell us everything. I never expected Amy to tell me *everything,* but surely she'd share the important stuff, like if she was worried, or upset. *Or scared about something, or someone?* Did I miss the subliminal messages in our phone conversations, was she trying to tell me something in her texts?

How well do we really know our children?

I'm still going over everything Amy said to me as we drive back to Worcester, and eventually end up thinking about everything that's happened. Events like this make you return to the past, because in truth, there's nowhere else to go.

Amy's illness impacted on me as a mother, and affected us as a family. For a long time afterwards, I would take her to the doctor's at the slightest complaint. A tummy ache, a fresh bruise all took on sinister connotations, and I'd lie awake at night just hoping to God she'd survive until the morning. Protecting her became my addiction, I was permanently on high alert, petrified the disease would come back and take her. I was told emphatically, and sometimes quite rudely, that there was nothing wrong with her – and it was humiliating, but for a while it was the only thing that gave me peace of mind. And even when my GP suggested I have a referral for my own mental health, I didn't care – I just kept taking Amy back to the surgery. It was the only place I felt we were safe. And I'm horrified to say that there were times when I'd wake in the middle of the night so scared that I'd make up a symptom, and call an ambulance. I just *had* to know she was okay and this horrible, insidious thing wasn't waiting by the back door in the shadows waiting to take her from me when I wasn't looking. But fifteen years on she was still clear, and I was almost beginning to think I could keep her after all.

Arriving back, we pull up outside the house.

'Funny how in just a few hours, everything's changed,' I say. 'I had a glimmer of hope when we left here this morning.'

Richard looks at me, the pain on my face reflected in his eyes as he reaches out for my hand.

'I naively thought that if we drove there, I could somehow conjure Amy up, that she'd be waiting for me, having returned from wherever she's been. I imagined us arriving, and she'd be there with everyone else around that little table eating pancakes, embarrassed but amused.' I smile at him, but the smile squeezes the tears from my eyes.

'Yes,' he says gently, 'and she'd call you a stressball, and laugh and this nightmare would all be over.'

'Oh, love, I think it's only just begun,' I say, leaning on his chest, reluctant again to leave the warm car and face the emptiness of our home. 'When she wasn't physically there it was bad enough,' I say, 'but now I can't face being in the house without her in it.'

'I know, darling, I know, but we must stay positive. The police are involved now and they will find her, I'm sure.' He goes to open the car door, just as my phone rings and I immediately see it isn't Amy, but an unfamiliar number.

'Hello? Hello?' I say, breathless, not knowing if this has anything to do with Amy, but expecting the worst.

'Mrs Ellis. It's Mark Mather down at Aberystwyth,' he says in his sing-song voice.

'Have you found her?' my voice is a whisper, I can barely form the words. I turn on the speaker of my phone so Richard can hear what they have to say.

'No, I'm sorry, nothing as yet. But we're checking CCTV and liaising with Worcester. I'm actually calling because Ahmed – one of the lads at Amy's flat – told us something after you'd gone.'

'Oh, really?'

'Yes. He said he recognised the older man who was in Amy's room on Friday.' He pauses, ominously.

I hold my breath. If I was standing up my legs would give way. 'Oh,' is all I can muster.

'And we've been trying to get hold of you or Mr Ellis to ask you about it.'

'Sorry, the signal's bad over the mountains,' I say 'we're back now, we can talk.'

'Well, Ahmed didn't like to say earlier when you were here, but I do need to tell you that he's adamant that the man he saw in Amy's room on Friday was Mr Ellis – your husband.'

# CHAPTER FOURTEEN

I hand my phone to Richard, who has a brief, rather monosyllabic conversation with Mather and says he'll go to Worcester police station to 'sort this out' before he ends the call.

'What the hell's going on, Richard?' I ask, my heart pumping, my breath sucked from my body.

We are both still sitting in the car. Zoe texted me a few minutes ago to say she and Jodie are in the house waiting for us, but this isn't something we can discuss in front of anyone.

'I wanted to tell you, Kat. I've been trying to tell you. On Sunday night when I got back from golf with Roger, I wanted to tell you. I called Amy, well I *tried* to call her on the Sunday night when I got back from playing golf. I went upstairs so you wouldn't hear and I called to say please phone your mum, she doesn't have to know we met up if you don't want her to. But she didn't respond. And then like you I began to worry that something had happened, so I tried to tell you when we were in her room at university, but you were so traumatised, you were manic. I didn't know what to do for the best but all the time I was protecting you.'

'I don't understand… so when you said you were on the phone to Roger about the merger you were trying to get hold of Amy?'

He nods.

'But why?'

'She didn't want to hurt you, wanted to sort out her feelings first…' He looks terrible, and his voice is breaking, I don't think I've ever seen him like this.

'Her *feelings*?'

Suddenly the porch light goes on, the door opens and then there's another flood of light from the hall as Zoe appears on the doorstep.

'She must have heard us pull up,' I say.

'Oh Christ, this is all I need,' Richard says, putting his head in his hand.

'What the fuck's going on, Richard?' I hiss. 'Why didn't you tell me you saw Amy on Friday? It doesn't make any sense.'

'Amy made me swear on your life not to say anything. I'm so sorry,' he's saying, and I'm so confused. My mouth's so dry I can barely speak. I want to talk about this, I want to hear his explanation. 'So many times I've almost said something to you. Last night at home, then today on the drive, but I kept thinking she'd be there, in her flat, and it would all be okay.'

'I don't...'

'Look, I'll go to the police station in Worcester now, sort this out before it gets silly,' he says. 'You just go in the house with Zoe and say I've got to deal with something at work. We don't want any whispers starting, she'd love a bit of scandal.'

'Scandal?'

'No... I don't mean...'

'Fuck! Just tell me what's going on?' I insist. I can't begin to imagine why he was there. Or why he hasn't told me, but Zoe's now walking briskly towards the car.

'No. I can't. Not now, not with *her* there,' he nods his head in the direction of Zoe, who's now a few feet from the car, leaning sideways mouthing, 'Any news, sweetie?' 'Just keep her out of *everything*,' he's saying. 'I'll explain when I get back, when she's gone home.'

'I don't care what she knows, it doesn't matter, she's my friend and she's concerned about me. At least she doesn't lie to me and skulk around my daughter's university without telling me. Or the police.'

'That's why I need to go now and sort this out,' he says, just as Zoe whips open the passenger door.

'Oh, I've been so worried about you. Darling, are you okay, what's happening? Are the police involved yet?' She's hurling questions at me, and I can feel Richard's irritation boiling over at the side of me, so I grab my bag, get out of the car and give the door a good slam.

Richard then sets off, wheels spinning.

'He's in a hurry,' Zoe says, putting her arm around me and walking me up the drive.

'There's a problem.'

'Oh?' Her face changes colour.

'At work.'

'Thank God for that, I thought it was Amy.'

'No. Nothing yet.' I sigh and we walk into the house together. Jodie greets us in the hall, and it looks like she's been crying again, this has really hit her so badly. I hope Zoe's keeping an eye on her, Jodie has anxiety and a couple of years ago stopped eating for a while. God, I hope this doesn't cause her to relapse, Amy will be so upset when she gets back.

'What's happening, Kat? What did the police say?' Zoe asks.

Where to start? There was no sign of Amy and her clothes were missing, but her flatmates are more concerned about eating pancakes and the police think I'm just an overprotective mother. Oh, but Richard drove to Aberystwyth on Friday to see her but didn't bother to tell me and nobody's seen her since.

'Nothing really,' I say, unable to go through it all again. I just want to sit quietly and think about everything while continuing to check and recheck my phone. 'To be honest, I think they genuinely believe she'll turn up tomorrow or the next day. Like she's just forgotten she was planning to come home – like she'd gone off and never thought to let me know.'

'Well, that could still be the case, love,' Zoe says as we walk into the living room. 'Josh is here,' she says, and despite feeling angry with him about breaking Amy's heart he's standing in the middle of the room looking so forlorn I push my anger aside, step towards him and give him a big hug.

'Oh, love, it's so upsetting, isn't it?' I say.

He looks like he's about to cry. 'I'm sorry – I feel so bad. When you left that message yesterday, I just thought she'd had a late one, hadn't texted you,' Josh says. 'I had no idea... I never thought that...'

'There's nothing to think, Josh, just because she hasn't been in touch doesn't mean something terrible's happened,' Zoe says, plumping the cushions on the sofa for me as I sit down. 'We mustn't jump to any conclusions.'

I nod, feeling like a child with a cold and an overbearing mother, but it's just what I need right now. Especially as Richard, who I thought was my rock, is now being questioned by the police in relation to Amy's disappearance. I need all the friends I can get.

'Jodie, go and make Kat a coffee, black,' Zoe instructs her daughter.

'I know Kat takes it black,' she snaps, 'you don't need to tell me.'

Zoe rolls her eyes at me, but I don't join in, I just wish Amy was here snapping at me.

We watch Jodie leave the room; my heart is breaking. Jodie's like a second daughter to me, she used to be round here most days before the girls went to uni. Richard had said she might as well move in.

He'd sometimes get grumpy when he couldn't listen to *The Moral Maze* on Radio 4 because two teenage girls were having a karaoke competition or gymnastic event in the living room.

'Why doesn't she go home to her own mother?' he'd ask.

'Because she prefers mine, and who can blame her?' Amy had joked. But if I'm really honest, I think there's some truth in that.

Zoe can be hard on Jodie and sometimes she just needs to be allowed to chill. I can see this is really upsetting Jodie, and I feel for her, like I'd feel for Amy if it were her friend missing.

'You okay, anything else to report?' Zoe says in a quiet voice, obviously trying to be discreet. Josh has followed Jodie into the next room while she makes my coffee. I get the feeling he's wary of being around me after what's happened with him and Amy.

Even now, with the police and everything, I think Zoe still believes that Amy's fine, that she'll walk in any minute. But if she knew about Richard she might feel differently.

Unwanted thoughts keep going round and round my brain and I feel that I want to tell Zoe about Richard. I feel I need another perspective and Zoe will offer that, but don't want to be disloyal to him, as he's specifically asked me not to tell her he's with the police. As yet I don't even know what there is to tell as he didn't get the chance to explain – but Richard won't have done anything, will he? I'm sure there's an explanation and I should wait and speak to him first. So I try to stay on safe ground, and hope I can keep this to myself until I know what happened.

'I'm touched that Josh showed up,' I say. 'It shows how much he cares about Amy. Apparently they broke up – I'm not sure what happened. But I wouldn't be surprised if, when she comes back, they get together again, they always seemed so happy.'

'Yes, shame, but it was just too much for them right now, the whole long-distance thing.'

'Oh, you knew that they'd finished?' I'm surprised Zoe knows when I didn't.

'Yeah, Jodie mentioned it.'

'Oh, of course.' So Amy had told Jodie. Why hadn't she told me? 'I don't understand it, they seemed happy, he was always so besotted.'

'Well, they're young, aren't they?'

'Yes, but she must have been so upset.' I try to stem the tears, I've cried too much today. 'They've been together for almost three years and I feel so guilty I wasn't there for her.'

'Don't torture yourself, Kat, she was probably trying to be emotionally independent. There comes a time when us mums have to cut the cord, you know?'

'I know, but I can't help but be hurt that she didn't tell me. That she was going through it and kept it from me.'

'There was probably a lot she was keeping from you,' she says. 'Same as Jodie, there's a lot she keeps from me. We just have to accept we aren't such a big part of their lives anymore.'

But Zoe's always been quite distant with Jodie, they never had that close mother-daughter bond, which presumably makes this whole university separation easier in a way. And it's why sometimes Zoe thinks I'm overreacting – because she wouldn't be so involved in her daughter's life. I respect that we both have different ways of parenting, no one is right or wrong, but I do sometimes feel as if Zoe's judging me – which is why it's taken her longer than it should to believe me since I first said Amy was missing.

'No, I know, but we should still be there to support them, and I wasn't.'

'She had her new friends at uni, she probably talked to them instead… and Jodie of course.'

'I suppose so. But I still talked problems over with my mother when I left home, and if she was still with us, I'd be talking to her now. Every day. You don't stop being a daughter, or a mother, just because you don't live under the same roof.'

Zoe shrugs, and changes the subject, she knows I'm upset and now isn't the time to discuss our changing maternal roles in our children's lives. 'So Richard's had a work emergency? It must have been pretty important, with how fast and furiously he drove off.'

'It's not like him,' I say, 'it's really getting to both of us.'

'Yes, but you don't need him losing it. That's going to stress you out even more.'

She knows there's more to it. Zoe has a sixth sense for these things, and she'll get it out of me, there's no point in hiding anything from her. I don't know why Richard didn't want me to tell her he was with Amy on Friday, but if there's a reason he wants to keep it a secret it will come out soon enough. Besides, he lied to me, and about God knows what else, so I suddenly decide he doesn't deserve my loyalty.

'Richard was in Aberystwyth on Friday,' I say quietly.

Zoe looks at me, slightly puzzled. 'You never said.'

'I didn't *know.*' I go on to explain about Richard being identified by one of Amy's flatmates as an older man who'd been in her room.

'What the hell was going on?' she asks.

'I don't know.' I see the look on her face and immediately regret saying anything. 'Like you said, we mustn't jump to conclusions.'

She clearly thinks this is dodgy, and I have to say I'm on shaky ground with this too. But I want her to do what she always does, soothe me, tell me it's nothing, that it's probably insignificant. But she doesn't.

'So why was he there?' she asks, her brow furrowed.

'I don't know, he didn't get chance to tell me, it could be nothing… But I'm hurt that they met up and neither of them mentioned it.'

'I'm sorry, Kat, but I don't like *that,*' she wraps her arms around herself and pulls her mouth down either side in a disapproving expression.

'Well, I don't know what *that* is yet. When he roared off in the car just now, he wasn't going to work. He was going to the police station. He needs to sort it out and says he'll tell me what happened when he gets back.'

She's looking at me with deep concern, and is about to say something when Jodie returns with drinks on a tray.

'Thanks, darling,' she says as Jodie hands me the cup of coffee. I get a whiff of Jodie's drink, and breathe in the sweet, heady peppermint, but it does little to soothe me. I'm so tender my heart hurts.

'Where's Richard?' Jodie asks, looking round. 'Does he want a coffee?'

'He's gone to work,' Zoe says.

'Oh?' She sighs, her face is pale, her voice is tearful. 'I thought he'd gone to look for Amy.'

'No,' says Zoe, looking from me to her daughter, concern on her face. Poor Zoe, she's caring for her best friend *and* her daughter. I feel guilty for putting this on her, but so grateful to have her here, someone I can trust, who is loyal.

'Sweetie, why don't you ask Josh to drop you off at home?' she says gently. 'All this is upsetting for you, and I need to stay with Kat a little longer, I don't want to leave her alone.'

'It's fine, Zoe,' I say, 'you take Jodie home.'

'No. Josh will drop her off.' In his silent presence it's easy to forget about Josh – he's clearly uneasy, not sure what to say or do, but he nods to say yes he'll take Jodie home.

Jodie seems okay with this and within minutes she and Josh are heading out of the front door.

'Thanks, Josh. See you soon, darling,' Zoe calls from the living room. 'And don't worry, I'm sure Amy's fine, just off on an adventure.'

I wish she wouldn't say things like that, I know she's trying to protect Jodie, but I feel like it might also be a dig at me. I don't know how long Amy has to be missing before people start taking me seriously.

As soon as the front door is closed, Zoe turns to me. 'So, Richard. What the fuck?'

'I don't understand why he didn't tell me,' I say. 'Zoe, what's he hiding?'

She shakes her head, as confused as I am.

'And why did he go to see Amy anyway? They get along, but she was quite grumpy with him last time she was home, said he was annoying,' I explain.

'Annoying?'

'Yeah.'

'Wonder what she meant by that?' she says mysteriously, causing my mouth to go dry. 'Thing is, he's a lawyer, he'll be able to squirm out of anything,' she adds.

'I'm not sure that's what he's doing… He just said he was going to sort it out. I'm sure it's nothing,' I start and Zoe begins to say something, then thinks better of it, but I know my friend, she clearly has an informed opinion on some aspect of this.

'What, Zoe?'

'No, I…'

'Tell me what you're thinking.'

'I'm not thinking anything.'

'Yes you are, please tell me.'

She covers her face with both her hands, and for a few seconds I hold my breath.

'What?' I ask.

'Oh, I don't know. I never gave it much credence at the time, but now I wonder.'

She's clearly trying to work out how to tell me something in the kindest, gentlest way, but I can't stand the tension.

'Just tell me, Zoe.'

'Jodie said once Richard was "creepy", and she felt he was looking at her – and at Amy – in an inappropriate way.'

'Inappropriate?' I say this hoping blindly that there's another meaning for this word than the obvious one. 'I've never ever felt—'

'Well, you wouldn't. I doubt he ever shows his true colours in front of you.'

'No. No. I would *know,* Zoe.'

'You're right,' she suddenly says. 'If you haven't spotted anything, then I'm sure Jodie was just imagining it.' But I can tell by her tone she doesn't believe Jodie was imagining it. 'You've been through enough, and you don't need me saying these things to you right now,' she adds, as if to draw a line under it. But I can't, because what she just told me is shocking, it goes against everything I've ever thought about my husband.

I've spent the last twenty-four hours wondering if I really know my daughter. But now I'm beginning to wonder how well I know my husband.

# CHAPTER FIFTEEN

Zoe left an hour ago and I'm sitting alone in the quiet of the kitchen when I hear the grating sound of Richard's key in the lock. It feels like the metal is being twisted into my gut. When I first heard that Ahmed had recognised Richard as 'the old guy' he'd seen with Amy, I was convinced there was some innocent excuse. Now Zoe's told me what Jodie said and I've had several hours to think about it all, I don't know anymore. I'm questioning everything. I know it's Richard in the hall, but I don't know *who* to expect when he walks in.

'Sorry,' he says. 'It took longer than I expected.'

'What's going on?' I'm not prepared to make small talk. I need to know. Now.

'Nothing – just a waste of everyone's time, that's all.'

'Okay. So, tell me... what were you doing with Amy on Friday?' I ask again.

After a few seconds, the silence prickles. I'm still looking at him, waiting for what he has to say. Of course for me there's a more pressing narrative regarding my daughter's disappearance, but I'm eager to hear this because it's also related to Amy.

He drops his head and says, 'I was stupid... stupid.'

My heart is thumping in my ears. All I can think about is Jodie's comment that he was 'creepy'.

'Richard? I don't understand...'

'At the time me going there to see her didn't seem significant.'

'Not significant? You are kidding me?' *She never told me. He never told me. What were they both keeping from me?*

'I mean it wasn't significant *before* she went missing, but as soon as I thought it might be, it was too late. I couldn't bring myself to say anything, I didn't want to throw up any red herrings, and as you know I didn't want to upset you.' He shakes his head. 'Kat, I was an idiot not to just tell you at the time, but then it was too late. Sometimes we do really stupid things that go unnoticed, and then something like this happens and they look odd, suspicious, when they aren't at all. And, Kat, I went to the station willingly.'

'But if they had you ID'd as the man with Amy on Friday, you had no choice.'

He looks weary, exhausted – but is it guilt?

'I *had* a choice, but I went willingly. And yes, I should have told the police as soon as we reported Amy as missing, but I honestly thought she'd turn up. I still do.'

'It doesn't make sense that she'd talk to you and not me – and why you didn't *tell* me.' Something isn't adding up, I'm on the verge of tears but I can't break down, I have to focus and get to the bottom of this. 'She wants *me* when she's upset, she'd never just run away.'

He tries to embrace me, but I pull away from him, my mind can't focus, the agony I've endured for the past few days now fusing with fresh pain.

'As far as I knew she was coming home, she wanted to talk to you. I thought she'd be back on Saturday. I know what you're like, if I'd told you I'd seen her, then you wouldn't be able to resist quizzing her about it and she'd guess you knew and she'd *know* it was me who told you. She trusted me, Kat – it was the first time she's ever confided in me. I realise it sounds stupid now, in the light of everything, but for the first time… I felt like a dad.'

I can't help it, this touches me. He puts his head down, runs his fingers through his hair the way he does when he's working on a difficult legal case and can't find any answers.

'Richard, what did she say?'

He looks at me and shrugs slightly, like he doesn't know where to begin. Then he moves and, wearily, heaves himself onto a stool next to me, both of us now leaning on the island worktop.

'The plan on Friday, as you know, was for me to go straight to the hotel in Cardiff, meet up with Roger and play golf. I had no intentions of going to Aberystwyth, or to see Amy, when I left here on Friday morning.'

I'm leaning on my elbows staring at the worktop, observing the flakes of glitter suspended in the black stone, remembering how much I'd wanted this. It was the most expensive stone in the kitchen shop, and I said we shouldn't – that it was too decadent. But Richard said I had to have it, and I remember thinking how bloody lucky I was to have a man like him. It seems like another life now, a life when all I had to worry about was what kind of kitchen work surface to choose. How shallow I was. Now I worry where my daughter is, and why my husband's been keeping things from me.

*I thought I was the only one in this marriage who had secrets.*

'I was on my way to the hotel when Amy called me,' he starts. 'She left a message, and it was only when I stopped for petrol at the services that I listened to it. She was crying…' He stops, and looks at me sideways, he knows this will hurt me.

I hold my breath and wait for him to continue.

'I'm sorry, darling…' he reaches for me, but I can't respond, I just want him to keep talking. 'She was crying, in the phone message,' he continues. 'She said she'd met up with her dad…'

'Tony? What did he say to upset her? How did he even find her?' *I knew it. I knew it.*

'Well, apparently he told her some stuff.'

'What stuff?' My stomach dips. *What the hell has he said?*

Richard shrugs. 'At the time I didn't understand, the message was quite garbled, and she was… distressed. So I called her and the first thing I did was to suggest she give you a ring. "Your mum always knows what to do when you're upset," I said. That's when she got really distressed and told me I mustn't say anything – that before she spoke to you she needed to know what the truth was.'

'So you offered to drop by?'

'Yes. I told her I was on my way to Cardiff. You know Amy's geography isn't her strong point.' He smiles. 'To Amy, Wales is Wales and she assumed I would be just down the road. She was so upset, I didn't like to say otherwise. So I took a slight detour.'

'Okay. But I still don't understand why she'd ask to talk to *you*?'

'I thought the same.' He opens his hands in a questioning gesture. 'Amy and me, we've never been all that close, I've always felt like a father figure – not the real thing, if that makes sense?'

It does. I think Tony's been a shadow over all of us, and it's impacted on Richard and Amy's relationship. I didn't want any more children after what had happened with Amy – I had this irrational idea that I should be there for her, that I couldn't be distracted by other children. Richard accepted this, but in later years I realised I was wrong, I denied him a child of his own, and perhaps that would have cemented us more, made him feel more secure because he was someone's father.

'So I collected her from her flat, and we went to a Pizza Express just down the road, she likes the dough balls apparently,' he says as an aside.

'Yes, she always has.'

'I didn't know that.'

I shrug. 'So what happened?'

'She told me she'd found her father, that they'd been in touch for a while, but then he'd apparently turned up at her uni on Friday morning, completely out of the blue.'

'So he's not in Italy?'

'No, apparently he's moved back here quite recently.'

'Oh no.' I put my head in my hands. Amy going missing just as Tony comes back here can't be a coincidence.

'If I'm honest, I was flattered that she felt she could share this with me,' Richard's saying as I try and get my head around the fact Tony's back and the damage he's probably already done. 'I was also relieved that there was a reason why she suddenly turned against me when she was last home,' he adds.

I nod. 'Yes, I just thought it was a late teenage rebellion. But he's clearly been poisoning her against you.'

This all adds up, it's beginning to make sense, how could I ever have doubted Richard? He wouldn't do anything to hurt Amy, he's not like that, he's straight and honest and upstanding. He's a bloody lawyer. No, Tony is behind all this disruption, and who knows what he's done. I look at Richard, who seems to have aged twenty years in the past twenty-four hours – how could I ever have doubted him? Richard would never do anything to hurt Amy, not like Tony.

'Yes, and I wanted to defend myself, defend you,' he's saying. 'And I felt like I was helping in my own, rather clumsy way, but now it's backfired spectacularly.'

'Mmm, you're a suspect in her disappearance, when it's probably him that's involved.' I decide not to tell Richard yet what Jodie had said about him being 'creepy' and 'inappropriate'. She'd obviously misunderstood or misinterpreted his behaviour. This kind of thing ruins lives, and the only person who can confirm or refute it is Amy – and she's not here.

'The police didn't *say* I was a suspect,' he points out.

'No, but by not being open and honest you've put yourself in a very difficult position,' I say, before asking, 'So what did Amy say… about Tony?' Just saying his name fills me with dread.

'That she'd met with him on Friday morning,' he says, recounting it like he's in court, telling the story to the jury. 'She asked him why he left, why he'd never bothered to get in touch with her, never came to see her.'

*This was never supposed to happen.*

'And what did he say?' I ask, scared of what had been revealed.

'He did what he always did, he told her lies, so I told her the truth. I pointed out that he'd never been in touch since the divorce, that no one would have stopped him reaching out to her. As I said, he can't turn up after all these years saying he cared, when clearly he didn't, if he had she'd have heard from him. I told her, "He missed your childhood."' He pauses and then adds, 'She asked me directly if you put her dad in prison.'

*Shit.* No. I really hoped we'd buried the past, but it's come back with a vengeance. I was only keeping her safe, I didn't want to hurt anybody, not even Tony.

'And you told her?'

'I said, yes, that he'd hurt you, that you were covered in cuts and bruises, and if you hadn't been so strong, and hadn't fought him in the courts, the outcome might have been very different. I had to. Kat, he'd said all kinds of things to her: that you'd lied about the violence, that you ruined his life, you were too possessive of her. He said you wouldn't allow him to be part of her life, even though he wanted to be.'

I nod. I'm already going through hell, and it just got a little bit harder.

'I knew he'd come back for her one day,' I say. Which is why I did what I had to do. I was protecting Amy, looking after her.

'I think he just happens to be back in the UK and wanted to cause some trouble,' Richard says. 'He said he'd wanted to see her, but you wouldn't let him. He told her that with my help you not only had him imprisoned, accusing him of things he hadn't done, but you took out an injunction, and then moved away so he couldn't find you. He said I colluded with your lies, that you and I are evil.'

'Did she believe him?'

'She didn't know what to believe. Bear in mind this is her long-lost father. He made her doubt everything, and everyone, especially you and me – her parents. He really messed with her mind, Kat. She said she'd always wanted to meet him, that she was so excited when he got in touch, and I think she wanted to believe him.'

'Yes, she's always had this fairy-tale idea about him,' I say with a sigh. 'When she was younger, if ever she was in trouble, or she didn't agree with us she'd say, "I'm going to find my real dad."'

'I remember,' Richard says sadly. 'It hurt.'

I suddenly feel so sorry for him, he's been through so much, and all because of me. 'I'm sorry you felt hurt, Richard.'

'Perhaps we shouldn't have been so scorched-earth about it. We could have allowed him to see her with a chaperone, so she wouldn't be in danger – she could have got to know him, and he wouldn't have been forbidden fruit.'

'Yeah, you're right, but I still wouldn't have trusted him. If he'd been a good father, a kind, loving husband, maybe things could have been different.'

'I think she retreated into a world where she had this amazing "cool" musician dad who would rescue her,' Richard adds. 'But the truth is quite different, and you must never feel guilty.'

*But I do. God, how guilty I feel.*

'She thought he was some bohemian singer who lived this nomadic and carefree life wandering the beaches of Europe,' I add, the guilt slowly wrapping around me like a cobra, suffocating me.

*What lies I've told. What harm have I done?*

'When you describe him like that, I can see why she sometimes resented her boring stepfather,' he says sadly.

'You were never boring,' I say. 'You rescued us from a terrible situation. God only knows what would have happened if it hadn't been for you.' He'd given us more than he even knew.

'Well, Tony clearly sees me quite differently, he harbours such a lot of hate. Oh, and another thing, he told her he'd sent her a gift and a card for every Christmas and birthday, and postcards from wherever he was. She said she never received them. I told her that's because he's lying. The audacity of the man.'

I look at Richard, unable to speak.

'He's lying – isn't he, Kat?'

For a moment I think about denying this, but I've told so many lies, I have to own up to it. Besides, some of the things Tony sent were recorded delivery and he probably has proof.

'No,' I say.

Richard looks shocked.

'He sent her letters, birthday cards and gifts – just little things,' I add.

He looks around the room, like he's searching for something, and then he looks back at me. 'He sent things to Amy, things *for* Amy. And you never passed them on?'

I take a breath. 'No.'

'Oh, Kat.' He's looking at me like I'm a murderer. Until now, Richard's always trusted me implicitly, and it was important that he trusted me, so he believed everything I told him. To suddenly discover that I've kept something like this from him is clearly distressing, disappointing. But there's so much more, and it makes me wonder if he could ever handle that truth. I hope he doesn't have to find out, but I can feel things coming undone.

'I know it was wrong, and I feel bad about it – but to give her the gifts and the cards was selling her the dream dad. I knew even if he did turn up in her life, he'd never be the father she wanted, she'd be disillusioned, he'd let her down again – and I couldn't bear to watch him destroy her like he did me.'

But more than that I didn't want her to look for him, I didn't want them to speak to each other. Richard thinks he knows why I don't want my daughter to meet her father – but he doesn't.

'You can't cover it all up, Kat. What he did was terrible, and she needed to know that. But you really should have passed on the gifts and the letters,' he adds.

'His letters were full of his lies… and I just wanted to keep her. I knew he'd come looking for her one day, and the gifts and the cards would have kept the channel of communication open. I know I was wrong, but I was thinking of her.'

We sit in silence for a while, I want to ask him more, but it feels like he needs time to digest what I've just told him. Here he was defending me to Amy, telling her Tony was the liar, when all the time it was her mum, his wife. It was me. And the truth is, he doesn't even know the half of it.

# CHAPTER SIXTEEN

Having walked out on us, Tony made the odd phone call to ask how Amy was, sent her a couple of postcards. In that time, I rebuilt my life, took freelance work writing for newspapers and magazines, and though it didn't pay much, I lived frugally and worked from home, looking after Amy, who was now thriving. She was physically well, and after two rounds of chemo there were no signs of the leukaemia, but it would be a long time before we could say categorically that she was clear and I wanted to be there every minute to check on her. So, six months on, our lives were more stable, and she was happier and much calmer without Tony around. But then, out of the blue, I received legal documents from his solicitor demanding full custody of our daughter. I knew he had little chance of gaining full custody, but he may have had a chance of caring for her for half the time, and even the odd weekend would have been too much for me – I was determined to fight it.

I was even more devastated when I found out through an old friend who was still in touch with him that he now had the money to see this through. Apparently he'd dumped the woman he left me for (who had his child, a son) and now he had a rich, older girlfriend. She was funding his musical career, and he was having a great life. But it seemed she couldn't have children, and was pushing him to get his pretty little girl back. So, true to character, this selfish waster had decided it would be fun to torture me and add a pretty little trinket to his life. I remember looking him up on Facebook at the time, photos of him and his new girlfriend on the Italian Riviera, flashy cars, the yacht, the drinking-and-dancing lifestyle he loved. Yet he had suddenly decided it wasn't enough – or his girlfriend had – and he now wanted his child to add to his list of possessions. There was no way this was ever going to happen. I'd only just got my daughter back, after months and months of treatment and worry. I'd been the one to care for her and she wasn't out of the woods yet, if the disease didn't return the chemo may have left some weakness in her immune system. She needed care and I was the only one who was going to do that properly.

Then, late one evening, when Amy was sleeping, he called to ask if I'd received his solicitor's letter.

'You must be joking if you think after all this time you can just take her,' I said. 'You haven't bothered to come and see her for eighteen months, I'm sure that won't go down well in court.'

'I didn't have the means,' he said, 'but now I do, and I live in Italy, I can give her a wonderful life – and I can't believe you'd get in her way. You just want to keep her in your miserable existence. You're so selfish, you'd deny her the very best just so you can cling to her, you sad cow.'

I told him I wasn't going to speak with him anymore, and my lawyer would be in touch. Even though, at that point, I didn't even have a lawyer, or any money to get one.

'I *will* have my daughter,' he said, before putting down the phone.

The very thought of losing Amy appalled me, and from being on the brink of getting my life back, and building a future for us – I was a mess. I had no money for a lawyer, I didn't know where to start with legal proceedings. I just hoped Tony would get bored and move on, like he always did.

But the following night I received another call. 'I intend to use everything I've got to get her…' he hissed down the phone.

The hairs on the back of my neck stood up as I slammed the phone down.

His campaign was in full swing. He called many nights after that, always late, always menacing, he was trying to break me down, and it was working. The problem was that during Amy's illness I'd taken antidepressants to get me through, and he was going to use this against me, paint me as some crazy, incompetent mother. 'I have the best lawyers and I want my daughter, so game on, you pill-popping bitch. Let's see who takes her home after the court case.'

I didn't sleep for a week. This was a very real threat. My heartbreak was being turned into some kind of insanity for him to present as a case against me. I was angry, but more scared, because I knew he'd ruin Amy's life. And even if he got partial custody, he'd take her away from me, her mother, to live in another country. There were no guarantees that he could even be trusted to bring her home on time, if ever, and if and when he got bored, who knew what would happen then? I wasn't prepared to risk losing Amy, not after I'd almost lost her once. I'd spent the eighteen months since her illness loving her, caring for her in every way, protecting her from germs, feeding her organic food, vitamin supplements, never allowing her to get too cold, or too hot. Yes, for a little while you might describe me as obsessed, but she was my child, she'd suffered a life-threatening illness. I couldn't bear to lose her, nor could I bear to countenance the thought of her being in another country with a man I didn't trust to look after her.

His new woman had lots of money, and they were tiring of the cars and the holidays, but I also guessed that Tony would soon tire of his girlfriend, he usually did, and if he had any kind of custody where would that leave my daughter? So, as determined as he was to have Amy, I was just as determined he wouldn't. I'd have done anything to keep her with me, keep her safe. It sounds dramatic, I know, but I even considered dying our hair, changing our names and moving to the Outer Hebrides. I seriously considered it, but Amy's well-being was always my priority and she had to be seen regularly for scans and blood tests and I wasn't going to compromise her health.

I knew that I couldn't handle this on my own, but I was a single mother with very little income, so I went to the first Legal Aid solicitor I could find in the phone book. He seemed kind, understanding and calm – his name was Richard Ellis. He explained everything clearly and patiently to me, and for the first time in a long time I felt that I had someone batting for my team. And when we won the case, I said I'd like to take him out to dinner to thank him, but I couldn't afford it, and suggested McDonald's. He said it was his favourite restaurant, and I brought four-year-old Amy along on what was to be our first date. We married six months later, and Richard told me he had fallen in love with me from the minute he heard my story, and wanted to make everything better. And he always has, until now.

He took on my case with enthusiasm, leaving no stone unturned and constantly looking for ways we could not only win custody but make sure it was watertight for the future so Tony couldn't come for her again. So much for the future being watertight – it wasn't. Tony has done what he'd always threatened and found a way to get to Amy.

So now, as a result of Tony's actions, we once again find ourselves in a horrible mess. I just hope to God Amy's okay.

'So what did you say to Amy?' I ask Richard now.

'I told Amy, as you told me all those years ago, that you cut her father from her life for her own good,' he says. 'I said, "Your mum loves you so much. She was worried he'd neglect or perhaps even hurt you if she allowed him to see you."'

It was exactly that, but so much more. Tony could barely look after himself, and there was also the small matter of the fact he'd moved to another country. For a long time Richard and I worried he might try to kidnap her, and we never left her alone for a minute if we were collecting her from school or gymnastics or ballet. She once asked to walk home from school with her friends and I said no, which caused a huge row. Even Richard had said it would be okay, that I could take my foot off the pedal: 'Kat, she's twelve and we haven't heard from Tony for seven years.' But I knew differently.

Richard continues, 'He told her you wouldn't even let her go to Italy for a holiday. She said that upset her; she wasn't even told about it, let alone given a choice.'

I didn't respond, just listened.

'I said, "Imagine as a little girl going to your dad's for a holiday. What if he never brought you back? You'd never have seen your mum ever again." She cried when I said that, she was so upset, so confused.'

I'm crying now myself. Huge tears are running down my face. Everything was going so well, I might have known he'd do this. Why did Tony have to turn up after all this time and ruin everything?

'I just want to hug her and make it all better,' I cry.

'It's okay, Kat,' Richard's saying. 'She was so upset – that's why I still believe there's a strong chance she's just gone away for a while.'

'But what if Tony's taken her… or done something?' He has reason enough to get back at me, and this would be the worst.

'He's messed with her mind and she's gone of her own accord, trying to work through it all, if you ask me.'

'Perhaps,' I concede, 'and I really, really hope and pray that's the case – but I don't think it is. I *know* she'd have wanted to talk it through with me. And even if she didn't, she'd say, "Mum, I'm going off for a couple of days, I'm fine, but don't contact me." She wouldn't be so cruel as to just disappear.'

'To be fair, she did say she was going to contact you on Saturday; she was going out on Friday night.'

'Yeah, she texted me on Saturday, but looking back there was something about that text…'

'What do you mean?' Richard asks.

'I don't know, it didn't seem like her – just a bit… flat.'

'She was still upset probably. I did my best on Friday and when we parted, she seemed happy, but who knows?'

'No, it wasn't just that.' The more I think about it there was something off about that message. 'She usually fills her texts with emojis and exclamation marks and witty comments, even if she's pissed off. But it was just, "Hi mum going for breakfast with the girls."' I think again about this text. 'When has she ever said, "the girls"? She'd say, "I'm going for breakfast with Becky, Tom and Emily" or whoever.'

Richard looks at me, his head to one side.

'I'm overthinking it again, aren't I?'

'Probably,' he says.

*But what about Tony?*

When she came home for my birthday, I realised Amy still had this romantic vision of her father – even after all these years. I didn't think it would be góod for him to come into her life just as she was starting university, so I'd given her the truth about her father – or at least some of it. I felt she was old enough to understand – but now I realise they were already in touch.

'It's Tony, isn't it? I knew he'd charm her, then break her heart if he found her,' I say.

'Don't worry, I've told the police everything, and they're going to locate and interview him.'

'Thank God,' I say, but deep down I don't feel appeased because if Tony's been with Amy all this time, he may have already destroyed mine and Amy's relationship. He will have told her I lied, and he'll do the same with the police and they may just turn their attention on me rather than finding Amy.

Later that night when I can't sleep, I come downstairs and make a cup of Amy's peppermint tea. It's 4 a.m. and dark outside, and as I wait for the kettle to boil I stand close to the frost-framed window, it looks so dark out there. I hope Amy's okay, hope she isn't cold. I'm beginning to hate it here, the wallpaper, the waiting, the landline ringing urgently during the day, people calling to ask if we've heard anything, the kettle boiling endlessly, steam and fear thrumming through the house. I'm living in a loop, and though it's now the early hours of Tuesday – three days since anyone last heard from Amy – I can't see an end to this. And when I think about the possible outcomes, I want to run away. But I can't – because as bleak as this is, and as low as I feel as each day dawns, I have to be here because I'm hoping against hope that eventually she'll come home.

My mind goes back to last night and I keep thinking about how both Tony and Richard were the only people who saw her before she vanished – is that significant?

# CHAPTER SEVENTEEN

Heather, the police liaison woman, is very nice, but I wish she'd fuck off. I haven't slept for days and I'm really not in the mood for a stranger in the house. She keeps offering to make me cups of tea, and encouraging me to talk about Amy, but I know what she's doing, she's trying to find out if I know any more than I'm letting on. Yes, there *are* things I'm not telling her, there's stuff that goes back years, but none of that matters now.

As I said to Richard, it's too little too late, Amy could be anywhere by now. If Tony's taken her, who knows where he's sailed off on his yacht, they could be on the other side of the world and we'll never find her.

Richard says I'm being paranoid because I'm stressed and sleep-deprived, and I just need to let the police to do their job. But what I really need is for Heather to stop playing the female lead in a detective drama. *There's nothing to see here, Heather.* She turned up yesterday, which was Tuesday, but the day doesn't really concern me at the moment, each one bleeds into the next and all I know is that today, Wednesday, Amy has been missing for four days.

I hate the waiting, the hanging around, the endless cups of fucking tea. I don't drink tea! Sometimes I have this urge to go back to Aberystwyth again, see if I can find Amy, walking along the wintery pebble beach, mustard jumper, red scarf, her hair flying behind her. I dreamt of this last night, and when I caught up with her, she turned round and said, 'Oh hi, Mum, I've been so busy,' and disappeared into thin air.

I wish I was there instead of here. I'm like an animal trying to escape pain, but it's inside me and I know I'll take it with me wherever I go. But for now I'm stuck here with Heather pretending we're best friends.

'How do you all get on?' Heather asked after she'd been here about four minutes, and 'What's Richard like as a father?' I told her, 'He's fine, he's a good father.' Then she started asking me all about my life with Tony, of which I gave her edited highlights.

I hate that our lives are being laid out on the police petri dish, infinitesimal flaws scrutinised under a microscope where every imperfection is magnified and made more significant than it really is.

This morning Heather's obsessing about the fact that I have 'a close relationship' with my daughter, and 'have been known to panic when she doesn't call for a matter of hours'.

'That happened, yes. I thought she'd drowned at the lido,' I say, knowing Heather had spotted my 999 call from last summer in the bloody notes.

'But she was fine,' Heather says, nodding.

'On that occasion, yes. I think as parents we all have those moments,' I say, knowing she thinks I'm unstable and blowing this out of all proportion. Everyone hears of the dangers of teenagers drowning in the summer – okay, it's usually in lakes or reservoirs, but I'd seen the number of people who congregated at the lido on those warm July days and the rather young, vain lifeguards who sat preening themselves rather than keeping an eye on the swimmers.

Of course, like everyone else, Heather's got me pigeon-holed as the mad mother. This isn't helped by the fact that both Richard and Zoe still keep stressing to anyone who'll listen that Amy's probably gone off 'to think about everything'.

'I have a daughter of a similar age to Amy,' Heather's saying. She isn't even dressed like a policewoman, she's wearing a powder-blue jumper and slacks, very non-threatening, and presumably worn in the vain hope that devastated people will think of her as a friend. And tell her everything.

*Not always they won't, Heather.*

'Good, so if you have a daughter, you'll understand what I'm going through,' I say. 'And if… what's her name?'

'Ella, her name's Ella.'

*We can both play the psychologist's game, Heather.*

'Okay, if Ella is anything like Amy, you'll know that she would not go AWOL without telling you.'

'I'm not so sure.' She's shaking her head and looking doubtful.

'Well, as far as Amy's concerned, I *am* sure. This is the girl who calls me at midnight to dissect a row she's just had over whose fridge shelf belongs to whom. She texts me updates of her day every few hours, from the sandwich she had for lunch, to what her lecturer said about her essay, to what a stranger said in the coffee queue at Starbucks – *everything*. And because we're so close I could probably tell you what she had for supper every evening last week, and who's on her in list and her out list, what she loves this week, or who annoyed her and what was said. I know that Becky is irritating, with the way she leaves her hair straighteners on the kitchen table. I know Emily is noisy in the bedroom, and that Ahmed bought her a muffin at the university canteen…'

I stop for breath, while Heather just nods slowly and smiles, seemingly unperturbed by my passionate diatribe. She's like my therapist – I'm expecting for her to say, 'And how does that make you feel?' any minute now. I suppose she's used to it; as a family liaison officer, it's her job to listen to the ranting of people driven insane by the loss of loved ones.

'What I'm saying is that I know my daughter,' I repeat, and an image comes unbidden of Amy meeting Tony without telling me, and Amy and Richard meeting up to discuss what had happened. And then there's the fact that Amy and Josh aren't even together anymore, and I had no idea. *Why so many secrets, Amy?* Then again, the fruit doesn't fall far from the tree.

'Yes, I hear you…' Heather says. 'I sometimes wonder though if mobile phones are a blessing or a curse. When I think about what I got up to at Amy's age, I'm glad I didn't have my mum calling me every five minutes.'

'No, they're a blessing. And as I'm not the kind of mother who calls Amy "every five minutes", it isn't a problem,' I add pointedly, aware she's still smiling and nodding. I feel like everyone has this theory that I'm an obsessive mother who won't leave Amy alone. Heather's not the only one who seems to be under this impression, but the poor woman's like a police punchbag; though it's frustrating to throw it all at her as she just soaks it up. I wish she'd retaliate, give me something to argue with, but everyone's treading on eggshells around me. I know they're all thinking the same, that Amy's escaped her smothering mother.

I glance at Heather who's paid to sit on strangers' sofas on the worst days of their lives and watch them spew their anger and fear. What else can she do but smile and nod in the face of all this pain and anguish?

I become aware of a noise, then realise it's me as a huge, racking sob starts deep inside my chest and pushes its way out.

Immediately, Zoe comes in, she's been in the kitchen making lunch with Jodie and Josh. She sweeps me into her arms and embraces me as I sob and talk and make no sense.

'I don't know what she had to eat for dinner last night,' I say, stuttering through the tears. 'And I… I know she hasn't been in the university canteen, because I've called them for the past two days and asked if there was a girl in there with long blonde hair wearing a red-checked scarf.'

'Oh, Kat, you're torturing yourself,' Zoe's saying, while Heather makes a discreet exit.

Eventually the guttural sobs subside and Zoe goes back into the kitchen, passing Heather, who's returning with more cups of bloody tea. She's carrying two mugs, gives one to me and puts the other on the coffee table for herself – it has the photo of a pug on the front. It's Amy's mug. I have to stop myself from asking her not to use it. I'm being irrational and I know it.

'The station just rang me, and CCTV can't place Amy at any of the railway stations she may have used to come home,' she announces.

'So she never set off for home?' I ask.

'Doesn't look like it,' Heather says, taking a sip from my missing daughter's mug. 'You *were* expecting her, weren't you?'

'Yes – I was,' I say, having been asked this question so many times I'm beginning to question myself. 'She just didn't specify what day or what train.'

'Kat, there's something else…' she starts to shift in the chair and I brace myself for what she's about to say. I've acquired a sixth sense in the time Amy's been missing – people, even police liaison officers – shift in their seat when they're about to ask or tell me something difficult.

'We checked Amy's bank records, and on Saturday afternoon all her money was taken out of her student account from a cashline in Aberystwyth.'

'Oh…' I don't breathe. 'What does this mean?'

'At this stage it's hard to tell, but it could place her in Aberystwyth at that time.'

'Yes – yes it could, couldn't it? Perhaps she took the money and left the area after all?' I say, relieved at this possibility, this chink of light in the darkness.

'Or it might be that her bank card has been used by someone else.'

Immediately I come crashing down. Of course, I didn't think of that in my current blurred state that only wants to hear what I want to hear.

We both sit in silence while I let this information in.

'What do you think has happened to Amy?' she suddenly says.

'I don't know.' I feel tied up in knots. She's making me paranoid.

'Do you know what happened to her, Kat?'

'No! Of course I don't, what are you trying to say?'

'Nothing, and please don't take offence. As I'm sure you'll appreciate that everyone has to be considered in this scenario.'

I'm not convinced that was just a routine question, and I'm not sure what I should or shouldn't tell her. I don't want to get into the whole birthday fallout – nor do I want to go into all the Tony stuff that I believe isn't relevant. So I just speak from the heart.

'As one mum to another, Heather,' I say, 'all I can tell you is that every nerve in my body is telling me she's been hurt, taken... and that's *all* I know.'

I've seen enough crime dramas to realise that as soon as someone goes missing, whoever they are, the family are the first focus. I know Heather's only doing her job, but I feel like I'm constantly defending everything about my life, the way I behave, my relationship with my child, my marriage. And even the fact that my daughter is actually missing!

*

'Do you think you worry too much?' Zoe says to me later.

We've just had a sandwich lunch and Jodie and Josh are in the kitchen on Jodie's laptop while Zoe and I are in the sitting room.

'Worry too much about Amy, you mean? I suppose I do. Richard says I wrap her up in cotton wool, but I don't.'

Zoe raises her eyebrows; she clearly thinks the same.

'Heather sees me as this mother figure straight out of a Stephen King novel. It's not like I make Amy pray for hours, wash her mouth with soap, ban boyfriends and deny the existence of menstruation,' I say, in an attempt to get this into perspective.

Zoe laughs at this. 'Not quite!'

'Not at all!' I say, surprised at the implication. 'You sound like Richard – just because he doesn't *understand* our closeness, it doesn't make it weird,' I add.

'Oh God, what an insult, I sound like Richard?' She laughs.

'No, it's just that Richard didn't have a close relationship with either of his parents so judges my close parenting by those standards – he just doesn't understand,' I back-pedal. 'And if I'm honest, Zoe, I'm beginning to question everything, even myself. Everything is a blur and I don't know what's real anymore. Heather asked me if Amy said she was definitely coming home, and I know she did – but the longer she's missing, the more the conversations we had become blurry.'

'Do you have a text from her telling you she was coming home?' Zoe asks, leaning forward, her elbows on her knees.

'No, that's it. We talked on the phone about it, and I'm only questioning it because everyone keeps asking me. I'm sure, really. She said she was excited about coming home – had loads to tell me.'

I see the way she's staring at me and I'm slightly uncomfortable.

'Kat...' she starts. 'Do you know more than you're telling the police – or any of us? Do you *know* where Amy is, love?'

'No, no... Zoe, how can you say that?'

'Sorry, love, I just had to ask. As your friend I had to ask.'

'Please don't ask me again,' I say, with tears in my eyes. And I see the tears in her eyes, the sympathy on her face and know she's just being a good friend.

'As uncomfortable and difficult as it was for me to ask – you understand why I had to?'

I just nod, unable to speak, because if I do I might cry again, and I'm not sure I could stop.

Later, when Zoe's gone, Richard's asleep in bed and everywhere's quiet, I scroll Amy's Instagram looking at the photos and allow myself to cry. Freshers' Week, just eight weeks ago, her Instagram spewed stories and photos with classmates, and flatmates usually in fancy dress. It began with selfies of perfectly made faces that seemed to disintegrate as each photo was taken as the evenings wore on. By midnight there'd be blurry photos and shaky videos of Amy and her friends hugging each other in the street, and by 3 a.m. they'd be falling out of nightclubs, lipstick and mascara a memory.

Those online photos – of this new, exciting time Amy was having – gave me great joy. I was happy because she was happy – and a 4 a.m. video of my daughter dancing in a dimly lit venue was strangely comforting. It meant she was okay, alive, and enjoying herself. And, trust me, the two magic words, "active now", on her social media, are the most wonderful words a mother can see in the wee small hours when her child's far from home.

'I just know her…' I murmur to myself, and think back to earlier when just before she left, Zoe had tried in her way to prepare me for what might happen next.

'Love – don't just assume Amy didn't do something because you don't *think* she would. Our kids surprise us, and at this age they change daily – your version of Amy might not be exactly who she is anymore.'

My version of Amy? I'm not even sure what that is now.

# CHAPTER EIGHTEEN

Zoe, Jodie and Josh are with me, Richard's pottering around elsewhere and we're talking about doing some kind of Facebook page. It's Jodie's idea, I think she wants to do her bit to try to find Amy. 'I just feel so helpless, Kat,' she said, when she told me about her idea. I understood exactly how she felt. Now Josh is showing me the 'Find Amy' page and talking me through it.

'Amy will love this,' I say, and he nods, awkwardly. I wonder how he feels about all this, I still don't know what happened between them, and perhaps I overreacted in blaming him. There are always two sides, and he's been so good coming over every day. I'm grateful for his help.

Heather walks into the kitchen and no one looks up, all four of us in a kind of huddle, keeping out the rest of the world. She pours herself a glass of water and leaves the room and I feel slightly guilty. Under normal circumstances I'd go out of my way to make this woman feel welcome in my home – after all, she's a guest – but events change you. And here I am again, being tested. I'm polite, kind, thoughtful, compassionate – and yet I'm not, because here in my home my own feelings encompass everything, and there's no room for anyone else's. Even Heather's. My filter went with Amy and now it's okay for me not to offer hot drinks to everyone who turns up at my home or ask how they are or provide cake and comfort. I only spend time with the people I want to, and I fill the space with Zoe, Jodie and Josh, because we all know Amy, and we all share the same feelings, the same desire for her to come home.

There's a certain liberty in my current situation, I'm the mother of a missing child and will be forgiven anything. I have permission to say and do what I like without being concerned about how it affects other people, because my pain is worse. I'm a different Kat, not the one I thought I was, and can focus only on the horror hanging over me like a dark, sticky cloud.

Through all this, Richard and I have operated in separate spheres, he's there but I don't feel his presence as much as I do Zoe, Jodie and Josh's, which has kept me sane. From the minute this started, they've been here listening to my rants, wiping my tears, making food and drinks. I've been so low, so desperate since Amy went missing, it feels like Jodie and Josh, these two kids, Amy's friends, provide the antidote; the house becomes a home when they're around. Without Amy, there's this big vacuum in my home and in myself and they distract from the void she's left, they bring the outside world in the way Amy does when she's here.

Jodie played me a song this morning on her phone, it was a new singer I hadn't heard before, he had an amazing voice.

'I love it,' I said, as she hummed along.

'I knew you would, you like a bit of Ed Sheeran and he's a bit like him.'

'That's something I miss now Amy's away at uni,' I said. 'She played music all the time, I don't hear it anymore.' She brought so much into this home – the music, funny videos on her phone, shared snippets about her friends, and the big stories from her day. My daughter offered these precious things to me in the same way she'd bring in a beautiful butterfly from the garden when she was small – fluttering colour cupped in her hands.

'Kat – I can always download you a playlist,' Josh offered.

I was so touched, I felt my eyes sting and I had to turn my head so they didn't see me cry. 'Thanks Josh,' I croaked, seeing the little girl in the kitchen doorway, cupped hands reaching out to me, that smile that makes everything worthwhile.

'I used to make playlists for Amy – until she went off me.' He'd looked over at Jodie and she gave an awkward laugh.

'I'm sure she didn't go off you, Josh,' I offered.

'Oh, she did. She hated me.' I see the sadness in his eyes and realise that perhaps things weren't black and white between him and Amy.

'No, that's not true – is it, Jodie?' I'd looked at her and she'd shrugged, and turned slightly pink. I hoped I hadn't embarrassed her, the last thing she wanted to get into was a discussion with her best friend's ex about what went wrong. I, on the other hand, wanted every little bit of information because it might just lead me to Amy.

'I think you and Amy must have got your wires crossed,' I said, turning to Josh. 'You were living far apart and sometimes conversations over the phone are open to all kinds of misunderstandings.'

'But this was when I went there, to see her. She just didn't want me around, I could tell.'

'It's difficult because when you haven't seen someone for a few weeks it takes a little while to get back to where you were. I mean, you've both been in different environments, you're bound to have different expectations…'

'Yeah, I guess,' he'd said. But he seemed doubtful.

I had said all of this for Amy, really. I don't know how she'll feel about anything when she comes back, but I'm sure she still cares about Josh. I just hope that he doesn't meet someone before she's home, I know it would break her heart. He obviously cares about her, he's been here religiously for the last few days, helping out and just being there. The other day I went upstairs and found him looking through the door into Amy's room. He'd jumped when I walked up behind him, but I told him not to be embarrassed – 'I'm always in Amy's room,' I said. 'It makes me feel closer to her.' He'd nodded and headed back downstairs, but it made me realise how much this is getting to him.

Today his focus is completely on this Facebook page – he seems desperate to find her. Does he blame himself, perhaps? I know that feeling. I'm permanently on high alert, anxious, longing for some news, some tiny flake of hope that never seems to come, and like Josh, I'm always looking for her in everything. It isn't hard to be *with* her in this house, because she's been away such a short time. Yesterday I came across a pair of her summer sandals on the shoe rack in the hall, they were slightly askew, just as she'd left them, and I didn't move them. It reminded me of last summer when the two of us went for afternoon tea in Malvern, a small town on the outskirts of Worcestershire. Rolling green hills, blue skies and scones with jam and clotted cream, Amy's favourite – and as I think about it I can hear her laughter and feel the sun on my face. For a few, blissful moments I'm not scared, the absolute terror of what might have happened leaves me, and I bathe in the past. Then Heather offers me a cup of tea, or Zoe tries to engage me in some gossip to take my mind off things, and I'm plunged back into reality. Horrible, dark reality.

The past twenty-four hours have been a mosaic of nothing. Lots of little bits of nothing stuck together to make another meaningless, heartbreaking day where there's no news. I constantly check my phone, my eyes are sore and my throat hurts from crying. Tonight Zoe makes a valiant attempt to inject some punctuation into this endlessness by suggesting we get a Chinese takeaway for dinner, but I can't eat.

'Love, you have to keep your strength up. You need to be well for when Amy walks through that door.'

'You know it's all I want, all I need,' I say, with a smile. I hear my voice cracking, tears prick my eyes.

Zoe understands. We met at the school gate thirteen years ago, when our little girls were just five years old, and became firm friends, just as our daughters did. We always said that being mothers of only children is what bonded us, we have to get it right the first time because we don't get a second chance. Later, our husbands were included in our friendship, and even though Richard has never been a Zoe fan, he kindly went along with social events. Now Zoe and Pete are divorced, things have changed, but our friendship remains incredibly strong, and these past few days have proved that – I don't know what I'd have done without her. It's good to have Jodie and Josh around too, I can see a lot of Amy in both of them, the way they live on their phones, speak their own language with the phrases they use, the way they react with WTF? And OMG! Every five minutes. And I love that they are here every day, because she isn't. Jodie's lip balm is the same, sickly sweet vanilla that Amy wears, and each waft gives me fresh hope that all will be okay again one day. The four of us have formed an unlikely little group, sharing our stories about Amy, and we spend hours discussing various theories of what might have happened, where she might be.

I can see what Amy saw in Josh. Before I always saw him as 'Amy's boyfriend', an extension of her, and someone I knew because of his relationship with my daughter. But in the past few days I feel like I've got to know him, and understand the kind of person he is independently of Amy. I know Josh's mother died of cancer when he was quite young, but it was fascinating to discover just how much her death has impacted on his life and his future.

'I want to be an oncologist,' he told me yesterday when we talked about next year, when he starts his university course. 'I know medicine is intense, it's gonna be hard, but if I can stop one kid like me from losing their mum, then it'll all be worth it.'

'Wow,' I said, 'I'm impressed.' And it struck me how mature he is for a boy of eighteen. It made me think about Amy saying he was 'a child' and really immature, and it doesn't make sense. She just wouldn't say something like that.

'You know that Amy had cancer…' I'd said.

'Yeah – it would be so fucking shit if anything's… happened. I mean, after all that.'

'Yeah, Josh, you're right – it would be *so* fucking shit,' I'd said. I find his and Jodie's honesty, their teenage lack of filter so refreshing. They just say what they feel, they don't keep asking me how I am, or hiding how they feel or talk in low voices around me like they're at a bloody funeral.

This morning, Josh arrived earlier than the other two and it gave me a chance to have a chat with him about Amy. I think yesterday our conversation was a little awkward for him with Jodie there.

'What really happened, between you two?' I asked.

Initially he seemed reluctant to say too much, but then he confided. 'Amy changed once she got to uni,' he said. 'I reckon she'd met someone else and she went off me.'

I found that hard to believe. 'I was under the impression she still liked you,' I said.

'When I went to see her, it just felt like she didn't want me there, I was supposed to be staying a few nights, but I came back early.'

'Oh, I didn't realise. What made you think she didn't want you there?'

At first he looks uncomfortable, and I don't think he's going to say anything, but then he just blurts it out. 'She said I was boring, that I was "a child", and that now she was at university she'd grown out of "little boys". I just felt so pissed off I came home.' I see a flash of hurt in his eyes, and I feel for him.

'Oh, Josh, do you think you might have been mistaken?' I ask.

He shrugged. 'She could be mean sometimes.'

'I'm sure she *can* be mean,' I said, subtly correcting his past tense, and feeling slightly irritated that he seems to be blaming Amy for the break-up. 'But perhaps she was feeling insecure. You know sometimes people play hard to get, or appear to be a little cold because they feel like *they're* the ones who are being rejected.'

He nodded slowly without making eye contact.

'Amy wouldn't be mean to anyone, let alone you. In fact the last time we spoke she told me she thought you were being off with *her*. These things can get blown out of proportion, you might have both misinterpreted what was said.'

'You weren't *there* – I was,' he says, and for the first time I see anger in his eyes.

'Oh, Josh, don't take this to heart – especially now. Let's just see what happens when she gets back, you two need to talk.'

He shakes his head. 'That's not going to happen.'

'It will if you *want* it to.'

'It can't. Not now.'

'Why – what do you mean?' I ask, suddenly feeling a little uneasy about this conversation.

'Nothing,' he says, standing up. 'Oh, I forgot – I have to go, Kat. I told my dad I'd give him a lift this morning to the builders' yard – I'm late.'

'Okay,' I say – and before I can say anything else, he's gone.

Now Josh has gone, I wander the empty house, checking my phone, picking up photos of Amy that are perched everywhere. I wonder what time Jodie will get here? It sounds weird, but she's the nearest I get to Amy, the similar mannerisms, the clothes, even that welcome waft of vanilla. She hugs me like Amy would, leans on me when I'm nearby and makes me consistently revolting cups of coffee and presents them with the sweetest smile – just like Amy does.

Everyone else, even Richard, seems uneasy with me in my agony, like I might blow up or spontaneously combust if they do or say anything out of place. Then again, I might. I feel like a balloon filled with water, wobbly, and unreal.

Richard isn't so comfortable with the daily visits from everyone – especially Zoe. 'That woman's so opinionated, so bossy,' is his usual comment after her departure. But I've always welcomed her strength, and so-called bossiness – especially now. Zoe has my back, she'll take control if necessary, and right now she's just what I need.

Zoe holds me, and like a sponge I can feel her soaking up my pain, my uncertainty. *Where is Amy? Will I ever see my child again?*

Heather eventually leaves for the day. As with every evening she's been here, she offers to stay if I need her. As with every other evening, I don't. Zoe's on the phone ordering Chinese, having told me that, 'When you smell that sweet and sour you'll change your mind about not being hungry.' I won't. Richard's finally joined us downstairs and, in the absence of a laptop or a golf club, has started watching an old black-and-white film on the TV.

'I don't know how you can focus to watch a film,' I say. I can't concentrate on anything, and every single moment not spent searching for her online or anywhere else is wasted in my view. I resent the fact that he can do something other than worry about Amy.

'I'm not watching the film. It's just washing over me,' he replies.

While Zoe is on the phone ordering enough Chinese for an army, I stand in the middle of the living room not sure what to do. I feel like an actress who's forgotten her blocking during a play. I am lost, what do I do next? I'm in need of a shower, I'm not wearing make-up, my hair's a mess, and none of this matters. I feel flayed by worry, and my skin hurts, the only things I can bear to wear are soft jogging bottoms and a huge jumper. I don't feel like me. I don't want to *be* me. Josh and Jodie left just after lunch, and I miss them, the place is quiet again and everyone's on their best grown-up behaviour.

'What's Jodie been up to this afternoon?' I ask Zoe as she comes back into the living room.

She sits down and looks at me. 'Actually, she's been talking to the police, Josh too – they were there all afternoon at ours,' she says. 'They asked really probing questions, it was quite gruelling. Jodie's in bits.'

'Oh, poor Jodie, she doesn't need this. She's finding it difficult enough,' I say.

Zoe nods. 'She just wants to find her, she'll do anything to help – she thinks the world of Amy.'

'I know she does.'

'She keeps asking, "Where is she, Mum?" It kills me.'

I hate that this is affecting Jodie, who can be fragile at the best of times. She's been checking the 'Find Amy' Facebook page all day, but of course so far no one has anything useful to say. Zoe said there are already loads of people following the page. I'm grateful for any kind of publicity – even if it does involve the participation of some people who don't wish us well, nasty trolls infecting all the good messages of hope and love. Over the years I've seen mothers on the TV begging their kids to come home, or asking whoever may have taken them not to hurt their child. I never thought of myself as one of those women – but I've now joined that select club. As soon as Amy was declared officially missing, the local paper called and asked if they could do a piece and I couldn't say no. Then the local TV news got in contact and worked with Heather to liaise with us and come over and film us asking what all those mothers have asked before. It was pretty traumatic, but has to be done.

*Please don't hurt her.*

I'm looking at the latest edition of the local paper now on my phone. 'No News on Missing Amy' is apparently the highest-trending news story. No news is news then? I'm a journalist so I understand how it works, but experiencing it from the other side is painful.

I'm suddenly shocked out of my thoughts by the sound of the doorbell, and though both Zoe and Richard leap up to answer it, I insist on going. I have this wonderful vision of me opening the door to Amy, she might be slightly dishevelled, a little tired, but unhurt and home after an adventure. I know it's more likely to be the police informing me of some horrific find, but I'm so numb with waiting I just want to *feel* something. I open the door with my heart in my mouth, holding my breath and for a split second I think my ridiculous dream has come true because instead of uniformed men with grim faces or women pretending to be my friend in powder-blue jumpers, it's a blonde eighteen-year-old. It's Jodie.

Both Jodie and I burst into tears and hug each other. 'Did Mum tell you about the police?' she says as I walk her into the house and close the door.

'Yes, and I'm so sorry, darling.'

'It's not *your* fault, Kat, I know the police have to ask questions, but...' and she starts to cry again.

'You and Josh must have had a horrible afternoon,' I say, hugging her close and shaking my head. Her hurt is mine too and I find it hard to see funny, sweet Jodie like this.

She sits down next to me and, looking from me to her mum, asks if there's any news. We both just shake our heads, it's hard to keep saying no to people. I've had so many messages in texts or online from friends and friends of friends asking – and I just feel like copying and pasting 'no news' so I don't have to keep telling them the same thing. It's kind of everyone to be thinking of us, but every time the phone pings or the Facebook icon shows a message, my heart soars thinking it might be Amy. Zoe realised this and she's sent a global text message and done the same on Facebook saying thanks for all your kind wishes and offers of help, but the police are now dealing with the investigation and we need to keep all channels of communication clear. I wasn't so sure about the blanket ban. 'What if someone has information and they want to tell me?' I'd said.

'Babe, they can go to the police, I'm not having you distressed every time that bloody text goes off. Jesus, it's giving *me* palpitations, so God only knows what it's doing to you.'

Zoe was right, and it's a great relief now the pinging has stopped. But I still keep checking and rechecking my phone.

'How's the page doing today?' I ask Jodie. She's so pleased to be able to do something to help Amy I want to take an interest, show how proud I am. Zoe's never been very strong on positive encouragement, she's always erred on the side of the stick rather than the carrot when it comes to Jodie.

'The Find Amy page now has two thousand followers,' Jodie says proudly.

'Wow, that's shot up.' Zoe smiles, proud of her daughter's efforts, and so she should be.

'Jodie that's brilliant,' I add, just like I used to when I picked the girls up from school and they showed me their drawings, or their crazy poems, or mad dancing.

'You two are both brilliant,' I'd say. 'But who's the brilliantist?' Jodie would ask, and I'd laugh, and try to be diplomatic and say they were both the 'brilliantist'. The problem with being the mother of an only child, is that you have to remember when another child is around. I once told Amy she was 'the most gorgeous girl in the world', forgetting little Jodie was there, and Jodie wouldn't speak to me for at least an hour.

I smile now, looking at her scrolling her phone, going through the Find Amy page to see if anyone's made any comments that might give her a clue to finding her friend. I remember the girls in their matching Disney costumes at eight years old. They both wanted to be Cinderella, so Zoe and I bought the costumes together so they'd be exactly the same, because if they weren't there'd be trouble. And now they're grown and Jodie's gathered together all these people in cyberspace in a valiant effort to bring her best friend home.

'I've put loads of photos on Facebook and if anyone contacts me with anything useful, I'll send it straight to the police,' she says. I'm so moved by what she's doing, and the fact that so many people are engaging.

'Actually, someone did say they'd seen a girl that looks just like Amy in London, walking through Camden,' she says.

My whole body starts to tingle, it isn't impossible that she'd be there, Tony loved London – he might have taken her there. 'Was she with anyone?'

'Not sure,' she says, 'I'm just trying to find it… here it is,' she offers me her phone and sure enough someone says they saw Amy.

'Can you send that to the police? I'll tell Heather too,' I say. It's another little moment of sunshine in a dark day.

She nods. 'Actually, Kat, I've been thinking…' she says. 'Would you mind if we printed some missing posters? People could put them in their cars, their windows, we can plaster them on bus stops. We could put them all over the Aberystwyth campus too.'

'Better check with the police first, Jodie,' Richard says, tearing his eyes from the TV.

Jodie's face drops slightly. She was so proud of her idea, I wish he'd have been more positive, or at least said it in a less lawyerly way. He made it sound like a reprimand, and despite the situation, I'm slightly embarrassed by his curtness towards her. She's trying to help, and at this stage anything is better than nothing.

'Richard has a point,' I say tactfully, because he does. 'But I think it's a great idea, what harm can it do?' I ask pointedly in his direction.

Zoe clocks what I'm doing and gives me a sly wink, a little thank you for saving her daughter's feelings.

'A local printer has offered to do them free of charge, I could get a few hundred done and we could start,' Zoe says, with a sidelong glance at Richard. I think we're all waiting for him to raise an objection in his bloody courtroom voice, but before he does, I leap in.

'Yes, let's do it,' I say, and for the first time since Saturday, I feel like I'm doing something proactive.

Later, when Jodie and Zoe have gone home, Richard and I look at each other and he asks if I'm okay. I find this to be a rather ridiculous question, of course I'm not okay – but I don't want to snap at him. I don't have the energy to fall out with him.

'I find it hard to go to bed,' I say.

He turns off the TV, says he had to 'drown out that woman', meaning Zoe, and I roll my eyes.

'Richard, not now… she's my friend.'

'She might be your friend, but she's also a bossy woman.'

In the middle of the horror, I have to smile. He sits opposite me in the easy chair, a fresh mug of coffee on his knee, he's just brought a camomile tea in for me and it's steaming fragrantly on the coffee table. His outrage at Zoe is vaguely amusing, she just winds him up, she can't help it and he can't help how he feels, it's just personalities clashing.

'What?' he's saying, as I shake my head.

'Poor Zoe can never do anything right as far as you're concerned. What is it about her that makes you so cross?'

'Every day in every way she makes me more cross. Tonight she force-fed me sweet and sour pork – and I don't even like it.'

I smile indulgently through the pain, and try to imagine, just for a moment that Amy is at uni, and this is like any other Thursday night. But as hard as I try, I can't. Because it isn't.

'I understand how you must feel regarding going to bed – and at the risk of sounding like a boring old sod, you must try and get some sleep,' he says.

'I know, but I can't. I hate turning off the lights and going upstairs. It's like saying goodbye to another day without her, like I'm accepting that she won't be back today. But I *can't* accept it.

I'll *never* accept it. I want to keep the lights on and the front door open all night.'

'Of course you do. But you need to be strong, you need to sleep and eat and look after yourself. When she comes home, you must be well for her – who knows, she may need looking after.'

I think about a conversation I had earlier with Heather. She asked me if I thought Amy might have run away, or be capable of doing herself harm. I was horrified at the mere suggestion, but it's an avenue I've been down in my head, and though at first I wouldn't have countenanced it, I'm beginning to wonder. What if she comes home and she's different? What if she's run away and doesn't want to come home? As Mather said a matter of days ago – that now feel like weeks, 'sometimes people don't *want* to be found.'

'It's the not knowing. I don't *know* where she is, or if I'm ever going to see her again. What if it ends badly, Richard?' I hear myself ask out loud for the first time. Of course I've been thinking it, I've had those constant intrusive thoughts that I've pushed away, tried not to see. But the perhaps inevitable conclusion to all this keeps knocking on my brain and pushing its way in, the unbearable idea that I may never see her again.

'I feel like I'm back in that hospital room waiting for scan results and blood tests. And every time the front doorbell rings, or the police phone – I dread the prognosis.'

Richard gets up from his chair, and bringing his coffee with him, sits next to me on the sofa. He puts his arm around me, and we both sit in silence, in our own heads, unable to say some of the unspeakable thoughts running through them.

# CHAPTER NINETEEN

It's Friday, and Heather's not here today, she's threatened to call in later if she can, but I told her I'm fine, which of course is a lie but her being here won't help. Richard's pottering around and Jodie's here, she turned up at 8 a.m. and set up her laptop on the kitchen counter and announced that the Facebook page now has over three thousand followers.

'Amazing,' I said. 'Oh, by the way, I asked Heather about the sighting in Camden. She said they'd received your info and alerted the police down there, but nothing. They asked in all the shops and homes near where she was seen and no one else saw her and CCTV showed nothing either.'

'Oh, gutted.'

'Yes, me too. She never said anything to you about running away to London did she?'

'No. But she loved London.'

'Yes she does, she likes the shops, we went there over the summer. I thought perhaps… Oh well, it doesn't look like a lead.'

'No, sorry – but there are a lot of sightings and I send them all to the police, but I think some are just trolls.'

'Yeah, I suppose so. Hard to believe anyone could troll a family who have a missing child, but it's a cruel world, Jodie.'

'Yeah,' she said with a sigh, as she went back to the laptop.

'It's so good of you, Jodie. You really don't have to do this you know. You have uni too – Amy will feel bad when she gets back if you're behind on your course.'

'We have to find her, and I want to be here, Kat. I love it at your house, it feels like home – and, I dunno, I just feel closer to Amy.'

I was touched. 'Of course you do, sweetie. It's like old times, you sitting there on your computer.'

'Do you remember when I used to come here dead early in the morning to finish off my homework?' she says now from behind the laptop.

I glance over at her and smile. 'Yes, you were such a skiver.' I giggle. 'Your mother would have had a fit if she'd known I was "harbouring a criminal" every morning, you desperately trying to do your homework while I made toast and tried to get Amy up.'

I'm sitting in the chair by the window, enjoying her presence, the smell of vanilla, the click of her keyboard, the way she throws her long hair over one shoulder like a one-sided shawl. Just like Amy. It makes my heart hurt.

'Yes, Amy always hated getting up.' She smiles at the memory.

'She has always hated it, hasn't she?' I say, unwilling to talk about her in the past tense. The adults are a little more careful, but in their youth Josh and Jodie seem oblivious to the implications of this.

'Yeah, yeah, that's what I meant,' she says, and I hope I haven't embarrassed her, but we all need to keep believing and hoping. Without that there's nothing.

Later, around noon, I heat us up some home-made onion soup from the freezer. We eat it together in big earthenware soup mugs Richard and I brought back from a holiday in France years ago.

'I love these mugs, you used to give us your home-made tomato soup in these on winter days after school. We'd walk across the field home, it was white with snow – and me and Amy would throw snowballs and you'd join in.'

'Mmm, I always came off worse, as I remember it,' I say. 'And you two would throw your snow-covered wellies all over the hall carpet.'

'But you never told us off like Mum did.'

'Well, your house is always spotless, I'm a bit of a mess. Your mum's far neater and more organised than I am.'

'More bossy too,' Jodie suddenly says, and I realise we're veering into territory we should perhaps steer clear of.

'Your Mum just likes things a certain way,' I say kindly, but assertively.

She shrugs. 'I guess. But sometimes I wish I could run away to the circus.' She half-laughs.

'Do you think Amy has run away?' I ask then.

Jodie pauses. 'I reckon she might have, she talked about it… once.'

'Really?' I put down my soup, suddenly feeling very full. I see the dimpling of Jodie's chin and know tears aren't far away, but I push on. 'What did she say? Was it the course, was she finding it too much?'

'I think so.' She nods, and drinks some soup, and I get the feeling there's something she isn't telling me. But if I push her, she'll never tell.

I change tack. 'So why do you feel like running away, Jodie? Are you happy on *your* course?' She shrugs. 'Is there something else you'd like to do?'

'Yeah, loads of stuff, but Mum wouldn't let me. She says I've already let her down. I didn't get the grades for medicine, so, as far as she's concerned, I failed, I'm already a failure.'

'I'm sure she doesn't think that at all,' I say gently, upset that she'd picked up on this. Zoe had spoken to me about her disappointment at the time, but who can blame her? Like all of us, she just wanted the best for Jodie.

'You haven't let anyone down, Jodie. It isn't like you neglected your studies, in fact you had good A-levels, just not good enough to get into the university you wanted to do medicine.'

'The university *Mum* wanted me to go to.'

'But you're happy nearer home, at Worcester, doing a different course?'

'It's more me, but Mum says I just want an easy life.'

I feel really uncomfortable when Jodie does this; she tries to bring me in on her conflicts with Zoe. I happen to agree that Jodie should do the course she wants to do, not the one her mother wanted her to. Jodie's never been academic and I always thought she'd struggle with medicine, but I have to outwardly stay loyal to Zoe.

'I think… as long as you're happy, that's what matters,' I say, avoiding anything that may be quoted and attributed to me the next time Zoe and Jodie have a row.

'You let Amy choose where she went to uni, you let her go out with Josh, you even let them sleep in her room together. My mum would never allow that.'

'Who knows, perhaps I should have encouraged Amy more to go to a nearby uni? Things might have been different if I had,' I say wistfully. 'Everyone's different, Jodie, and I can't speak for your mum, but it's her decision, and you have to respect that.'

'I guess,' she says, and I feel sorry for her. Jodie's the kid who got the short straw, she's the quiet one, who seems to struggle with academia. 'Let me make you a cup of coffee,' she says. 'I know exactly how you like it, a heaped spoon, black, no sugar.'

I remember the girls being eight years old and making me a cup of coffee – both arguing about how much milk to put in and Jodie saying in Zoe's voice, 'Amy, she takes it bloody *black*!'

Zoe and I laughed about that later, when I told her. 'I bet you talk like that to Pete,' I said, referring to her husband at the time.

She'd laughed. 'I bloody *do*! He needs someone to sort him out. Honestly, I do everything in our house, from cleaning to pulling him out of scrapes at work, because, as you know, my husband has no filter. And when I'm not saving his career, I'm talking Jodie through her friendship issues, and homework.'

Like me, Zoe went through a difficult time when Jodie was little. She was born prematurely and for a while there were concerns about her lung and brain development. Zoe wasn't able to hold her baby until she was about six weeks old, and I can only imagine the agony she went through. But ultimately Jodie thrived, and although she's protective of her daughter like I am, she's a little harder. 'I think I've pushed Jodie more because I always had to,' she told me candidly, 'she developed later than all her peers, so I had to hothouse her just to keep up.'

And, to Zoe's credit, she transformed Jodie, a child who in the early years of primary school seemed to struggle with the most basic academic tasks. I remember the flash cards, the impromptu maths and spelling tutorials. Zoe would set Jodie mental maths tests as the four of us walked home from school together. Later, with exams looming, Zoe hired a tutor for maths and English just to help her daughter get decent grades. Poor Jodie has always had to work twice as hard as everyone else, and in my view it's a blessing she didn't get the grades for the medical degree – it would have been far too challenging, though, of course, Zoe doesn't see it that way.

When Jodie was born, she needed so much care. Zoe decided to take a career break to look after her daughter, but when she tried to go back years later, things had moved on. She found herself a job a couple of years ago but didn't get on with the boss and was recently made redundant. I think she feels like she failed, which is why she'd hoped Jodie would become a doctor one day and redeem her, make what she refers to as her 'career sacrifice' worth it. I know Jodie sometimes resents her mother's involvement, what eighteen-year-old wouldn't? But one day she'll realise what her mum has done for her.

I hope Amy doesn't resent *my* involvement in her life. I had to leave work as a feature writer for a magazine when Amy became ill. Despite continuing to work on a freelance basis, Amy became the focus of my life, and she had to come first after the illness. I'd been delighted when Amy decided to do an English degree because I'd done the same. At the time, Richard said I had to let her make her own choices, and not live my life through her. We argued about it.

'You always talk about your life in London working for a big magazine but how you never went back because of her,' he'd said.

I'd never put it quite like that. When Amy asked me why I worked at home, I'd wanted her to know that I'd once had a career. I wanted her to feel she could have one too and told her I'd only stopped because I loved being with her. I hoped it would make her feel special, that I gave it all up for her, but Richard reckoned I'd made her feel guilty for being ill.

'Can't you see, Kat, she's now going to do what you couldn't? She's doing it for you,' he'd continued.

I'd been angry with him at the time, but this has been playing on my mind over the last couple of days. Since Amy disappeared, I've had time for reflection – too much reflection, really – and the more I think about the way Zoe can be with Jodie, the more I wonder if perhaps I'm guilty of using Amy to fulfil my dreams too. Had Amy felt pushed into doing the same degree as me? Was she struggling? Did she feel she'd made a mistake taking the course but didn't like to say for fear of disappointing me?

Earlier today one of Amy's university tutors called our landline. Her name is Laura McKenzie and she wanted to say she was thinking of us. I was touched that she'd taken the trouble and I also wondered if I could perhaps get a feel for how Amy was coping. I know the police have all spoken to the relevant university staff and students, but as a mother I feel I can ask more pertinent questions and might pick up on something they miss.

So with Jodie clicking away at her computer in the kitchen, and Richard sweeping leaves in the garden, I take the phone into the sitting room and call back to talk to Laura McKenzie.

# CHAPTER TWENTY

Laura McKenzie sounds lovely, she has a Scottish accent which rolls around softly on her tongue. I find it comforting. She asks me how I am and I say what I always say, 'I'll be better when Amy's home, thanks.' I don't want to make small talk, it just ends up in a bunch of pointless clichés, so I come out with it. 'Can I ask, was Amy okay? Was she coping with the work?'

'Amy was… *is* a good student,' she says, immediately correcting herself.

'And was she was coping with the work, with living away, as far as you could tell?'

'Yes. Initially she was very enthusiastic and seemed happy with her degree choice,' she adds, like this has been rehearsed.

'But…?'

'But?'

'You said she was enthusiastic *initially*?'

'Did I?'

'Yes, did something change?'

'Not as such, but… it's hard to say, Mrs Russo.'

'I'm Ellis now, my ex-husband is Russo. I remarried.' I offer an incoherent jumble of words, but she seems to understand. Even after all these years, I hate that Amy and I have different surnames – it's like we're not related – but Tony would never allow it, like he'd never allow Richard to adopt her.

'Ah, I see.'

'So, did you notice anything different with Amy?'

'Are you referring to Amy's pastoral welfare?'

'I suppose so.' I'm finding her quite frustrating to pin down. 'I'm just so desperate to know anything and everything in case something is significant and might lead me to her.'

'I understand.'

She isn't offering anything so I go for a simple question, one she can't slither out of.

'Did she seem… *happy* to you?'

'Happy? I don't know.'

It may be my current intense state, where I'm too aware of everything – lights are too bright, voices too noisy and everything that's said seems to have a subtext – but I detect a pause, a flicker of doubt in Laura McKenzie's response.

Then she starts talking again. 'Perhaps I shouldn't say this, but Amy seemed… distracted.'

I feel my heart hammer in my chest. 'In what way?'

'I'm not really the person who should be talking to you about this.'

'But you called me,' I say. 'I know you just wanted to say you're thinking of us all, but you've just told me she was distracted. Can you explain what you mean by this? I need your help, Laura,' I add.

She doesn't respond. I'm worried she might just go and it sounds as if she has something to share so I have to keep her on the phone. What is she trying to tell me?

'If… if you aren't allowed to say anything – is there someone who can tell me why she seemed distracted?'

Another noticeable pause.

'There were rumours…' she says and leaves it with just those three words.

Oh God, I think I'm going to vomit. This is so frustrating and painful.

'Okay,' I say to myself as much as to her, in an effort to ground myself, to be prepared for what she's going to say. 'So what were these rumours?'

'Amy is a beautiful and very bright student, she showed great promise, her contributions in lectures and tutorials were brilliant and I have to say we were very impressed within the faculty.'

'I'm glad she shows great promise,' I say, aware she's ignored my question and wishing people would stop referring to my daughter in the past tense. 'She's always loved literature… but the rumours?'

There's a pause then before Laura speaks again. 'Yes. Controversially perhaps, one of the books on this year's course is *Lolita*… by Nabokov?'

'Yes… yes, I'm familiar with the book,' I say, suddenly feeling quite unsettled. 'In fact it was a set text on my English degree many years ago.'

'Oh, you did English too?'

'Yes… yes,' I say urgently. I don't want to talk about me, I need to know about Amy, but I feel we're dancing around this and I don't want to be rude and *demand* information because I get the impression she might just put down the phone.

'Well, this particular aspect of the course covers controversial twentieth-century literature and in tutorials Amy showed a mature and considered approach to the themes. She said that in *Lolita* she loved the way Humbert, the stepfather's, psychology is laid bare…'

'Oh…' I'm not quite sure what to make of this. *Is it significant?*

'Actually, I'm paraphrasing, I'm not her lecturer for twentieth-century lit, that's Dave Olsen.'

'Oh, do you think he may be able to shed any light on how she was last week at uni?'

'Yeah… thing is, Mrs Ellis, Amy was quite taken with Dr Olsen.'

'Sorry?' I can't get my head round this. Is it something to do with the rumours she'd alluded to?

'It happens a lot,' she continues. 'A young girl or boy away from home, an older person they look up to… they can become, infatuated, fixated even.'

I'm not sure what she's saying, then again, I know exactly what she's saying.

'Are you implying Amy *liked* this Dave Olsen in a romantic way?' I'm not prepared to use the condemnatory language she's using to describe Amy's feelings. Infatuated and fixated have such negative connotations. 'Perhaps she just found him interesting.'

'I think it was more than that,' Laura McKenzie replies.

'I find this very hard to believe.'

'I think you should talk to Dave Olsen. He's a senior lecturer in the department. I'm sure he'll be able to talk you through it.'

'I will, I will talk to him, but… can you tell me, what you mean when you say "fixated"?' The word has unsettled me, and I wonder, in all the turmoil with her father's reappearance, had Amy become slightly unstable?

'I can't really say, but Dave spoke to me about it earlier this week, when we heard that Amy was missing. He said that in the first few weeks, like the rest of us, he'd been impressed by her intelligence, her maturity when dealing with difficult themes. He encouraged her and enjoyed their chats after lectures, sometimes going for a drink, usually with other students,' she adds.

'And this became an *infatuation*?' I asked, struggling to use the word when associated with my daughter's feelings about her lecturer.

'It would seem so. He said it happened slowly, and before he realised, she was turning up at his room unannounced. Apparently, she was being very forward, suggestive, and he made it very clear he was a married man and not interested.'

'This can't be true, you must be mistaking Amy for someone else – she wouldn't,' I say snappily, offended on Amy's behalf, but then I think about what Josh said – that Amy said he was immature and she'd grown out of little boys. Oh God.

Silence.

'How old is he, this Dave Olsen?'

'He's in his forties. I can assure you I'm not mistaken. Earlier this week, when the story about Amy's disappearance was in the newspapers, Dr Olsen was forced to tell his wife about Amy's obsession.'

I don't believe for one minute Amy was interested in this man, whoever he is – nor am *I* interested in any conversations he's had with his bloody wife about it. 'Has he told the police about the situation with Amy?' I ask, because if he hasn't I sure as hell will.

'I don't know. The police are all over the campus, they've spoken to most of us, I'm not sure if they've spoken to Dave.'

'I will mention this to the police myself,' I say.

'Oh, well, if you feel it's necessary, obviously I can't be involved.'

'No, well, I just feel I have to pass this on. I'm grateful, really grateful that you called me,' I say.

She doesn't speak for quite a few seconds, then she says, 'Mrs Ellis, just so you know, this isn't the first time a young woman has become "obsessed" with Dave Olsen. And it never ends well.' With that she clicks off the phone.

I feel a shiver run up my spine. Was she telling me that this guy has had lots of affairs with his students... was she saying they get hurt? Emotionally, physically, what?

I press 1471 and try to call her back, but it rings and rings and there's no answer, so I make a note of the number – it looks like a mobile. I immediately call the university number and when I eventually get through to the department, I ask to speak to Dave Olsen, but he isn't available, so I ask for Laura McKenzie. I wait to be put through, then the voice on the other end tells me, 'Laura McKenzie is on long-term sick leave, I'm afraid.'

'Oh. Do you know when she'll be back?'

'She's been on sick leave for six months, and we have no return date as yet I'm afraid.'

# CHAPTER TWENTY-ONE

'It *must* be a hoax,' Richard says when I go upstairs to tell him about the conversation with Laura McKenzie. 'That doesn't sound at all like Amy. And how does this woman know anything if she's been off for six months?'

'I agree. It's all a bit weird that she talked about Amy like she knew her when she can't possibly because she hasn't been there. And yes, I can imagine Amy falling for a slightly older boy. But a man old enough to be her father?' This reminds me the police were supposed to be tracking Tony down several days ago and he's the prime suspect but we've still not heard anything. I make a mental note to ask Heather about it.

'Obsessed? Fixated?' Richard shakes his head, clearly questioning the words I also found hard to associate with Amy.

'No, it can't be true, but why would someone say that?' I ask, still confused by the conversation I just had and the news that Laura McKenzie is on long-term sick leave.

Richard puts his hands on his head, and I see the last few days have deepened the furrow in his brow. 'I don't know. But the police are on campus and they should already have spoken to this lecturer. If there's anything at all that indicates there was some kind of infatuation, it's his duty of care to report it to them. But I think we should mention it just in case…'

And then I remember something and my heart almost stops. 'Amy mentioned a lecturer, said everyone called him "Professor Perv".'

'Oh Christ,' Richard says, then backtracks when he sees the concern on my face. 'It might be nothing, Kat. But we have to report this.'

'Yes, of course. I'll call Heather,' I say.

I call Heather from Richard's office and tell her about the phone call with Laura McKenzie. I ask whether a Dave Olsen has been interviewed, and if they've looked into the backgrounds of Amy's lecturers. Heather, as ever, keeps things close to her chest, promising that the police will 'pursue all lines of enquiry' and we'll be 'informed immediately of any developments'. Honestly, it's like one big brick wall with Heather repeating the same phrases over and over, until I threaten to contact Dave Olsen myself.

'No, no, no. Don't speak to anyone at the university. It might muddy the waters,' she'd said, panic in her voice.

'What about the woman that called me?'

'Laura McKenzie? No, don't speak to her either. Just be reassured that we're on to it.'

I report back to Richard, then leave him to his work. It seems to be his way of coping, whereas I'm placated by being in the kitchen with my trusty band of supporters, each of us finding the safety net we need to get through all this.

When I get back downstairs, Jodie's still in the kitchen and Zoe and Josh have arrived, I say hi and we hug, but my mind is filled with Dave Olsen and the phone call. Is it true? I can't believe it is – how did I miss it in those long, late-night phone calls with Amy when I thought she was telling me everything? I'm constantly assuring everyone that Amy wouldn't run away because there was nothing to run away from. But now I wonder if perhaps she felt there was.

I'm in two minds whether or not to share any of this news with my little support group. If Amy didn't even tell *me* about Dave Olsen, then it either isn't true or it was a big secret; she'd kept it from those she loved and never asked for advice or help.

There may have been another angle – is he a predator? Did he proposition her, or worse?

'It never ends well' were Laura's last words, and though Richard said it was 'rather melodramatic', it gave me chills, and I needed to share this. Perhaps I *should* tell my trusty little group about the call? I wonder if Jodie or Josh already know something and can tell me more about this, help me to understand what happened.

'How are you bearing up, sweetie?' Zoe asks. And that's it – I just collapse into floods of tears, a reaction to the phone call now I've had chance to digest what was said.

Zoe and Jodie's arms are around me, while Josh stands awkwardly close by. This highly charged atmosphere is too much for him to handle; Richard's right, he's very young and it's a lot for him to take on. I just hope what I tell them doesn't hurt him any more than he's already been hurt.

'I've just had a phone call, from someone at Aberystwyth,' I start.

'The police?' Jodie says, her face white.

'No, the university,' I say. 'Did Amy ever mention a lecturer to either of you? A Dave Olsen?'

Jodie and Josh both shake their heads, but I see a look pass between them.

'Was he Amy's lecturer?' Zoe asks, looking a little puzzled.

'Yes,' I say, turning from Josh and Jodie to Zoe. I then go on to tell them what Laura McKenzie said, and when I'm finished, there's a silence.

'Wow!' Zoe says.

'I know. It doesn't sound at all like Amy, but the woman who called me said *she's* one of her lecturers, but she can't have even *met* her. And I remembered after the call that Amy once told me about this lecturer everyone calls 'Professor Perv' and I wondered if it might be him.'

'What the hell?' says Jodie. 'This is giving me the creeps, I mean – who is this woman? And if Amy had the hots for her lecturer – he might…' She looks at Zoe, who does an almost invisible shake of the head, and she stops talking.

'Hey,' I say gently. 'I know you're trying to protect me from any unwelcome thoughts – but trust me, I've thought them all. Amy might be in danger, she might be hurt, she may have been kidnapped by her own father or been forced somewhere with her middle-aged lecturer. But in a way, the idea that someone she knows might be involved gives me some hope – because they might not hurt her.'

'Yes, I'm sure you're right Kat – we have to stay positive, but at the same time be prepared…' Zoe pauses and I see a look of hope pass between her and Jodie. 'Has Amy ever mentioned this guy to you?' she asks Jodie, looking at her a second too long.

'No… I don't think so.'

'Are you absolutely sure, love?' she's saying, almost pleading now. I wonder if she thinks Jodie knows more than she's saying.

Jodie's now red in the face and flustered, and I don't want to add to the pressure, but I'm now staring as intently as Zoe – and from her reaction I think she might know something.

Jodie looks at Zoe, and Zoe nods. 'It's okay, love, you can tell Kat if Amy ever talked about this to you. I know you feel like you don't want to betray a confidence – but think about it, this guy could have information about Amy, he may be involved in her disappearance.'

Jodie looks extremely uncomfortable but eventually she speaks. 'She told me she fancied one of her lecturers…' Then she looks at Josh. 'Sorry,' she murmurs and he nods.

'Anything else? Did you get the sense that she was scared of him in any way?'

Jodie doesn't speak at first, she's obviously finding this very difficult. 'A bit… yes. She once said she was scared of him.'

'Did she say why?' I hear myself ask.

Jodie just shakes her head and looks at the floor.

*

I'm still thinking about Dave Olsen an hour later, when I hear Jodie calling me urgently from the kitchen. 'Kat! Hey, Kat, come here!'

I'm immediately propelled out of the constant loop in my head and plunged back into reality. I run into the kitchen to where she and Josh are sitting.

'Someone says they saw a blonde girl in a red scarf at the station in Aberystwyth!'

'Oh God, really?' I'm looking from one to the other and they are as excited as me. 'A blonde girl… a scarf? That *has* to be a proper sighting,' I say, pulling up a stool at the kitchen counter and joining them.

I'm so excited – this might actually lead to something, perhaps the police will be able to use the information and finally get somewhere. I find it incredibly painful to think Amy might have just jumped on a train and left without telling me – but it's far less painful than the alternatives.

Josh is screwing up his face at the laptop screen as Jodie continues to click the keyboard.

'What would I do without you?' I say, putting my arm around her. She leans into me and I kiss the top of her head, sweet vanilla fills my nostrils and makes me want to cry. 'Honestly, both of you, thanks for everything,' I say, putting on my glasses to read the comments. 'I know Amy will be really touched.'

I read the comment about someone who looks like Amy being spotted at the station. 'On Saturday afternoon?' I say. 'That would fit in with when she texted me.' I'm elated. This might just mean that she left of her own accord after all. 'Maybe there were reasons for Amy to be upset and jump on a train? And she wouldn't have told me because she knew I'd be upset too,' I say, to comfort myself as much as anyone else.

'I miss her so much,' Jodie suddenly says.

'Me too,' I say, feeling my eyes prickle, but I can't break down in front of them, we all need to be strong together, so I change the subject and go back to the page. 'I can't believe you've managed to get so many followers,' I say, peering again at the pictures of Amy through tear-blurred eyes. I can only just make out the photos of her, some I haven't seen before, and I'm reminded again of how Amy had her own life before she even left home. I thought I knew everything about her, but I'm constantly being reminded that I don't.

'We can't take credit for the followers, seems like people are kind of drawn to stuff like this,' Josh says.

'Well, it's so scary, so awful. It could happen to anyone.' I sigh. I never expected anything like this to happen to us. I thought I'd made us safe, that our home would protect her from illness and danger, but seems I was wrong about that.

'We've had some weird comments. Some of them haven't been… complimentary,' Jodie says.

'You mean about Amy?' I ask.

'Yeah.' She nods. 'And you and Richard,' she adds, clearly uncomfortable about this.

'Oh.' I'm shocked. 'But surely if someone has joined the Find Amy page, that's what they want to do?'

'Yeah, mostly, but people who don't know Amy just join these pages to be weird,' Josh says.

I suddenly feel hurt. How could anyone be unkind about a missing girl and her parents? Perhaps it's easier to hear a story like ours if you think there's something wrong with the family, it makes it easier to think, 'That happened to them because they're strange – it won't happen to us.'

'Don't worry, Kat, it's just trolls,' Josh says, seeing the look of concern on my face.

'It's just… I don't want you seeing something that might upset you, Kat,' Jodie says.

'I know, sweetie, but I'm a big girl.' I smile, and look at the screen. Even with my glasses on I can barely see the words.

In my time as a journalist on a local paper, I remember the ghouls coming out of nowhere telling their version of a story just to be in the newspaper. That was long before the internet, and times have changed, but people haven't.

'Just be careful if you get any private messages. Know who you're dealing with, Kat,' Josh says. 'People aren't always who you think they are.' I feel a shiver go up my spine. I'm sailing in unchartered waters here in this fast, teenage world of hormones and hate, fuelled by Snapchat and Instagram. Yes, I have a couple of social-media accounts, but I don't live through them as my daughter's generation do, and this is why I need Jodie and Josh around. They can tell me who are followers and who aren't – friends or foes, likers or haters. They can also translate messages, posts, comments and all the abbreviations, emojis, opening up Amy's online life in a way no one else can. Mind you, the deeper we go, and the more I discover, the less I feel I know my daughter.

And now Josh is looking at the screen. He murmurs something under his breath, and Jodie nudges him to shut up.

'What?' I ask.

They glance at each other.

'This is the kind of shit I'm talking about, Kat,' Jodie says, turning the screen so I can see it clearly.

'Just trolls,' Josh says, 'delete it, Jodie.'

'Sorry, Kat,' she says, and deletes it, but it's too late – I've already seen it.

*The stepfather did it.*

# CHAPTER TWENTY-TWO

I used to do ten thousand steps a day – that's almost five miles – and now I barely walk a few feet every day. It's Friday afternoon, and since our brief visit to Aberystwyth on Monday, the path between my living room, kitchen and hall is well trodden. I wander into the kitchen, treading the loop between living room and hall, and for a golden moment, there she is, standing at the sink. She has her back to me, blonde hair caught up in a messy bun, narrow shoulders, narrow, teenage hips.

'Amy!' I gasp, and as she turns round, she drops one of the glasses on the floor. It smashes into a million pieces – along with my heart. 'Oh, Jodie, I'm so sorry… it's just, from behind you look so much like her…' I try not to, but it's impossible and I burst into tears.

Jodie stands clutching the tea towel, her bare feet surrounded by lethal shards of glass. Her head's to one side, her eyes filled with pity. 'Kat, I'm so sorry I've upset you,' she says, and begins to negotiate her way out from the jagged circle of glass.

'Don't move, you'll cut your feet to ribbons,' I say, rushing towards her, and reaching for the dustpan and brush. 'And don't apologise,' I add. 'The likeness threw me a little, not your fault.' I smile, in an attempt to keep it light. I'm trying so hard to seem normal, but I'm falling apart. And now poor Jodie is standing amid a million shards of broken glass. She stands on one foot as I gather all the prickly splinters into the dustpan, and before I allow her to move, I wipe the floor with a damp cloth to remove any remnants.

'I should wear my slippers in the kitchen,' she says. 'Mum's always telling me to, but I like to feel the floor under my feet.'

'Yeah, Amy likes to be barefoot too. Always loved the sand in her toes when she was little,' I say, imagining her on a beach somewhere, young, pretty, happy – but then an unbidden image of an older man appears, then Tony, and I have to push it away.

'Me too,' Jodie says, with a smile.

'I remember,' I say, thinking back to those days when we were able to keep our children safe, including their hearts. I don't know Amy's life anymore, and yearn for a simpler time, when at the end of the day, I could tuck her up safely in bed.

I finish wiping the floor around her. 'There, you should be safe to put your foot down now.'

'Sorry I broke the glass.'

'It's fine, it was my fault,' I say as she grabs two mugs and begins to put coffee in them both. I watch her make the drinks and think how since that conversation with Laura McKenzie my mind has been going round and round and now I'm here alone with Jodie, I have to ask.

'Jodie, do you know why Josh and Amy finished?'

She shakes her head but doesn't look at me.

'Jodie, I've lost Amy, I can't find her. Nothing you tell me now can ever be worse than that. So please don't spare my feelings, love.'

I can see this is as distressing for her as it is for me, but I have to try to find out what happened there.

'You guys were still in touch, she must have told you. Did Josh finish with Amy or was it the other way round?'

She shrugs and screws the coffee jar lid back on slowly without looking at me. 'I don't know.'

But I think she does. I think she knows more than I do. But for some reason, right now she isn't telling me. But am I being paranoid? Perhaps the secrets she's keeping are just those melodramatic teenage things girls share. Maybe when all this is over

Amy will tell me herself and we'll laugh about it. It's not Jodie's fault and I'm grateful for everything she's done, even if Richard still doesn't appreciate how good Zoe and Jodie have been during these terrible few days. He can't bring himself to say anything nice about either of them. Just last night he was grumbling about Zoe.

'She's such a gossip,' he was saying, 'and Jodie's probably the same, I bet they're spreading all kinds of rumours about Amy, and us.'

'Zoe's been amazing, she's been there for me through all this and I'll always be grateful to her and Jodie,' I said, refusing to buy into his prejudice. 'She's a true friend – I'm such a mess, I don't know what I'd have done without her this week,' I say making the point that she's been here for me when he hasn't.

'Mmm, she likes it when people are a mess. Gives her more control over everything.'

'She's not like that, she has a good heart.' Richard is irritating me with his constant picking on Zoe when she's done nothing wrong at all. I don't understand him – our focus should be much more on finding Amy.

'A good heart? You told me yourself that she's got a mean streak. I remember you saying that if she ever had other kids to tea after school she'd go through their homework bag to see how well they were doing so she could gloat or seethe. If that's a good heart and a true friend, then God help us – and don't think for one minute that Amy's school bag was excluded from that little ritual.'

I'd almost forgotten that, I wish now I hadn't told Richard, because clearly he's still using that anecdote to judge Zoe. Richard's always looking for a reason to criticise her and she definitely picks up on it. 'Your Richard doesn't like me,' she once said. I was so embarrassed, but assured her she was wrong, but she's become quite defensive in his presence, and this comes over as prickly to Richard. And I've noticed that Jodie's quite stand-offish around him too, which is causing real tension and making me think about her comment to her mother about finding Richard 'creepy'.

'I feel uncomfortable in my own home,' Richard had continued. 'And Jodie should be at university, not hanging round here, pretending to be Amy – you shouldn't encourage it, Kat, it's not healthy. Jodie will never be Amy.'

'I know that – Jodie could never replace Amy either, but I just want to be with her and Josh because somehow I feel they hold the key… Jodie has this best-friend connection with Amy and a few clicks of her keyboard and taps on her phone and she can tell me what Amy was doing on any given day. Josh is the same, and between them they can give me a map of Amy's life until she disappeared. It's vague and blurry, but it's better than staring down into the abyss.'

'The truth according to Jodie,' he'd muttered, but I'd ignored him. He disapproves of her Facebook page and, for that matter, any kind of media intervention – he says, as a lawyer, he's seen how it can have an adverse effect on an investigation or a prosecution. As a journalist I know the way law and the media works, but I sometimes think with Richard it's more about *who's* doing it. He doesn't like Zoe or Jodie and resents their involvement; he just can't see how much I need them here.

'You've encouraged Jodie to virtually move in,' he'd added, 'and it's the same with Josh… you're surrounding yourself with kids.'

'How dare you criticise me for allowing Amy's friends to be here,' I said, tears coming, but they were angry tears.

'It's not just that. They're here all the time, listening to conversations, adding their theories, getting involved in stuff they don't understand.'

'They care as much as I do. They want her home.'

'No one cares as much as you about Amy coming home,' he'd said gently. 'You're her mum and that's how it should be. But what you don't see is that I also care very much about Amy, and I don't feel that filling our home with her friends is the answer. They've set up this web page with the best intentions, I'm sure, but social media is a mixed blessing, it can be as dangerous as it can be good.'

'I don't agree, the police have followed up several lines of enquiry after Jodie passed on information from the Facebook page.'

'But, Kat, those "lines of enquiry" have come to *nothing*! And what about the lunatics, and the trolls saying "the stepfather did it". And did you see that one saying, "Ask her uni lecturer, he knows where she is."'

'No. I hope they passed that on to the police,' I said. 'I'll check with them.'

Richard had sighed. 'My point is, Kat, you'd only just told them and Zoe about the phone call regarding the lecturer, so it's no surprise that some troll then posts it.'

'I don't understand.'

'Jodie and Josh, they're on their phones all the time, they probably told friends, who told friends, and before you know it, the rumour becomes fact and it's on Facebook.'

'They wouldn't repeat what I told them,' I say, desperately hoping I'm right.

'I'm not suggesting they'd do this in a malicious way, but it's a leaky bucket, Kat.'

'It isn't. I mean, sometimes they don't even tell *me* what's on Facebook, let alone their friends.'

'But that's my point, Jodie and Josh are suddenly in this crazy position of power, where they're controlling the narrative coming in and out of this house by the bloody Facebook page. Along with possibly sharing information with people they think they can trust, they're telling *you* what they think you want to hear, the stuff *they* think you should know. But they hide from you any comments about Amy's life, her relationships and anything they don't want you to see.'

'I don't want to hear this, you're overreacting,' I'd said, something he always accuses me of doing.

'I don't believe I am overreacting. And what concerns me most, is that two teenagers are the conduit from the public to the police.

They are just kids – they aren't equipped to know what's significant and what isn't. Jesus – talk about fake news!'

'I get what you're saying, but without the Facebook page people wouldn't make their comments.'

'No, they'd go to the police, like they're supposed to, like everyone used to, before all this,' he said raising his voice and waving his arm in the direction of my laptop sitting on the counter like it was the source of all evil.

'But surely the good outweighs the bad?' I'd said.

'Like the woman in the green jacket, seen walking with Amy in Worcester, who turned out to be a mother shopping with her daughter, and all the other so-called "sightings". A total waste of time.' Richard had shaken his head.

'You can't *say* that. If nothing else it makes me feel like she's loved, like people care about her. There are good people out there… it gives me hope.'

'Hope can be dangerous in the wrong hands. How many times in the last few days, since they started that damn web page, have you had your hopes raised by something, only to be dashed again?'

'You're doing that to me now,' I'd said then, 'dashing my hopes.' My eyes rested on boxes of freshly printed missing posters lining the wall of the living room, an idea of Jodie's.

'I'm sorry, darling, that's the last thing I'd ever want to do,' he'd said more gently. 'We have to stay positive. But I really think Jodie and Josh should be mindful of what's happening, should care about Amy, but not feel under pressure to give up their own lives.'

'Are you saying that *I* put them under pressure?' I'd asked.

'Not exactly. I feel like you don't have to try to put pressure on Jodie, she'll do what she thinks you want her to do.'

'She doesn't. That's not true.'

'You underestimate yours and Zoe's influence on your daughters,' Richard had said. 'I think you may have been too close to the situation, Kat, but Jodie can be as manipulative and controlling as her mother, and I think she's doing this to please you. I also wonder if it suits her purpose.'

'What do you mean?' I'd asked, curious at his remark.

'I wonder if being here to "work on" the page is her escape from the university course.'

'No, not at all. I asked her about her coursework, told her not to get behind – but she said she had to find Amy. Richard – her heart's in the right place.'

'I don't doubt her good intentions, God knows, she clearly misses Amy. She's in tears half the time.'

'Yes, I think Jodie lost her direction a little when they went their separate ways.'

'Mmm, she probably didn't know what colour to dye her hair.' He'd laughed. 'Do you remember when Amy dyed her hair pink, Jodie dyed hers?'

'Yes, and there were times when she even bought the same outfit. It used to annoy Amy sometimes, but I used to say she should be flattered. I suppose there's always a mini alpha in a friendship even when you're young, one that sets the trend?'

'I remember you telling me about the scarf you bought for Amy, the one in the photo,' he'd gestured towards the pile of missing posters on the side.

'Yeah, I remember saying to Amy, "That's something Jodie can't copy, because it's the only one like it."'

It's one of the reasons why I love that photo so much, because it represents Amy's independence, from her old friends, her school. From me. The scarf is unique, and so is my daughter – the way she smiles with one dimple, the way she loves chocolate so much she makes herself sick, the way she makes Harry the cat dance on his hind legs and the way she faced death and came through. These are the things that make Amy, Amy. I'm aware that in just a few days she's being defined as 'Missing Girl Amy Russo' and 'Missing Teen Amy' and she's so much more than that. I wanted to tell the local newspaper all about her when they called me to ask if there was any update today, but they were more interested in the police investigation.

As far as I know there's been nothing significant yet as a result of the interviews I've done. But I live in hope, and Heather says it's a proven way to get good, solid information, keep the 'story' out there and get genuine leads. God, I hope so. She calmed me down, helped us with the questions, and after the crew and reporter had gone she asked me some questions of her own, that were far more difficult to answer than anything the press had asked me.

'Kat, we've been looking over some information received from the A & E Department at Worcester Royal,' she started, and I knew where this was going. 'It seems that Amy was taken to the hospital several times over a short period between 2005 and 2010?'

I explained about my anxiety at the time and that I had therapy for it. 'I think it was a perfectly natural reaction to Amy's illness,' I pointed out. 'But everyone else seemed to think I was going mad.'

Heather didn't know what to say to this so I asked her questions about where the investigation was at to change the subject. She just kept answering from the same script: 'As soon as anything turns up that's relevant, I promise you'll be the first to know.'

But so far nothing has, and it's this lack of information that makes Amy's Facebook page even more vital, along with the fact Jodie's here, bringing a little sunshine into my day. And Josh has come over to help too, he's sitting with Jodie now, looking at his phone, they're discussing poster distribution and it's great to see them getting along. Jodie and Josh seemed to always be at loggerheads, I wouldn't be surprised if they were each a little jealous of the other one with regard to Amy. It makes me think. *Is he the jealous type? Is it a coincidence that she went missing just two weeks after they split?* But then I kick myself for being so bloody stupid – we've known Josh and his family for years, and after his mother died I welcomed him in. Like Jodie, he was often here at meal times and always such a lovely boy, polite, friendly, funny. No I must wipe any thoughts about Josh being the jealous type straight from my thoughts, I never saw that – and Amy certainly never mentioned anything about him being possessive.

Josh smiles, and I immediately erase this thought from my brain. I mustn't let Richard's suspicious nature infect everything I see.

# CHAPTER TWENTY-THREE

It's Saturday morning, I can't believe it's a week since I last heard from Amy. It's been the longest and most painful seven days of my life, and I've tortured myself with all the possibilities of where she might be and why. Heather says they are looking into all the lines of enquiry, including Tony, who I think would be very capable of doing something to cause me great pain as an act of revenge. And of course there's Dave Olsen who is a shadowy figure I didn't even know existed until after Amy went missing. And there's Amy's relationship with Josh, which according to him seems to have been far rockier than she let on. Looking back, I realise that this time last week I felt like I was holding Amy's hand, guiding her home – this morning I can feel it slipping from mine.

I still can't sleep, though eventually drifted off about 5 a.m. this morning, and when I woke at nine-ish Richard had left a note to say he'd gone to the supermarket. I can't even think about food – the fridge is empty and where once I enjoyed grocery shopping, I'm not remotely interested and have no intention of leaving the house in case something happens.

I wander the rooms, silent, no teenagers – no Amy. The Find Amy page has, as Richard predicted, had to be suspended at the request of the police – it happened late last night, and I know it makes sense, but as I have said, it gave me hope – and I feel bad for Jodie and Josh who'd put so much time and energy into it.

I go upstairs, feeling like a ghost in my own home, and wander into Amy's room, sit on her bed, and I do what I have been doing every day this week. I text her. I tell her what's happening, how the case is progressing, how annoying Heather is, how I wish I could talk to her because I miss her so much. I also tell her what she'd say is 'the vital shit', like which celebrity relationship has collapsed/reunited/started, and the scandal surrounding any of these. I press send and sit and wait for the 'OMG!' or 'NO!' at my Z-list revelations. We're both aware of the meaninglessness of all this, but somehow these people and their stories bond us over the miles – I hoped they always would. But as the silence creeps through her bedroom and wraps itself around me I know today will be the same as yesterday, and the day before. Nothing. I check her social media, and then I check Tony's, which seems to be filled with stuff about some sad band he's in and I can't bear to look at it. My days have no structure, I'm constantly searching for clues and finding nothing, and sometimes I feel so scared I have to put my fist in my mouth to stop myself screaming.

I lie down on Amy's bed, stretching out, breathing her pillow, pretending she's fine and enjoying her new student life. I'm falling asleep but something wakes me and coming round I hear a tentative tap on the door, which I think might be in my head, then it comes again and I sit up. In my heightened state I imagine it's Amy at the door, but the door slowly opens and it's Jodie, she's tearful as always and, when she sees me on the bed, she starts crying again.

I move to the end of the bed and put my feet on the floor, still drowsy and disorientated, but before I can say anything Jodie's standing in front of me, wiping her eyes.

'Kat, I've got something to tell you.'

'Okay,' I say, trying to sound calm, unflustered, but I have to stay seated on the bed, braced for what she's about to say. Some new piece of information about my own flesh and blood that might floor me, or petrify me, or both.

'It's Amy… it's all my fault,' she sobs.

'Jodie, you can't keep blaming yourself.'

'No.' She puts her hand up to stop me, and I see a flash of Zoe – strong and assertive – she has some backbone after all.

'I think she ran away because of something I did.' With that, she almost falls next to me onto the bed. She's so distressed, I think she may be having a panic attack and I don't know what to do.

'Jodie, Jodie, it's okay. Whatever happened you can tell me,' I say gently. I'm holding onto her shoulders, looking into her face, a million things are running through my head. I'm trying to make her focus, and eventually she looks at me.

'Go on… you can tell me.' I nod, grabbing a tissue from the box on Amy's bedside cabinet, which Jodie takes from me.

'I went to the pub a few weeks ago… with a load of our old school friends.'

'Yes?' My heart's thudding, how on earth can this lead to Aberystwyth and Amy?

'Josh was there.'

'Okay.'

She looks up to the ceiling, her hands twisting at the tissue, her mouth quivering, not knowing how to tell me what she has been holding in all this time. 'He's lovely and kind and… he said Amy was being mean to him and… I was drunk, and he was drunk.'

I'm not sure I want to hear the rest, I don't know how to feel. But I need to know, for Amy's sake.

'So you're telling me that you and Josh hooked up and…'

She nods. 'Yes, and… now we're together.'

'Oh.'

'But Amy didn't want to be with Josh anymore, Kat,' she says, reaching for my hand. I let her take it, but I suddenly see things quite differently. 'You heard what he said the other day, she was mean to him, didn't want to know once she'd gone to uni.'

'That's not… I'm not sure that's true Jodie,' I say, but I don't *know*. I'm feeling like the wronged woman on my daughter's behalf. My feelings towards Jodie are – not surprisingly – mixed.

I am reconfiguring the closeness I've noticed between Josh and Jodie over the last few days. I thought they'd just been working with each other to bring Amy home, but perhaps they weren't so selfless after all and just wanted to spend time together. Eventually I come up with a question for her, but I can't smile.

'I don't want any details, but why would Amy run away because of you and Josh? Wouldn't she just tell me or one of her other friends, cry a bit, then realise he's a shit boyfriend, she's lost a best friend and move on?' I say bitterly.

'She told me she was going to leave,' she says through tears. 'She said she'd just jump on a train or thumb a lift and get away, she said she hated me, and Josh and she never wanted to see us again and would never come back to Worcester.'

'I don't blame her,' I say, feeling anger towards Jodie. Despite my mother's fury I have to remind myself they are teenagers, and that this is all a storm in a teacup in the great scheme of things. But then to Amy it was probably so much more. I hate the thought of her feeling betrayed by her best friend and boyfriend, how horrible it must have been for her.

'When you and Josh spoke to the police, did you tell them all this?'

'Yes.'

'Well, hopefully they're pursuing that line of enquiry,' I say snappily, which seems to upset her even more. Jodie's always needed approval and usually she gets it from me, if not her mother. I know my disapproval has hurt her deeply and I have to be careful, because however much her being with Josh has hurt Amy, Jodie is extremely fragile.

'Kat, I'm so, so sorry, I wouldn't have started seeing Josh if I thought Amy was still into him, but she told me she fancied someone at uni.'

'Who, the lecturer?'

She shakes her head. 'I don't know… probably.' Now she's in floods, rocking backwards and forwards and I realise it's time to be the grown-up. I imagine Amy was very hurt about Josh finishing with her, and pissed off with Jodie – but there were other things going on. As much as I'd like to think she ran away, because that means no one's harmed her physically, I don't buy it. Other people are more likely to blame for Amy going missing, because that is the only explanation for her lack of contact.

'Jodie,' I start, in an attempt to calm her down. 'If it makes you feel any less guilty, I don't think Amy just walked away from her life.'

But what *has* happened? And why? Seven days missing and still there are more questions than answers – I don't know how much more I can take.

Jodie asks me if I'd like her to leave, and I really don't want to hurt her, she's just a child. So I suggest she goes home for a while, just to give me time to adjust and take in what she's told me.

'I will be okay with this – eventually,' I say. 'It's just that Amy isn't here to tell me her side, and obviously I'm on her side. You understand, don't you?'

She nods and, shoulders slumped, leaves the room; a few seconds later I hear her going downstairs and closing the front door. Then it's my turn to burst into tears.

Eventually I stop crying, and tell myself Amy may be crying for me somewhere and I'm achieving nothing. So I check my phone, nothing new – my email box is full and, on automatic pilot, I open one telling me how many shopping days I have before Christmas. Another informs me about the latest ways with turkey and a third offers me twenty per cent off Christmas decorations. Christmas. What's Christmas without Amy? What's anything without Amy? How can life go on? Why are people planning for Christmas when Amy is missing? It's weird to think that outside this house other lives are continuing as they did before – whereas inside everything is on pause. These days that are so long, and yet so short, the November night stealing them just after four thirty and plunging us into darkness on every level.

# CHAPTER TWENTY-FOUR

I wanted Jodie to go, and it's only been a few hours, but now I want her to come back. She's still the nearest thing to Amy that I have, and it's so quiet here without her and Josh. I feel like I did just after Amy left, when I missed that sudden late-afternoon injection of after-school life in my now too-quiet house surrounded by trees.

We came here for the seclusion. I didn't want Tony to find us. I had to make a fresh start, just like he had. Amy didn't need to know his truth, she knew mine and that was enough. So I married Richard and we moved to paradise, away from the past, into leafy Worcestershire, by the River Severn, and for a while we lived happily ever after. Amy was six years old when we came here. It's the perfect family home to grow up in, Richard and I were happy and I continued to make Amy my life. Now I wander aimlessly through the days with only the memories – I hear the sound of all the children's birthday parties, barbecues in the garden, cold white wine and distant laughter. Amy with her friends on the trampoline, pink lemonade and paddling pools, girls' giggles as they splashed and screamed, the wonderful sounds of summer.

That first year, we began our family traditions that we've continued over time. We bought our first real Christmas tree from the nearby farm. Amy and Richard went together to collect it, dragging it across the lawn, Amy falling in the snow and Richard flopping down next to her, the two of them hysterical. I watched through the window and laughed along, bottling those few seconds in my brain like perfume.

I open the bottle now, a heady mix of nostalgia and Christmas – I hear them thundering into the hall, wellingtons heavy with snow, a tree drenched white. Months later, Richard came home with a fluffy kitten in his coat. 'He was just wandering in the road,' he'd said. The minute Amy clapped her eyes on the kitten, I knew we were done for, and when they both named him Harry spontaneously, I also knew I'd been had. This wasn't a lost kitten, Richard hadn't *found* Harry, he'd *bought* him for Amy – it was an elaborate plan they'd cooked up together. She'd been desperate for a kitten, but I'd never allowed it – too worried about germs and her health. But Richard found a way of bringing Amy what she wanted, and I couldn't begrudge either of them.

'You two plotted to get this kitten,' I'd said, and laughed as Amy held the tiny little thing in her arms.

'Please can we keep him, Mum, please?'

And I'd agreed, my concerns about my daughter's fragile immune system deleted by her happiness. This was my dream, my family – and against all the odds, we were slowly rebuilding our lives and erasing Tony from the picture.

Now it's all so different. Our house is like another place, the walls come in on me and the ceiling threatens to crush me. Richard and I both wander through the house, sometimes passing in the hallway, sometimes I see his closed office door, and at times he'll open Amy's bedroom door and find me there. Just now we met in the kitchen and he's put the kettle on and we're just going through the motions, a couple so close, and yet pulled apart by all this.

Throughout this horrible week, I've been drawn back into the past, some happy memories and some horrible. When Richard won the case and I got full custody, I knew Tony would be bitter, and I couldn't take any risks. So we married and moved to a house in the Worcestershire countryside and tried not to make too many friends.

Here I was able to relax for a while, no more late-night phone calls scaring me with my worst fears, and though I still kept an eagle eye on Amy, we were able to live our lives. Until one lovely, sunny spring morning when the postman knocked on the door, and handed me a parcel. I took it from him and he remarked on what a nice day it was going to be, but when I saw the Italian postmark and the handwriting on the brown paper, I knew it wasn't going to be a nice day at all. Tony had found us, and though I knew he was still in Italy, he was suddenly back in our lives.

That first gift was a teddy bear in a dress, something that Amy would have loved – but she never saw it. I couldn't open that door and allow her to walk through, because I knew her father would charm her and take her away from me.

God knows how he ever found us, but from that moment I was on red alert. But as the years went on, he never actually called, or turned up – and I convinced myself that, despite the gifts and cards, he'd moved on, he'd accepted that he couldn't be part of her life.

I watch Richard as he opens the cupboard searching for sugar, when I can see it on the worktop in a jar marked 'sugar'. He looks at me, about to ask where the sugar is and before he speaks I point to it. That's what happens after years of marriage, you don't need to talk, you read each other's minds, and I feel a sudden sweep of emotion run through me.

'Thank you… for everything,' I say. He turns back to me, the sugar jar in his hand, surprised, I think, at my gentle tone.

'I know it's rough at the moment, and you've been on the ropes. But I can see how you just wanted to help Amy and at the same time didn't want to betray her trust – that means a lot. From what I gather, Jodie and Josh had also caused her some anguish, I didn't know at the time because she didn't tell me.'

He puts down the sugar jar and looks at me for a moment. 'She didn't mention any of that when I saw her, but I think she was more concerned about Tony, to be honest.'

'And now he's back and she's missing,' I murmur, seeing his black leather jacket disappearing once more down another white hospital corridor.

'We can't put two and two together, Kat. They don't always make four,' he warns.

'I know, I'm just frustrated that the police haven't tracked him down yet.'

We know he's met Amy, and he must have seen the news – must know she's missing – so if he isn't involved, why hasn't he contacted the police? He must know he's a person of interest. I don't think he'd hurt her physically, but he may hurt her emotionally. I worry about what he's told her; what horrible things has he said about me? And what did Amy think of her mother when he asked her if she liked the space hopper he bought for her ninth birthday? It's still in its box in the attic, along with the teddy, the doll, the puppy Nintendo sent by special delivery on her thirteenth birthday, and there's the necklace when she was eighteen. I haven't thrown away these things; I always imagined giving them to Amy one day, but it was too risky, she was too vulnerable. It's my job to protect her, even if that means protecting her from her father. But did I do enough? Tony found her in the end, and who knows what poison he laid.

As much as I wanted to protect Amy from her father's influence, in my defence I didn't keep him a secret from her – I wanted her to have a sense of identity, to understand where she came from. I never denied his existence and gave her a framed photo of the last photo they had taken together, on that holiday in Spain. In her own, childlike way she's always loved Richard, how could she not? He's a brilliant lawyer, but as a father he's sometimes a bit clumsy, and slightly inarticulate, especially when it comes to dealing with a teenage girl. They got along better when she was little and he could play 'trains' with her and take her swimming, but, like most girls, she drifted away from him when bras and boys came into the picture. Meanwhile, the idea of Tony seemed to grow in those teenage years, to her he was the unattainable knight in shining armour. But to me he's always been the dark shadow over our lives, the person who wanted to destroy me and take away the person I love most.

So I stopped telling her how he used to throw her up in the air, and sing to her in Italian, and if she asked about him, I kept my answers to a simple yes or no. I didn't elaborate or add any colour, because it made Tony seem exciting to a little girl whose stepfather didn't wear an earring or play in a band.

So when she came home on her last visit, and started to say how she wanted to meet her *real* dad, that Richard was boring and had only ever worked in an office, I gave her some home truths.

But she didn't want to hear these, she'd suddenly developed this deep resentment for Richard. Now I can see her mind had been poisoned by Tony, and she saw Richard as the reason she couldn't be with her dad. He'd finally made contact and it looks like he's been peddling his lies and half-truths. But then again, who am I to criticise a liar? I'm a bigger liar than Tony ever was.

I watch Richard making my coffee just the way I like it, my favourite mug, two measured teaspoons of instant, and I wish Amy realised what a good person Richard is. Being a great dad isn't about sending expensive gifts every now and then. He was there for all the big stuff when she needed him. I wish she could see how much he cares for both of us, and how he saved us back then, when everything was so bleak.

Amy has a far better life, emotionally and materially, than she ever would have had with Tony, and Richard's kind and caring and loves her as well as any father could. And when she comes home I'll remind her of this and tell her that Tony might be her real father, and he might tell her Richard's boring and evil, but he isn't. Richard's been there for the cuts and bruises of life, and only ever been good to her. And we both owe him big time.

*

It's late and I'm sitting with Heather in the living room, talking about the sighting at Aberystwyth train station.

'We couldn't find anything on CCTV,' she says. 'I hate to say it, but we think it's probably just someone making mischief.'

'The woman who made the comment was called Sandra,' I say. 'Sandra Wilson. Can't you check her out?' I'll never forget that name, I planned to send her thank-you flowers when we found Amy.

'Sandra Wilson probably isn't even her name, people make fake accounts, it's a nightmare.'

'The Facebook page, it seems to have brought up more red herrings than leads,' I say, echoing Richard's earlier comments.

Suddenly Heather's phone rings. She answers it immediately, and as she listens to what's being said on the other end, she's looking at me – fear claws at the back of my throat. It's clearly some news regarding Amy and I ache for Heather to come off the phone and tell me what. I'm terrified and wonder if I'll survive, will my heart hold out? Heather nods and talks, jotting down a few words throughout the conversation, her face revealing nothing, and all the time I'm preparing myself for the possibility that I might never see my daughter again. What if she's been found and she isn't alive? What if the last time I'll ever see Amy was when we waved her off on the train two weeks ago after my unhappy birthday? I steel myself, ready for whatever Heather's going to tell me when she gets off the phone.

As usual, she's being painfully discreet – it's so frustrating – lots of monosyllabic yeses and noes, but then a glimmer of hope when she glances over at me.

'I'll ask her,' she says.

My heart soars, but at the same time is ready to dip. I look up eagerly. 'Is there news?' I croak.

She nods, slowly. 'We've got some CCTV footage.'

'Yes?' *Just tell me. I am dying here.*

'It shows a girl we think might be Amy walking along the promenade at Aberystwyth on Saturday afternoon, 4.10 p.m.,' she says.

'Saturday afternoon?' My heart's lifted just hearing about Amy.

'Yes. And she's taking money from a cashline.'

I want to scream for joy, 'So it wasn't someone else using her cashcard? It was definitely Amy?' *Am I finally allowed a flicker of hope?*

'Amy was at the cashline – *she's* the one who emptied her bank account?' I just want to make this clear before she adds the 'but'.

She nods, tentatively. 'Well, we need confirmation. CCTV footage can sometimes be blurry, but it matches her description and apparently the girl in the video is wearing a red scarf and a mustard jumper.'

I try not to leap up and embrace Heather at this news. Never has a mother been so elated to discover her daughter has emptied her first-term's money from her student bank account and run away.

'We may need you to take a look at the footage, and confirm that it's Amy.'

'Yes, yes, but that *must* be her.' I grab my phone and show Heather the screen, my daughter smiling. Mustard jumper, red scarf, perfect white teeth, thanks to regular dental visits. *See, I'm a good mum.*

'The police have this photo,' I say, 'I gave it to the Welsh police when she first went missing.' It seems like years ago, her little room, the desk, the two policemen who really thought she'd gone on some kind of bender and I was overreacting. I was right to trust my instincts – as much as I wanted to be wrong, I was right all the time.

'Could be legit.' Heather nods into her phone as I continue to hold mine up for her to see. I'm desperate. I feel like a pupil in class with her hand raised. 'Mum has a photo here and she's wearing that combination of clothing.'

'Excuse me, Heather.' I grab her arm.

She keeps the phone to her ear and lifts her hand in a 'wait' gesture, then tells the person on the other end to hang on. 'Mum's just asking me something.' She looks at me.

'Was she wearing a purple padded jacket in the footage… bright purple?' I repeat. 'Only, it's missing from her room, she'd definitely wear it in this weather – I did tell the detective in Aberystwyth. It's new,' I add unnecessarily, not wanting to leave any detail to chance.

Heather asks the question and waits for a response, I look into her face for a clue, but her eyes are down, all I can see are her lids. 'So as far as you can see she's not wearing or carrying anything purple…?' She shakes her head at me. 'Yes, Mum says it's missing from her room,' she adds, and after a few more yeses and noes she puts down the phone.

'What do you think?' I ask.

She looks at me for a few seconds. 'Hard to say. We're trying to piece together Amy's movements on Saturday, and this is promising, but I'll say what I always say – don't get your hopes up until everything's confirmed.'

'I know, I know, but surely this is a good thing. It means she was alone and alive on Saturday afternoon and took money from her bank account.'

'Yes, but there are still other unanswered questions, Kat. She hasn't been on her phone since Saturday, her last text was to you, and we can't trace any activity on her phone since.'

'Maybe she threw it away, if she really felt pissed off about her life for whatever reason – she might have just decided to get rid of it.'

'Mmm it's possible. I promise, as soon as we have something solid, you'll be the first to know.'

Except I feel like I'm the last to know. It's so frustrating, complete strangers know things about Amy that I don't. I feel like the more people that become involved, the more they get between us and that we're growing more distant from each other as the days pass.

Later I call Zoe with the news, she sounds as delighted as me. 'Oh, love I feel ten years younger hearing that – I can only imagine how *you* feel,' she says. And we chat about the different possibilities and what the sighting might mean, and then suddenly she goes quiet.

'Can I come over?' she asks.

'Of course, you don't need permission.'

'Yeah, but Jodie told me about – the situation between you and her about Josh and...'

In my excitement about the CCTV footage, I'd almost forgotten about my anger towards Jodie. This positive news has put everything into perspective, my priority is to get Amy back safe and sound, and some teenage lovers' tiff or friendship fail isn't important.

'It's fine, I was just surprised – upset for Amy,' I say.

'I wanted to say something, but didn't feel it was my place. I told Jodie she had to tell you, however hard it was.'

'She did the right thing. It wasn't easy to hear, but you know how I feel about Jodie, love her like my own.'

'I know, and she does you. I just... I'm just relieved, because if... if anything ever happened to Amy – well you know Jodie's...'

I can't let her finish her sentence, can't bear my pain or hers, because I know she's feeling this as much as any friend can. 'I know, love,' I say. 'Tell Jodie to come over whenever she wants to. I'd love to see her – and Josh,' I add.

'Thanks, Kat, you're amazing, she's been so upset, you mean a lot to her and your acceptance is everything. And as always, my love, I'm here – I can't begin to imagine what you're going through, but I *can* hold your hand while you're going through it.'

This is so typical of Zoe, she is a hand holder. And she doesn't pretend to know how I feel, because she knows she can't; even Zoe can't comprehend the visceral, animal pain of losing your child, or not knowing where they are and having that threat hang over you. My brain is mashed, my emotions are raw and I can't rest, nor can my mind, which conjures up a new image, a fresh horror, every few seconds. I'm aware that Richard's feeling it too – he keeps himself to himself during the day, working from his office upstairs, but yesterday I heard him crying. I'm not the only one suffering, and at night, when I only sleep for minutes at a time on top of the covers, fully clothed, we talk about Amy to each other in the dark. Everything from her favourite bands to her birthday parties, to funny, endearing things she's said and done, like the Father's Day card she made for Richard when she was six.

'Sequins and feathers on a pink background.' He laughed. 'Do I seem like a pink, sequin and feathers kind of guy?'

I smiled. 'To Amy you were. I reckon that was a compliment, you were her tribe.' He gripped my hand, gave it a gentle squeeze, and I knew he was trying not to cry.

I've promised myself I won't sleep under the covers or put on my nightwear until Amy's found, it feels self-indulgent to do that, or even have a long soak in the bath. For me, everything is on a perfunctory level until she's home, how can I do anything remotely pleasurable or comforting if she's in pain or danger… or worse?

# CHAPTER TWENTY-FIVE

It's 8 a.m. on Sunday morning, and I'm shocked awake by a heavy knock on the front door. I'd eventually fallen asleep last night and immediately sit up and look across to see an empty space next to me. For a moment, I'm disorientated, until I remember that Richard left early to get some paperwork from the office so he can continue to work from home – he says it stops him from thinking. I feel more alone than ever, and wonder if it might be Zoe – but earlier this week I gave her a key, so she'd let herself in. Could it be a stranger?

At a time like this, a knock on the door could be devastating news – *that* news. I can't even comprehend this, uniformed police at my door, or Heather with a look on her face that tells me it's over – I've got to know her and I can imagine the expression on her face. I look for it every time I see her in case she gives something away. She never does.

There's another knock, each bang feels like a punch to the stomach and I'm so petrified, I can't move my legs. My brain knows I should get up and deal with it, but my body won't. I wait to hear if whoever it is calls through the letter box, but after a couple of minutes, no one does – I think they've gone, maybe it was a journalist after some sensational backstory. If only they knew. I breathe a sigh of relief.

I force myself to move, to get out of bed, find my dressing gown and I'm just wrapping it around me when there's another knock, this time sharper, more urgent – more aggressive. It makes me jump. Whatever it is, whoever it is – it's not a friend. And they aren't giving up.

The sound jars my body, fills me with electricity and the panic and adrenaline push me from the bedroom and down the stairs to the door, almost against my will. My instinct is to go in the opposite direction, head for the back door and run away across the frosty morning lawn in my bare feet, my robe flying behind me. But as scared as I am to open the door, I'm even more scared to leave the house.

Is this sudden knock the final piece to a jigsaw I'm dreading? Has Amy been found? Has something been discovered?

Fighting my desire to flee, I walk towards the door and see an outline of a man through the glass, a tall man wearing black. Please God, I hope it isn't Detective Mather who's found something and come all the way from Aberystwyth to tell me. I wish Richard was here, or Zoe – and where's Heather to soothe my nerves, to prepare me? If ever anyone can be prepared for something like that.

A strange rush of adrenaline propels me forward and against all my instincts I walk towards the impatient man waiting behind glass. He clearly has no intention of leaving until the door is answered, and I pull my robe tighter around me as I open the door. But when I see who's standing there, my mouth opens in shock – a 'wow' emoji made flesh. I'd never expected *him*. A man I'd hoped I'd never see again. Tony. My first husband. Standing on my doorstep.

I gasp, stepping back, almost falling, but he doesn't reach out to save me. He never did, not his style. All I see is pure hate on his face, and I almost expect him to spit on me as he stands there.

'Where IS she?' I hiss.

'Are you going to let me in?' he asks. It's that voice that terrified me, that threatened to take the thing I loved most.

I daren't refuse him, what if he has Amy? I don't meet his eyes as I reluctantly step back for him to walk past me into the hallway. *The magpie in the nest.*

I've dreaded this for fifteen long years, been plagued by the thought he might turn up here one day. And that day has come. He knows me well, knows what will hurt me, what he can do to inflict the most pain – and as we stand now in the living room, facing each other, I think, just for a moment, about killing him. It's fleeting, but it's there, and the poker by the fire is close enough to reach for and bash his brains out. If he's done anything to Amy, that's what I will do. His presence still fills me with fear and resentment, his mental torture never went away, like a stain on our lives. Even after he'd gone, my moments of happiness were tainted by the thought of him returning and wrecking everything. I can't remember the good times, he obliterated the few we had. I still don't know why I ever loved a man like him – all that's left are the scars of what he tried to do to me. To us.

Since I last saw him, Tony's changed little. Still slim, still the handsome face but slightly fuller, more worn the full head of thick, dark hair now also peppered with grey. It's in Tony's interests to stay fit, attractive, relevant – his life is probably still one long indulgent self-preserving orgy of young women and pleasing himself. But the leather jacket, the jeans low on the crotch and the bracelets are clichés of a man in his late forties desperately trying to relive his so-called glory days. I wonder if Amy saw him in this way, or did she see him as some cool, fun-loving, wannabe-rock-star dad?

'Why are you here?' I ask, my face giving nothing away.

'My daughter's missing.'

The look in his eyes is pure loathing. I think back to the last time I saw him. We were in court with our solicitors, the police had been involved, he'd been charged with Actual Bodily Harm. Much of it is now just a blur. Despite pleading not guilty, he was given a twelve-month jail sentence and I remember feeling relief, standing in court, despite my black eye, and smashed cheekbone, with older injuries caused when my hand was smashed by a car door. Nothing changes, he looked at me then in court as he's looking at me now.

'Oh, *your* daughter? So, suddenly, you're here to play the concerned father.'

'I *am* the concerned father,' he spits.

I'm blinded by resurrected rage. How dare he turn up after all this time? After abandoning us in the hospital on the darkest day, when it seemed there was no hope. Leaving me to fight alone, to fend for myself and my baby.

'Do you have Amy?'

'Don't be stupid,' he says.

'The police have been trying to track you down, you went off the radar just after Amy disappeared. Don't try telling me you're not involved.'

'I'm not. I went back to Italy for the weekend, took a flight Saturday, didn't know anything about it until Interpol were on my doorstep. You trying to pin this on me too?'

'I told the police about you, yes. I knew you'd be a prime suspect.'

He shakes his head, a slow, unhappy smile creeping across his face. 'I've talked to the police,' he says, 'I was out of the country when Amy disappeared. But looks like your husband is a person of interest.'

'Rubbish. Amy called him. He took her for pizza.' I snap.

'On the day before she went missing?'

'The only reason he was there and has got caught up in this is because you'd forced her to meet you and really upset her. She was distressed and she called him and he went to her – like a real father and daughter. Why… why after fifteen years do you just turn up and ruin everything?'

'I wanted to see my daughter,' he says.

'But all you did was cause her distress. You're evil, I never want you anywhere near her.'

'But you let that pervert near her?'

'Richard is her stepdad, he's a good man,' I say, horrified that he's gunning for Richard. 'I'm damn sure the police are more concerned about the fact Amy disappeared just a day after you tried to inveigle your way back into her life,' I say through gritted teeth.

'When this is over, I'm going to make sure he doesn't come within an inch of her.'

'Fuck off, Tony. You tried threatening me before and you were locked up – just try it. Richard's a good father, that's why he went to Aberystwyth last Friday, because he loves her – like a dad.'

'I love her like a dad too – and I'd have been there for her, I *am* her dad – but *you* wouldn't let me.' He's seething.

'You would have been a shit dad, a liability.'

'And what does that make you? You're a psycho, couldn't keep her away from the doctors, the hospitals…'

'My daughter had *leukaemia*, for Christ's sake!'

He shrugs. I remember the time he accused me of 'enjoying the attention' of Amy's illness. I try not to think about that now, because if I do I may lose it.

'You never really got it, did you? The life-threatening nature of what she had was lost on you. You hated the inconvenience of having to be at the hospital day and night when you could have been out shagging whichever woman you had on the side at the time.'

'I was there then and I'm here now, but as usual you're so obsessive you won't let me in.'

'Don't kid yourself. Tony Russo doesn't stick around for sick children, so I doubt missing teenagers are your bag.'

He just sneers at me. 'I didn't "stick around", as you put it, because of *you*. I was never allowed into your little world with Amy, no one else was, you were neurotic, no one was good enough to take care of her. And now look what's happened.'

'Yes, you're suddenly here and she's suddenly gone. *That's* what's happened,' I snap, clinging to the narrative I'm convinced is the right one. The more I think about it, the more I'm convinced of his guilt. 'What have you done to her, Tony? Have you told her lies, made her go away just so you can hurt me and keep us apart?'

'You wanna talk about lies, Kat? You and that bent husband of yours? You really wanna go there?'

'I don't want to go anywhere, I just want to know Amy's safe. If you've harmed a hair on her head, I will kill you. And you *know* I mean that,' I say, my face showing no emotion. I stare at him. He knows I mean it.

'I haven't harmed her, and I don't intend to. I have three kids, I see the other two all the time, they're fine.'

'Yeah, how unfair is that? You were a shit father who went on to have other children you didn't deserve,' I say bitterly.

'You know what I love about having *those* kids? That *you* don't get to decide if I can see them or not,' he says, taunting me with that ugly half-smile. 'Oh, or are you still playing God? Do you have something up your sleeve to stop me being a father to my other kids?'

'I don't need to. I'm sure their mother or mothers have done that – and if they haven't, then they aren't good mothers. There's only one thing worse than no father – and that's a bad one, and that's why I did what I did.'

He doesn't answer, he doesn't need to. I know from the short conversation we've just had that Tony hasn't changed, he hasn't learned from what happened. He still puts himself and his own feelings before those of everyone else – including his child. And now, I know his bitterness, his failure and his deep resentment for me shaped him. I was right to do what I did and I'd do it all over again if I had to.

I sit down, exhausted and, after a few seconds, Tony looks around the room, then he picks up the photo of Amy wearing the mustard top and red scarf. As it's the last one I have of her, and probably taken the day she disappeared, I'm anxious as he holds it. Concerned he'll try to take it, like he tried to take Amy. I can feel my fingers itching to snatch it from him, and when his fingers touch her face, I want to yell at him to stop.

I don't like him being here, I don't know what he'll do. He has good reason to hate me and I'm worried he may take his revenge, especially as I'm on my own.

'Kat, we can't change the past,' he suddenly says, looking up from Amy's photo, his eyes a little softer. 'We can't do things differently, but I'm here because whatever happened between you and me, she's my flesh and blood. She's an adult now, you can't stop me seeing her – and you can't stop me looking for her… you can't send me to prison this time.'

What can I say? I don't want him in my home, or anywhere near me, but my biggest worry is when we find Amy, he'll still try and take her away from me, either physically or emotionally. If I antagonise him too much, he could make things very difficult for me, or Amy if he's involved in her disappearance. I have to play along – at least for now.

'So,' he says, slowly putting the picture back, making me feel nauseous as he caresses the frame one last time, 'no one knows where she is?'

I shake my head.

'Even the last person to see her – your husband?' He looks at me, waiting for my response, but I look away. He wants to bring me down, destroy me after everything that happened. I can't let him do that, I have to be strong for Amy.

'Richard wasn't the last person to see her. According to the police there's some CCTV footage of her walking along the front late Saturday afternoon.'

'But Richard's been hanging around the uni, hasn't he?' he says his name like it disgusts him. I can't bear him being here. Hurting me isn't enough, he wants to hurt the man who replaced him too.

'No, he hasn't.'

Tony's now weighing everything up, his eyes all over personal family photos, all over our home, taking it all in. I feel violated, but I tell myself I can polish the photo of Amy when he's gone.

'Big garden,' he murmurs, gazing out onto the lawn. I'm on the verge of tears when he adds, 'You did well getting with the solicitor – I mean, it worked for you on several levels, didn't it? Nice crib… and I've seen your Facebook page. You go on fancy holidays, don't you, Kat?'

I don't respond to this, I mustn't get into personal stuff; I don't want him ruining the present like he has the past. I hate the idea of him looking at my Facebook photos though. I don't like the thought of him peering into my life, it makes me feel exposed, violated. Perhaps he did come here today because of Amy, but I can't help but feel he also came to see how my life turned out. In his shallowness, his misplaced values, he envies me my lovely home, the big garden and the long-haul holidays. I wonder if he feels so resentful of me going to the police, so ruined by what happened, he's lost control of his life? And might that loss mean he wants to make me pay for what I did even more?

'Still suffering PTSD after me?' he suddenly asks, fingering a vase of roses Zoe brought me yesterday.

I don't answer him. I won't discuss what happened with him, because I can't be sure he won't use it against me.

'Yeah, you certainly landed on your feet with boring, straight Richard.' He walks towards me. 'But it looks like he isn't that boring or straight after all, doesn't it?'

I'm suddenly aware of how vulnerable I am. Alone in the house, I'm still sitting as he stands over me, my phone is in the kitchen, the poker is by the fire. I can't reach it, I have no way of defending myself.

Tony stares down at me and slowly grasps my chin with his fingers. Never taking his eyes from mine, he holds my face. But as threatened as I feel, I stare back, knowing the minute I drop my eyes, he will see this as victory. For quite some time, we stay like this, a tableau of the past, the dynamics of our once-marriage laid bare for any onlooker. Except there aren't any onlookers, we're alone, and that's the problem.

Flashes of the past play through my mind, the hammer crushing my cheekbone, blackening my eye. The agony of my hand jammed in the car door. All the blood. My head banging against the brick wall of our house. Trying not to cry out. Not allowed to make a noise. Someone might hear.

'This isn't the time for you to come and intimidate me again,' I say, twisting my face away from his hand. 'All I want is for Amy to come home safely. If you know anything, or can help the police in any way, then please do. My liaison officer is due any minute,' I add as a warning. 'But if you can't help, then please don't try to be part of this because you don't belong here. I've cared for Amy all her life, without any help from you.'

'Yeah. Nice job, Kat,' he says, sarcasm dripping from his voice.

I feel another rush of rage. 'Oh God, are you hoping this will give you the fame you always craved? *Father of missing teen writes song in her honour?* Or will you be subtle and just make it a photo shoot desperately searching the campus with a team of cheerleaders?' I ask. So much for not antagonising him. But he has this effect on my usually forgiving and calm nature.

He feigns a look of surprise. 'Do you really think so badly of me, Kat? Let's face it, no self-respecting media outlet would want to interview me after the lies you told. Your hack mates on the local paper were bad enough, *Musician Who Walked Out On Dying Daughter Beats Wife.* I mean, where do we start? I was a pariah – I had no money, no work. Then my band, who said they'd weather the storm with me, suddenly decided they didn't want a singer. Turns out they didn't want *me* as their singer – domestic abuse wasn't part of the branding. I was a mess, it was so hard to pull myself out of the abyss, the black hole *you* sent me down. I couldn't get a job anywhere, I had community service, and so for a while I couldn't even leave the country. People shouted "wife-beater" when I walked in the pub… *my* pub, the one where everyone knew me. But suddenly no one wanted to know me.' Then he puts his face right in mine. 'You bitch. I lost everything.'

His face is on mine, I can't move, I won't move, and just when I think I can't take any more and I'm reaching for a stone bowl on the coffee table, Richard comes rushing in.

'What the hell is going on?' he yells, immediately realising who it is and grabbing Tony by both shoulders, pulling him away from me. 'Do you want another restraining order?' he's shouting at Tony, who always claimed to be a lover not a fighter. I think of him as a coward, as he allows Richard to physically manhandle him down the hall, me following to help, in the unlikely event that Tony finds some courage between here and the front door.

Richard's just pushing him out of the house, when Tony says something that takes my breath away.

# CHAPTER TWENTY-SIX

'Just one thing, *Dick*,' Tony says, making it sound like a body part, rather than a name, 'I've been to Aberystwyth, been doing a little investigation of my own.'

Richard is still holding him by his leather jacket, about to hurl him through the door, but he stops.

Tony continues. 'Was just about to tell Kat all about it… Spoke to some of Amy's flatmates. They say you were round there all the time. In and out of her room, turning up late at night, creeping out first thing in the morning. And all the time you thought you were getting away with it.'

Richard's trying to push him with even more force now, and Tony's looking back at me.

'Don't worry, Kat,' he says, pushing back against Richard. 'I've told the police everything. He's going down.' He turns back to Richard. 'And when you do, I'll make sure my mates in prison make you pay for what you did to my little girl, you filthy, vile BASTARD,' he yells, as Richard finally manages to force him out and slams the door hard.

'Christ,' Richard says, turning round and walking back up the hall towards me. 'He is evil, so bloody evil.'

He comes to me, his arms outstretched for a congratulatory hug, expecting a heroine's thank you for saving her from the bad man. But that isn't how I feel. Doubts are beginning to take root.

'What was he talking about, Richard?' I'm trying to assimilate the words I just heard.

'That idiot? He was talking rubbish, laying his poison, like he always did.'

'But he's spoken to Amy's flatmates. They *all* said that you visited late at night… creeping out in the morning. What was that about?'

'It wasn't *anything*.' His eyes are laughing, his arms outstretched. He has this incredulous look on his face, like he had in court when Tony denied hurting me all those years ago.

'I don't like this, Richard.'

'Neither do I, but you know what he's like – a proven liar. Jesus, Kat he even lied in court, tried to say that it wasn't him who gave you the black eye, that he never touched you. He's a *liar*.'

'I think *you* might be the liar, Richard,' I say.

By the expression on his face, it's clear he can't believe I'd think this, but I can't help how I feel, and right now I feel uneasy.

'But we've talked about this,' he looks anxious, nervy.

'Yes, and I naively accepted your outright denial.'

'You don't believe that. You know me, Kat.'

'I've heard other things too. Jodie said you've behaved inappropriately. She said—'

'Jodie? I can't believe this. She's an attention seeking—'

'Oh, give it a rest, Richard. Stop trying to point the finger at someone else. I'm sure it works in court, but it won't work with me – not this time.'

'How can you even…?' For once he's lost for words.

'I don't know anything anymore. You're used to playing a role in court, Richard, and I don't know what to believe, or how I feel.'

And as he stands there, looking at me in absolute shock, I finally face the fact that Jodie might not have misinterpreted his actions, because it ties in with what Amy's flatmates saw – and they can't all be wrong. What other reason could there possibly be for Richard's nocturnal visits, for him keeping secrets from me?

As hard as I try to think it through, the same question keeps hitting me in the face. Has Richard been abusing Amy? He might have been doing it for years, here in the home I created to protect her. Has he continued this since she went to university? Is that why she wanted to move so far away?

I find it impossible to believe, but I've written magazine articles about women who've been through this: intelligent, aware mothers who marry a man who wants them for one thing – their children. And having talked to some of these women, it's clear these men are so clever, the mothers are usually the last to know.

'Kat, you're going through a terrible time, and I realise you're probably confused, desperate. You just want to find Amy and I do too – but this is crazy. Thinking this of me isn't helpful; it will just destroy you – and me – which is exactly what Tony wants, he's probably paid those kids to say they saw me at Amy's room.'

'I'm sorry, Richard, I'm confused. I know you're right about Tony, but he isn't the only one who's suggested…' The horror on his face stops me from saying any more. 'Look, I'm not accusing you of anything, but I can't stay here with you until I know for sure what's been going on. I'm going to pack some things and—'

'No. No. This is your home. It's the place Amy will come back home to and when she does she will tell you the truth. I'll go.' He has tears in his eyes, and so do I, but I have no choice.

He looks at me, waiting for me to say something – but I have nothing to say. Is he my husband or is he a stranger? After a few seconds he leaves the room. A little later, I hear him close the front door behind him. And for the first time ever, I am truly alone in the home I have shared for the last fifteen years with my family. A home I thought would keep us safe, but what if the danger had been inside these walls all along? I imagined this house was strong, secure, but today Tony brought darkness into my home, a reminder of a horrible past, a time when I was driven mad by fear of losing my only child. I did some things back then that I'm not proud of and a part of me wonders if there's such a thing as karma. I was so desperate to escape Tony, to find salvation, I fell into Richard's arms. I trusted him with my life and that of my child's. But given my track record with men, perhaps my instinct with partners is far weaker than my maternal instinct. *Perhaps I didn't protect my child after all?*

I'd prayed when she was two years old that she'd survive to go to primary school, then that she'd attend high school, go to her prom. I was so desperate to have my baby for longer, that I'd have sold my soul for fifteen more years – and in a way I did. Perhaps I got greedy, I wanted her forever, I wanted her to myself and I did everything I could to make sure that happened. That's why I did what I did, why I said what I said. Perhaps I didn't deserve to keep her, because I was dishonest, I told lies, but Amy was so precious. Was that so wrong? Did it make me a bad person or just a desperate mother doing everything I could to protect my child?

Now I'm doubting Richard, and wondering if I missed something I shouldn't have. No one is the perfect parent, we all do things we regret, say things to our kids that perhaps we shouldn't, but in seeking a better future, a better family life, did I overlook something? Did I miss what was staring me in the face? That Richard isn't who I thought he was? Had I kept Amy safe from her father on the outside while trapping her *inside* with someone even more dangerous – her stepfather?

# CHAPTER TWENTY-SEVEN

Later on Sunday, I call Zoe and tell her that Richard's gone. I don't tell her why.

'Jesus, love, is it because Richard was in Aberystwyth?' she guesses. 'Do you think he was involved?'

'No, no. We're just under so much strain, we thought it best to have some breathing space.'

'Okay.' She doesn't believe me, but I really don't want to get into it about Richard, it's too painful. I can't bear to talk about this, don't want to hear myself say the words, it makes it too real and I'm not ready to share my stupidity, and my failure as a mother.

Minutes later I'm glancing through the front window and see Jodie's little Fiat pootling along and I've never been more pleased to see anyone – except Amy, of course. I go to greet her at the door.

'Are you okay, Kat?' she asks, as she gets out of her car on the drive.

'I'm glad you came, Jodie.'

'I'm so sorry. I feel so bad about Josh and…'

'No. *I'm* sorry. I just want us to be friends again.' She walks towards me and I hold out my arms, she immediately responds by grabbing me round the waist and burying her head in my neck. We hug on the doorstep for a long time. It's comforting to feel her narrow frame and breathe in the familiar smell of vanilla lip balm and green apple shampoo. It's almost like hugging Amy.

We go in and I close the door behind us, I don't want anyone or anything else to come inside.

'I'll put the kettle on,' I say, still shaken, but trying not to show it.

I take a packet of digestives from the cupboard and put six of the golden wheat discs on a plate. A tornado has torn through my world, my daughter's still missing after eight days, and here I am calmly placing biscuits in a neat circle on a deep-blue plate. The distraction of this simple, pointless act provides a familiar kind of comfort as the kettle boils, and Jodie opens the fridge for milk. I watch her and wonder if perhaps there was more to what she'd said about Richard than just a feeling? Has he ever done something to her too? Or tried to?

She puts down the two mugs she's holding, and as she pours hot water into them, she looks up, but not before a slight pause, and I wonder what awful secrets she and Amy shared.

'Kat, about Josh and—'

'Look, it's happened and, of course, I'm sad for Amy, but I suppose you can't help your feelings,' I say, taking the mugs, putting them on the tray and walking towards the French windows, where two easy chairs sit looking out onto the lawn. Richard likes to sit here and watch the birds. Today there's a robin, I point it out to Jodie and she smiles.

'Come and sit down with me and have your coffee,' I say.

'Amy and I may have drifted apart, but we're *still* best friends, always will be, Kat.' She reaches out and touches my hand, I feel my eyes brimming with more unshed tears. I thought I was all cried out, but it seems there are always more waiting.

'Of course, sweetie. You two have grown up together – gymnastics, brownies, ballet… and…'

She smiles. 'Yeah, Amy was always better than me. She was so agile, so flexible. I always felt a bit wooden next to her – in fact the gymnastic teacher used to say to me, "Be more like Amy."' She laughs at this, but I can't imagine it was much fun for her to be told she should be like someone else.

I remember Zoe once saying to her, 'If Amy can do the splits, why can't you?' Jodie's little face had crumpled, and my heart broke – no one wanted to do the splits more than Jodie, but she just couldn't. I'm biased, but it was obvious that Jodie didn't have Amy's confidence, her intelligence, and Amy was prettier too. Jodie has always wanted to be like her – was something happening with Amy and Richard, and Jodie decided to copy Amy in that too?

'Jodie, is there anything you're not telling me – about Richard?' I ask now, trying to force down a biscuit – it tastes like cardboard in my mouth.

She shakes her head and bites on her own biscuit.

'What about Richard? Do you think he might be somehow involved in this?'

Jodie puts down her biscuit and takes on a demeanour that's so familiar to me.

'Jodie, I know that face. You can't hide it from me. I've known you for so long, you're like my second daughter.'

She's distressed, and I won't get anything out of her like this, so I lighten the conversation – an old journalistic trick: let the interviewee think you've moved on, change the subject, and pounce again later.

'When you were little and your mum asked you a difficult question, like "What are you hiding in your pockets, Jodie?" You'd get that closed-in look.'

'It was usually contraband sweets.' She smiles. 'But I didn't realise I was so transparent.'

I nod. 'Well you are to me.'

We sit together in the silence, watching the robin bob about the garden.

'What do you think has happened?' I ask her. 'If you had to give a scenario – what would it be? Richard, Tony, the lecturer? Or do you still believe she ran away because you and Josh began seeing each other?'

Jodie takes a deep breath. 'I think you were right about me and Josh – she would have got over it, called you, talked it through. I think someone else… possibly Richard, upset her… and she ran away. She's probably having a really cool time and doesn't want people looking for her.' Sweet Jodie as always takes her time to find the kindest words to tell me the cruellest things.

We both sip our coffees and I consider what Jodie said. It just all hurts so much. It doesn't matter how people dress up Amy's life for me, it's beginning to look like she was in pain, and I don't know why. I find it hard to believe Richard is involved, and I find it hard to believe Tony isn't. Then there's Josh and Jodie – she must have been hurt but she didn't even tell me about it. There are so many secrets, so many possibilities. Some of them too dreadful to contemplate.

'Kat, I don't think anyone's hurt Amy,' Jodie suddenly says.

I take another sip – hot, tasteless water in my mouth. 'Thanks for being so kind,' I say.

'You've always been kind to me, that's why I feel so bad.'

'I've told you, you have no reason to feel bad.'

She slowly shakes her head.

'Guilt is a destructive thing,' I add, knowing from experience.

'I feel guilt about loads of things,' she says.

'Like what?'

'Oh… Amy, and my mum.'

'Why your mum?'

'Because I'm not doing medicine at university. Mum's always telling me how she sacrificed everything for me and I should have worked harder to get good A levels. But I just find it really, really hard. I hate the course I'm on now and *that's* supposed to be easier.'

I get up from my seat and put both arms around her. Jodie is so like Amy, just another lost little girl trying to find her way in the world. The difference between them is that Amy had me, and I think my way of parenting provides more choices – Zoe's way does have more of the boot camp about it at times. It's hard but you have to give them the freedom to choose what they want to do, and live the way that makes them happy.

'You need to talk to your mum before it's too late,' I say.

'She doesn't want to hear it, Kat.'

In spite of my current situation, I'm concerned about Jodie – does Zoe really think she'll survive three years of university? I don't.

She finishes her drink and asks if I mind her studying. 'I'd rather be here,' she says.

'Of course – like old times.' I smile.

She goes to her laptop, and I think how ironic it is that we're both here now, thrown together by some horrible fate – Jodie needing a mother, me needing a daughter. And I'm drawn again to the photo of *my* daughter, smiling in the wintry sun, red scarf against blonde hair, the mustard jumper reflected in her face like sunshine. Young. Pretty. Happy. *Where did you go, Amy?*

She has to be out there somewhere. Her vanilla lip balm, ASOS-ordering, Snapchat bubble still exists and I cling to the sweet, sticky fragrance that permeates the home – for me it's the scent of hope. I have to believe she'll be back soon to reclaim her world. And when she does, will her world be the same one she left? And will Amy be the same girl who disappeared?

I'm suddenly dragged from my Amy rainbow by Jodie's voice.

'Oh, Kat, someone's posted something *horrible* on your Facebook account,' she's saying. I immediately walk over to where she's sitting so I can see.

'My personal one?' I ask, getting up from my chair, horrified.

'Look,' she says, pointing to the photo of Amy, the missing poster I put on my own account, hoping someone, somewhere would see it.

I put my glasses on and lean in: *Ask your husband, Kat – he knows exactly where she is!*

# CHAPTER TWENTY-EIGHT

'What the hell?' I say. 'Is it a troll? Can we find out who it is?' I can't help but wonder if Tony's now taking his fight online.

'No,' Jodie says. 'It's okay though,' she says kindly, 'I'll delete it.'

If only it were that easy, I think.

She deletes the troll's message and turns to look at me, concerned. 'It's so hurtful,' I say. Richard's always been my saviour, the man I trust, my rock. How did I get it so wrong?

My eyes fill with tears and Jodie opens her arms, pulling me into her. It's pure role reversal – I've done this so many times with her. I soothed her when she dropped her ice cream, when she fell off the trampoline, and the time when Amy was mean to her and played with Freya Robinson instead.

When I eventually stop crying, she nervously says, 'Kat…'

'Yes.' I blow my nose and emerge from the tissues. 'What?'

'Oh, nothing.'

'You can't do that Amy, you can't just say "nothing", not now… not with all this…' I snap.

'You just called me Amy,' she says, and I could kick myself.

'Sorry, love, I don't know my own name at the moment, let alone yours. It's tough.'

'Yeah it is. And I don't want to add to all the stress you're under, but I feel there's something you should know. It's just…'

'Yes?'

'Amy always said that she'd find her real dad one day… I don't think she liked Richard.'

'I think her… Tony had confused her.' But had he? I just don't know anymore.

'I don't think it was just that, Kat. It wasn't her father who upset her, it was Richard,' she says, and glances at me before staring ahead into the garden.

'Oh?' *Please don't tell me anything else about Richard.*

'I wasn't going to say anything,' she starts, 'but after seeing that Facebook post on your account it looks like other people might know anyway.'

'Go on,' I say, wanting to put my fingers in my ears.

'Amy once told me… something.' She hesitates, looking at me with her head to one side. I almost don't want to know what she's about to tell me, but I've braced myself, literally – I've put my mug down in front of me and I'm discreetly holding onto the kitchen counter with both hands. I may not want to know, but I need to.

'Tell me,' I croak.

'Amy said this thing…'

She looks away, she knows what she's about to say might upset me, and I can see she's finding this hard. She feels sorry for me and she's trying to choose her words, but I beg her to continue, to finish what she's started to say.

'Look, Jodie, whatever it is, I can handle it. You can tell me anything,' I say. But I don't think I mean it.

I watch another robin springing around the greenery still covered in frost, it's cold again today. I shiver. *Is Amy out there somewhere in this freezing cold?*

'Anything?' Jodie asks.

'What?'

'You said I can tell you anything.'

I nod.

'Okay, well, she said that… Richard used to watch her when she was getting dressed.' She ends this difficult comment in the way teenagers sometimes do – with an upward inflection, making it sound like a question. I don't respond, I don't feel strong enough for this today, but I know I have to hear it.

'He walked into the bathroom without knocking… she said he did it all the time but pretended it was an accident.'

'Were you there, Jodie?' I ask.

'No. Amy was pretty upset about it.'

'But there's a lock on the bathroom door, and Amy's been using the lock since she was about ten. I can't see how that happened,' I say, desperately trying to bat it away. I thought this whole 'inappropriate' comment Jodie had made to Zoe was about her own interpretation. I didn't realise Amy had discussed anything with her.

She shrugs. 'I don't know, Kat, I'm only telling you what Amy told me. She said she also saw him peeping through the crack in her bedroom door.'

I shake my head. 'He may have been checking she was asleep but didn't want to go in and wake her.'

'Yeah, but he'd sometimes say things about her when you weren't around.'

'*Things?* Like what?' My heart's thumping in my chest, I can feel blood rushing to my head.

'Just like how cute she was, and how she was looking good.'

'*Cute?* Cute isn't a word Richard would use about *anyone*,' I say, unable to conceal my horror at what she's telling me. I mustn't let anyone think this is even a possibility, Richard deserves a chance to defend himself, this is a horrific accusation… but this is Jodie telling me, not some stranger or some troll on Facebook.

'I don't mean he said that word *exactly*, I don't know. I wasn't there – it was only what Amy told me.'

'This doesn't sound at all like Richard.' I look at her doubtfully, but feel sick. The cardboard digestive biscuit is in my throat and I want to vomit. 'Do you think Amy could have misinterpreted this?' I ask Jodie, but she gets that closed-in look and decides there's an urgency to tidying away. She picks up both our mugs and goes over to the dishwasher.

I didn't think things could get any worse. But they just have. I desperately try and work through what she's said. At the moment what I have is that Amy's five flatmates say Richard stayed over – and even brilliant lawyer Richard would have a problem coming up against five witnesses. And now this, Amy's best friend, who I've known all her life, telling me that Amy had caught Richard snooping on her.

'Did Amy ever say Richard… *touched* her?' I ask, hearing Richard's voice in my head, *You're leading the witness, Mrs Ellis.*

'Yes. She didn't like it.'

I don't want to know any more, but the question of the nature of Richard's feelings for my daughter makes me feel numb. I don't want to open that up and look at it, because if I find out it's the truth, then I'm the one to blame for everything.

Later, when Jodie's gone, I'm alone again. I feel wretched, and scared. I think I see the shadowy figure of Richard standing under a tree in the garden, but when I look again he's gone. Every bump, every slight crack of the trees in the wind makes me jump. It's cold and dark outside, and it suddenly feels cold and dark inside too. I have to get away, I don't want to stay in the house tonight, and Zoe's kindly told me I'm welcome there any time, so I'm going to take her up on her offer. I leave a key under the usual plant pot for Amy, along with a note telling her where I am, just in case she comes home tonight. I'm ever hopeful. It's Sunday night – it's been eight days – it feels like eight years – I've lost all track of time, and it feels strange to be leaving the house. Outside, it's freezing. The cold hits me hard after being inside for so long. I haven't driven for days, so even the pedals feel strange under my feet. Everything looks the same – but nothing's the same.

When I get to Zoe's, just minutes down the road, she's so pleased to see me. I didn't even call ahead, I just threw some clothes in a bag and landed on her doorstep. And, like a true friend, she welcomed me with open arms, the kettle is on, the coffee brewed and within minutes I am sitting at the table in her Shaker kitchen with the Aga and the gingham blinds and it feels like home.

'So, Richard's gone?' Zoe says, placing a mug covered in pink hearts in front of me.

'Yes. I asked him to leave. I'm beginning to think he might be lying after all about visiting Amy.'

'Finally!' she says, looking up in the air like she's thanking God.

'I talked to Jodie. Keep an eye on her, she's still very upset.'

'I will. She'll be okay, she's tough underneath all those tears,' she says, putting her own steaming mug on the table. Have to say, I wondered when you'd come to your senses. I wouldn't trust him as far as I could throw him.'

I know they've never seen eye to eye – but I'm still surprised at her vitriol.

'He may be innocent, it might be nothing, Zoe.'

She sits down, folds her arms and raises both eyebrows. 'No smoke without fire is all I'm saying.'

Perhaps Zoe has known all along, or had a feeling. Perhaps Jodie told her a long time ago. But I don't want to ask, I'm not strong enough, I still can't bear to think about what may have happened, let alone vocalise it. I have to let the police do their job and when it all comes out, I'll deal with it then. I'll need Zoe's support, because if Richard isn't telling the truth and something horrific emerges, then my life has been a lie – and I'm going to need my friend to get me through it.

'You did the right thing cutting out the poison from your life,' she says. 'I've been waiting for you to realise...'

'I know, I know.'

'Sorry, sweetie, I do go on sometimes, don't I?' She smiles.

'Yes you do, but it's only because you care.'

'I'm overprotective, really, but you're a big girl and you know what you're doing.'

'I am, but I feel like a child at the moment – and after kicking Richard out, I just didn't want to be alone tonight. It's excruciating to sit there longing for news and at the same time dreading it,' I say, as she gets up and produces a half-eaten cake from under a glass dome.

'Lemon drizzle?' she asks, and I shake my head. I can't even think of eating. Zoe cuts me a slice anyway.

I take the plate and tell her all about Tony's visit, Amy's flatmates saying they'd seen Richard there and what Jodie told me earlier.

Zoe just sits back on her chair with a knowing look on her face. 'Kat, I told you the other day that Jodie finds him creepy. And now this stuff about him being at the flat when he shouldn't have been – it isn't exactly a revelation, is it?'

'It is to *me*.'

'Really? This is the man who lied to you about where he was when he was with your daughter last week. He just sat there while you were going crazy with worry and never once mentioned the fact that he'd seen her on Friday.' Zoe throws her hands in the air.

'Yes, but the reason he didn't tell me is because he promised Amy he wouldn't, and until she went missing it wasn't an issue. He's a lawyer, Zoe, he keeps confidences all the time,' I say, wondering why I'm defending Richard.

'Even if that means lying to his wife?'

I don't answer. I can't. She has me on the ropes. 'Jodie's said things to me in the past.'

'About Richard?' I ask.

Zoe suddenly looks uncomfortable. 'Only about him being close to Amy, the way he looked at her, that kind of thing. I've seen it myself, I can't put my finger on it, just… something not right.'

'Oh, Zoe.' I start to cry. 'Why didn't you say something to me?' I trust her judgement – not only is she my best friend, she's a mother too, we're finely tuned to danger – or we should be. What a blind idiot I am.

'I didn't want to cause trouble if it wasn't true,' she explains.

'I understand, but you could have hinted, pointed me in the direction. I can't believe I missed it.'

'I didn't want to upset you,' she says. 'And I had no real proof – Jodie didn't understand it, she was too young, so I didn't get much out of her, just the odd comment that got my radar going.'

'If you had a partner and I felt he was behaving inappropriately with Jodie, I'd tell *you.*'

'I'm sorry, love, I just wasn't one-hundred-per-cent sure. What if I was wrong? I might have harmed your marriage, lost your friendship, and I wasn't prepared for that to happen. Why don't you discuss all this with Heather?' she suggests.

I nod. 'I will. Richard's been questioned already, and most of the time when I tell Heather something they seem to be a few steps ahead of me, or that's the impression she gives. I assume he's been vetted…'

'They might be watching him, see if he slips up.'

'That's possible, but I think they'd want to speak to Jodie – and probably you – about him watching her and all that.'

'Of course, if it stops some other young girl being abused…'

'We don't know that… yet.'

She rolls her eyes.

'Zoe, look – thanks for being here for me. It feels like a bloody horrible big knot I'm trying to untangle and it really helps to talk… I'm not angry with you for not telling me. I'm angry with myself.'

'I understand, and I am here for you. You were there for me when I was going through my divorce – bloody hell, I owe you big time.'

'Mmm, looks like I might be heading that way myself depending on what happens with Richard.' I sigh.

'I hate to say it, Kat, but I've never been happier since Pete went. And as for Richard – he's always seemed shifty to me, but then I've never really been a fan.'

She knows Richard's never been a 'fan' of hers either; he didn't hide it as well as she did.

'Let's see what happens,' I murmur, 'until I have real proof, like Amy telling me he did something. I really thought I would have known… it's like Amy being fixated on her lecturer, I just don't see it.'

Zoe raises her eyebrows. 'Sometimes we can't see what's right in front of us, Kat. Everyone has secrets, even the people we love, the people we live with.'

'I just find it so hard to think… Richard… Really?'

'I'm telling you, we don't know who we're sharing a bed with. Let me introduce you to Pete, the nicest, sweetest man in the world,' Zoe starts, 'and we all know how *that* turned out. Bastard was sleeping around, had the morals of an alley cat – and people tried to tell me, like I'm telling you now. But did I listen? Did I hell.'

'But this isn't about sleeping around. This is about so much more and I never saw it, I *never* saw it. Richard's so… so decent. He's a lawyer, for God's sake.'

'Just because someone appears to *be* something, doesn't mean that's who they *are*. Just make sure you talk to Heather.'

It crosses my mind that Zoe might know more than she's letting on. She's keen for me to tell Heather – therefore the police – about Richard, which makes me think Jodie might have told her mum more than she told me. *Has he hurt Amy?*

'Thing is, we all go along, living our lives, getting through the day, the week, the year – but, like I said, sometimes we don't know *who* we're living with,' Zoe's saying now.

I can't argue with that. Richard thinks he knows everything about me, and yet the first words from my mouth on the day we met were lies. I've felt bad about the way I lied to Richard – but it looks like I may not be the only one in this marriage who's lied, and I'm wondering if my husband, the man I have trusted with my and my daughter's life, is a liar and a stranger.

# CHAPTER TWENTY NINE

Zoe and I are sitting close at the wooden table, the warmth from the Aga is thawing me, and I take a deep breath. I feel like I'm finally able to relax. 'I wish I'd done this days ago, it's just what I need… apart from anything else, I know Tony will never find me here.'

'Oh God, I hope not. Imagine that psycho turning up, his face pressed against the window, I'd be straight onto the police. I don't even know why you let him in.'

'It was stupid. I just felt scared when I saw him, he made me feel like I used to feel, and I won't ever go back there.'

Zoe knows my story – not everything, but she knows how unhappy Tony made me, and how I hid from him for years. She puts her hand on mine, and looks into my eyes. 'I know it's all so hard, but I'm here, love, and you're welcome to stay as long as you like.'

'Thank you. The house has become so oppressive, it's like a waiting room, but until now I felt I couldn't leave in case Amy came home, but I left her a note.'

'Just in case,' she says with a sigh, and pats my hand and gets up to cut herself some more cake.

'I know Richard would say I'm being melodramatic,' I say, 'but I wonder if Tony told her to empty her bank account, dye her hair black and he's smuggling her to Italy – or perhaps I've seen too many made-for-TV movies?'

She smiles kindly. 'Oh, Kat, I think anything's possible with that twisted bastard. He just never let go, did he?'

'No, and I know he loves Amy in his way, but this is about him winning. He feels like I won all those years ago when he was found guilty and lost custody and he's still out for revenge.'

'God, it must be horrible, constantly trying to work it all out, and with men like Richard and Tony in the background, I don't blame you. I wouldn't trust either of them.'

'Mmmm. I just hope that wherever Amy is, she went willingly…' I say, welling up. 'I can't bear the thought of her being hurt.'

'No, of course not.' She leans on the table, resting her chin on her hands. 'Kat, you know me, and I'm the last person to bring you down, take away any hope…' I look at her, wondering what she's going to say. 'But it's been over a week now, love… and the longer she's away, the more likely it is that… she won't come back.'

'But I can't think like that, I have to…' I'm nowhere near ready to give up, I never will be.

'No, no, you mustn't give up hope. I'm not suggesting she's… gone… just that you have to prepare yourself, for anything and everything. She might have made another life for herself.'

I take a deep breath, and nod slowly, I know what she's saying, but she's doing it gently. 'But a week's nothing, is it? There's still a chance?'

'Absolutely. But the thing is, if she's run away, managed to stay hidden for a week, given the police search, and all her friends at uni and on Facebook looking for her, posters everywhere… I'm just saying you might have to accept that she doesn't *want* to be found. Now that might be because of someone else… Tony, or Richard…'

'Or me?'

Zoe looks at me with such pity I want to cry again.

'I doubt she was running away from you, love,' she says. 'You weren't the monster she was escaping.'

'And mothers have to protect their children from monsters, wherever they might be and however old they are. She might think she wants a new life, she might think things are easier somewhere else, that life won't touch her there, but it will – I'm her mum and I know best. I have to find her, Zoe.'

Again, I see the pity on her face. 'I know you do, love, but… I just want you to be prepared.'

'I'll never be prepared for something like that,' I say.

We talk some more and after a while I notice the big clock on her wall says it's almost midnight.

'It's late, it's been a long day, do you mind if I go to bed?'

'Of course, you don't need to ask. I'm tired too,' she says. 'Jodie's already fast asleep.'

We both get up and I follow Zoe upstairs, where she takes a small stack of clean towels from the airing cupboard.

'There you go, love, have a bath, a shower or both – whatever – just make yourself at home. The spare room's waiting and available for as long as you need it,' she adds, which is a very comforting thought.

'You're such a good friend,' I say, hugging her tight, almost breaking down.

Just about holding myself together, I make my way into the second room on the left, painted in calming shades of cream, with a soft, downy duvet sprigged with blue flowers. I lie on the bed fully clothed and, exhausted, I drift off into sleep.

When I wake a few hours later the room's dark, and the duvet is over me, Zoe must have covered me up when I dropped off. It makes me feel cared for – how like another mother to do that.

I do what I always do and check my phone to see if Amy's been in touch. She hasn't and I need to go to the bathroom, so I climb out of bed and, on my way, I'm aware of the delicious, sticky sweet smell of vanilla lip balm and, glancing over at Jodie's room, I see the door is ajar. There's a lavender light coming from inside, and I tiptoe across the landing, so I don't wake anyone. I peep in to see the lavender flower fairy lights around her bed and smile to myself remembering Amy's outrage when Jodie dressed her headboard with exactly the same fairy lights she had.

It's a dog-eat-dog world, but Amy hadn't experienced that in the way poor Jodie had – Amy always found school and friends and life so much easier. Amy liked Jodie, but she also felt her pain and felt sorry for her because she struggled and her mother was always making her do things she couldn't do. I felt the same. When Amy excelled at gymnastics, Jodie's desperate attempts to make her mother proud fell flat when she couldn't even get on the horse in the gym. At the gymnastics club's open day when – helped by the coach, who virtually had to lift her in the air because she was so scared to jump – Jodie awkwardly, and painfully, followed Amy's leaps and rolls it was embarrassing. The poor girl humiliated herself because her mother was so desperate for her to be as good as the other girls, when she physically couldn't be. I watch her now sleeping in her version of Amy's room, with similar colour scheme, the same posters, and I realise that Jodie's always been scared to jump. That's why she needs Amy – and now she doesn't have her, she must feel so lost.

Jodie stirs, and I turn to leave the room when I see something peeping out from the wardrobe. It's the strap from a rucksack, a bright-yellow rucksack… just like Amy took to university. My first thought is: *She'll go mad when she finds out Jodie's bought the same one*. 'Honestly, Mum, we're not even in the same town anymore and she's checking out my social media to see what bag I've got.'

I smile to myself about this, I understand Amy's frustrations, but I think it's sweet. I go to the bathroom and wash my hands and face, looking at myself in the mirror: sunken eyes, dry skin, extra crevices carved into the flesh of my forehead. A week ago, this would have mattered, I'd have put 'anti-ageing moisturisers' into Google and ordered what I *had* to have online. But now I see the haunted face of a woman who doesn't care how many lines she has, all she wants to know is where her child is. I am now a woman whose life, whose identity, whose future will be shaped by this, whatever the outcome. When people see me in the street they won't think, 'There's Kat,' they'll think, 'There's Kat, who never found her daughter.' Or worse. I continue to look in the mirror seeing only her, and knowing my face is irrelevant. Everything is irrelevant until Amy comes home.

I leave the bathroom, and walk back across the landing, unable to resist sneaking another peek at Jodie. In the semi-darkness, I can make out her blonde hair like a halo on the pillow, I breathe in the smell of vanilla and pretend for just a moment that she's Amy. My eye catches the yellow rucksack strap again, and I don't understand it, but I'm suddenly compelled to take a closer look – another reminder of Amy, I suppose. So I quietly head into Jodie's room and move towards the wardrobe. As I start to open it, the wardrobe door squeaks, and Jodie turns over. My heart's in my mouth, if she wakes up and sees me standing here, she'll be so freaked out. Whatever she thinks Richard was doing in Amy's doorway is nothing compared to how she'd feel waking at 3 a.m. to find her best friend's mother face deep in her wardrobe. But I'm so close to the rucksack now. I wait a moment, until I'm sure Jodie's not going to wake, and then I slowly and carefully feel the strap with my hands until I reach the bulging bag. I grab it firmly and am relieved to discover it's lighter than I'd thought, and as I lift it I see something pushed into the top that makes my heart almost stop.

It's the red, hand-knitted scarf – the only one of its kind. The one Amy was wearing on the CCTV when she walked out of her life.

I am so confused, I don't know what to do. My instinct is to grab the bag, take it back to my room and go through it. But what if it's actually Jodie's bag? I was with Amy when she bought it before leaving for uni – we bought it from a chain store and there were loads of them. Jodie might simply have seen it and bought exactly the same one as Amy. But the scarf? Why is the scarf here in this bag? It doesn't make sense.

Everything else Amy was wearing on the CCTV could have been worn by any other teenager on any other day. But she was definitely wearing the scarf, it's how I knew it was her on the footage, no one else has one. Either the woman in Selfridges was lying to me about its uniqueness – or something's going on here.

I'm standing in Jodie's room, clutching the scarf in one hand and the yellow rucksack in the other, and I just can't think straight. I don't want to wake Jodie and ask her now – I'm upset and tired and it might all be a horrible mistake on my part. I need to think about this calmly first, so I push the scarf back in the bag and, holding it to my chest, I head for the spare room as quietly and quickly as I can.

I dash in, breathless with exertion and nerves, and quietly close the door behind me. I'm desperately hoping I haven't woken anyone. I know Zoe's a light sleeper and she might wake at any time and, if she hears me, she might pop her head round the door to check I'm okay. How would I explain the fact I've taken her daughter's rucksack from her room and I'm now rooting through it? But as I pull out the scarf, I know it isn't Jodie's bag, because inside is the mustard jumper, black jeans and a pair of Converse trainers. And if I was still in any doubt as to whether these belong to Amy, I suddenly see the rainbow sticker on the outside, big and bold, applied in a wonky fashion, just the way Amy did it.

# CHAPTER THIRTY

I sit on the bed, the contents of the rucksack in a small pile next to me. I bury my face in the jumper, hoping to recognise my child's scent, like an animal might know her young. But all I get is the overpowering hit of vanilla lip balm – something both girls use. *What the hell does this mean?* Are the girls in this together? Have they staged Amy's disappearance for some reason? Why else would Jodie have Amy's clothes and her bag? Perhaps Amy's so upset about something, she's had to leave and Jodie's harbouring her somewhere. I'm confused, tired, and exhausted – am I thinking straight?

I hear a noise on the landing and keep very still, quietly turning off the lamp so whoever's there can't see the light under the door. The floor creaks, and whoever it is, is standing outside my room. I'm still sitting on the bed, I daren't move because that will give me away. So I barely breathe, just stay rooted to the spot until they seem to move away. I wait for total quiet, and sit in the dark, clutching my missing daughter's belongings, big tears dropping down my face.

I could be completely wrong about this… except for the scarf, the scarf is the one thing I keep coming back to. *It's the only one like it.* And it's giving me hope that Amy may not be as far away or as lost as I thought. I'm also filled with something like joy… it's sweet and warm in my chest; because if the scarf is here, I think (irrationally, perhaps) that means Amy's safe – somewhere. I caress the red wool, telling myself she was wearing this when she left. So why is it here? Is *she* here? Can I even dare to hope this might mean my daughter didn't leave us forever when she walked along the promenade at Aberystwyth on that bright, but freezing, November morning eight days ago?

There may be an innocent explanation, something I haven't thought of in my muddled, exhausted state, but I can't sit here all night in the dark wondering. I have to ask Jodie.

I turn on the light, creep across the landing, and when I get into her room, I go and kneel by her bed, still clutching the rucksack and clothes. I tap her on the shoulder, whispering her name. I want to ask her without Zoe being involved, because if Jodie and Amy have cooked something up between them Zoe will go mad. I don't want her screaming in Jodie's face and scaring her while I'm trying to find out where Amy's hidden.

But Jodie's fast asleep, and as much as I pat her and as loud as I whisper, she isn't waking, so I say her name louder, causing her to stir, while patting her on the shoulder. 'Jodie, Jodie.' I'm saying it louder each time, and eventually she sits up with a start and a loud yelp. 'Sssh,' I'm saying by the side of her bed.

'What…? Kat, what are you doing here?' She sounds distressed.

'It's fine, sweetie, I'm staying tonight, and I'm sorry to wake you…'

She rubs her eyes and looks at her phone. 'Shit, Kat, it's four o'clock in the morning.'

'I know, I know, but I had to wake you because this is driving me mad.' Our eyes are both becoming accustomed to the light, and I'll never forget the look on her face when she sees what I'm holding. *She knows, she bloody knows.*

'What are you doing with that?' she asks nervously.

I respond calmly, gently, I don't want to scare her off, but inside I'm screaming. 'I found it, love – what's it doing in your room? Where's Amy?'

Jodie's pulled herself into a sitting position now, but she's looking at me like I'm about to murder her. 'Kat, why are you in my room?'

'No, you don't get to ask me questions, Jodie. What's going on? Are you and Amy both in on this?'

She's shaking her head vigorously. 'It wasn't me. It was her... It was her...' I feel her anxiety bubbling, I need to keep her calm, but I'm not holding back anymore.

'Amy?'

'She told me I had to pretend to be her, I had to dress up in her clothes and...'

'What's all the noise?' A booming voice makes us both jump and a light goes on. We both turn to see Zoe standing in the doorway. 'What's going on?'

Jodie is now sobbing into her hands, rocking back and forth – I don't know what to do.

'I... I'm sorry, Zoe, I didn't want to cause all this upset, but' – I lift the rucksack – 'Amy's stuff, it was in Jodie's wardrobe.'

And there it is. The look on Zoe's face changes everything. *She knows.*

'Oh, love.' She gives me what I think is meant to be a sympathetic look, but Zoe can't hide her feelings. Her face is red, her gestures are suddenly quick, like a bird, as she flits across the room and tries to take the rucksack from me, but my natural instinct is to grip it tightly.

'Zoe, what are you doing? Why is it here? Tell me why it's here – you know something, don't you? You *know!*'

'Kat, there's nothing to know. The bag's Jodie's, you know what she's like – if Amy's got one, Jodie has to have it.'

'No, the clothes...' I protest.

'All Jodie's.'

'Not the scarf. The scarf is Amy's.'

'It must be Jodie's; it's in her bag,' Zoe says, her voice raised, high-pitched. She's glaring down at me and I suddenly feel vulnerable.

'No. No it isn't. You *know* it isn't,' I say, standing up to face her. She steps back suddenly and bangs into a shelf, knocking a glass candleholder onto the wooden floor.

'Shit, shit,' she's saying, and I can hear tears in her voice.

'Zoe, leave it, it doesn't matter – it's a bloody candleholder,' I say, aware that Zoe seems to be stalling for time. But now I'm scared. What *is* this about?

Surrounded by broken shards, she's on her knees, grabbing at them manically, like a woman possessed.

'Mum, tell her… Tell her,' Jodie cries between sobs.

'Don't be stupid, Jodie, there's nothing to tell, calm down!' Zoe barks, looking up from the glass, then turns back to me, her voice gentler now. 'Kat, you're confused, love.' She glances at the bag and I instinctively clutch it tighter. 'Come on, let me make you some coffee, you're getting yourself into such a state.'

'Oh no. I'm not in a state – I just don't know what the fuck's going on, but *you* do.' While she's here playing games, Amy could be in trouble. 'SOMEBODY TELL ME. WHERE IS SHE?' I cry, looking from one to the other.

'Mum!' Jodie whines. '*Please,* Mum, tell Kat what happened.'

At this, Zoe stops moving, and slowly, silently brings her head up. 'I have no idea.'

'You do. You do. I don't know what's going on here but you'd better tell me.' I turn to Jodie. 'Was Amy running away from someone, something, and you helped her? Is she hiding somewhere?' I walk away from Zoe and move towards Jodie, who seems to be on the brink of telling me. 'Jodie, *please*?' I'm on the verge of tears, someone in this room *knows* where Amy is. *And they're not telling me!*

I can see Zoe slowly getting to her feet, out of the corner of my eye – she doesn't speak, just stares at me, I feel quite unnerved. Jodie has her head in her hands, unable or too scared to respond to me.

'Kat, I don't think we should be having this conversation in here – in front of Jodie. She's been through enough, I'm sure you understand?' The voice is the same, she looks the same, but Zoe's different. I see it in her eyes, a blankness I've never seen before. I don't want Jodie to be any more distressed than she already is, so I agree to go downstairs with Zoe. I follow her into the kitchen clutching the rucksack and scarf close to my chest.

# CHAPTER THIRTY-ONE

'Coffee?' Zoe says, as if I've popped over for a bloody chat.

'NO. I don't want *fucking* coffee, are you *mad*?' I yell. 'I want to know where Amy is, and don't tell me you don't know. What's going on, Zoe?'

She almost throws herself into a chair, puts her elbows on the table and rests her head in her hands. When she eventually emerges, she's crying.

'What, what?' I'm crying too. What is it that she can't tell me? Is it too horrible to reveal?

'Oh, Kat, why have you done this? You've made all this fuss… Why couldn't you just believe that she ran away? Amy ran away…' She's looking at me through her tears, nodding.

'*Has* she run away? Did Jodie help her? You can tell me – you *have* to tell me. Where is she, Zoe?' I'm shouting now, close to hysteria, I can't take any more of anyone's lies and secrets.

'It was all a horrible mistake. Jodie didn't mean… she didn't mean it. I'm so, so, sorry, Kat.'

'I don't understand. If Jodie helped her run away, I don't understand why you didn't tell me. I DON'T KNOW WHY SHE RAN AWAY! TELL ME!' I'm screaming in Zoe's face and she's a mess.

'KAT – STOP! STOP!' she screams back.

We're both stood now, facing each other, crying and shouting and then she slowly sits back down and I wait too long for her to say something.

'She didn't… run away. Amy had an accident.'

'What kind of... What are you saying?'

'Jodie was with her, she went to see her in Aberystwyth. They argued...'

'Okaaayyy...' I say slowly, not asking questions, eager for her to speak.

'Jodie was so upset. When she'd started seeing Josh, Amy had taken it badly.'

'Yes, yes,' I say gently. 'Just tell me what happened and where Amy is, Zoe.'

She looks straight at me. 'Kat, I *told* her. I said, "Jodie don't go on a long train journey to Aberystwyth, Amy might not want to see you. Wait until Amy gets home and you can tell her how bad you feel then." But no, Jodie didn't want that. To be honest, Kat, I think Jodie was worried if Amy came home, she might see Josh, and Josh might fall for her all over again. Jodie was used to being second place to Amy,' she adds bitterly.

I don't respond, so she'll continue.

'She didn't mean for it to happen, Kat. It's not like our Jodie planned it. God, it was all so horrible. She called me last Friday at midnight in tears, and instead of telling her to sort her own shit out, I did what I always do – went and cleaned up her mess.'

'Mess?' I can barely speak, my head's spinning.

'Yes. She kept saying, "I killed her, I killed her." I thought when I got there that Amy would just be unconscious and I'd bring her round and tell them both not to be so silly. But Kat... when I got there...'

'She was... dead?' I hear myself croak, like I'm in an echo chamber.

She nods. 'I'm sorry, love. So, so sorry.'

'No.' I burst into tears – my baby, the child who'd cheated death, who grew into a young woman with all that future ahead of her. The endless hours of waiting and hoping in hospitals, and now the absolute torture of this not knowing, but hoping – and it's all come to nothing in a moment. The light's gone out. Life is suddenly meaningless.

'I know, love, I know.' Zoe stands up. But I don't want to hear her pretending to care. 'They argued, over Josh – Amy was mean,' she adds, like that somehow justifies what happened. 'And Jodie pushed her… she slipped.'

I'm suddenly aware that she's trying to give me a bear hug, but I'm resisting; I don't want her near me, her breath in my face, her sickening apologies, her disgusting attempt to somehow make this defensible. I still can't process what she's told me. I stand with her arms around me, I'm holding the yellow rucksack to my chest – it's all I have of Amy.

'I'm calling the police,' I say, but realise immediately my phone is still upstairs. And now she's gripping me to her, but what was once the gesture of friendship has changed.

'No police, love, no police,' she's saying, her arms around me tight, squeezing me. Too hard. How quickly my friend has become my foe.

'All the time, all that time – you knew, you fucking *KNEW*!' I scream in her face and struggle to escape her grip, but she's stronger, bigger than me. 'You watched me go through hell… you were with me, you were supposed to be my friend… and all the time…' I break down, unable to process what's happening.

'Give it up, my love. I know how hard it is, but think about Jodie – you said it yourself, she's like a second daughter to you.' Her face is in mine, her teeth are gritted, she's talking fast, her voice eerily high-pitched, and she doesn't sound like Zoe, my funny friend, anymore.

'Get OFF me!' I say, desperately trying to struggle, to push her away, but now she's pushing me against the wall, leaning her weight against me, squeezing the breath out of me. I'm tired, weak, I don't have the strength to push her off.

'Don't call the police. Please don't throw her to the wolves, Kat. Please, please, *please,* she's my baby, my only child,' she's saying. 'Don't, don't do it, for Jodie's sake, don't tell the police, don't tell the police.' Her words merge into each other, repeated, unfinished, one garbled sentence bleeding into the next. 'Amy ran away, please say she ran away, she was scared of Richard, he was touching her, tell them he was doing things to her.'

'NO. NO. Because he wasn't, was he?' And it's all becoming clear, I feel as if I've been walking through a forest and suddenly reached a clearing. Things are beginning to make sense. 'Richard always said you were out for yourself, but even Richard never thought you'd be capable of this… this… horror,' I cry.

'I know, I know, I know.' Again garbled words attached to each other, repeated like a mantra. 'As one mother to another, think of me, think of Jodie – she'd be a child in a women's prison.'

'WHERE IS AMY?' I shout loudly and clearly in her face.

But she's not listening, she's in her own world, her voice urgent, incoherent. She's still pushing me back against the wall, her face pressing on mine. Each word burning into my brain. 'Amy's dead, it's too late for her, but it isn't too late for Jodie. Amy's gone now, love. She's gone. It's too late. Nothing I could do,' she says, the parody of a smile of sympathy plays on her face – she is terrifying.

I can't speak, can't get the words out, as I push against her with one, huge effort, every muscle in my body forcing me forward. But as I do, she raises her hand, and I see the milk bottle, as it comes crashing down on my head.

She stands back, one arm in the air, still holding the remains of the jagged glass bottle, the rest is in pieces in my scalp and on the floor. I look down, scattered shards twinkle like tiny stars on the slate floor, and as she lets me go, I lunge for the table to hold myself up, but my legs give way beneath me. I look up and, through blurry vision, see she's standing over me.

'That's right, love, Amy was unhappy and she ran away… just like you're going to. You'll throw yourself into the River Severn, late at night. Jodie and I moved Amy's body, we can move yours too. I mean, if Amy isn't here anymore, you won't want to be here either, will you? Especially after what her stepfather did – pompous, arrogant bastard that he is. I was never good enough for him, and Jodie was never good enough for your precious daughter – precious, precious.' She's hissing in my face, her arm now across my throat pinning me to the wall again. 'Always had to be the best, didn't you? You and your daughter, your clever, pretty daughter,' she adds as if the words taste nasty on her tongue. 'Life's always been easy for you and her. You've had the same, nice man with a bit of money to see you through life, a good friend like me, always there when you need her. "Ooh, I broke a nail. I must call Zoe, she'll come over and listen to me wail for an hour about it,"' she sneers.

'And when our Jodie got Josh, your perfect daughter couldn't believe he'd dump her for someone like Jodie… but he did, and I was glad, I nearly threw a bloody street party. For once our Jodie won at *something*!'

And there it is, her jealousy, her self-hatred and low self-worth passed on to her daughter. How could I have missed it? This competitive, resentful mother who on the outside congratulated and smiled, but on the inside seethed at everything me and Amy had that she and Jodie didn't. From a faithful husband to good A-level results, she's been so jealous – and taught Jodie to feel the same, causing her to covet everything Amy had, including her boyfriend.

'Everyone will understand, the heartbroken mum…' she's saying. 'I'll make sure they know what a wonderful mother and friend you were, my darling… my best friend forever, forever.' She's wheezing in my face, breathless, filled with so much hate that's been boiling up for years.

And then, just as quickly, the wild eyes soften, the hand comes up to my cheek and she's looking at me and smiling.

I reach out to try to push her away, but I can feel myself slipping, falling.

And now she's just standing over me, nodding slowly. 'There, there, my love, it'll be over soon,' she says, still watching me, as I fall, defeated, floored by the pain in my head and the agony of knowing my child is dead.

I'm lying on the floor but feel like I'm underwater, desperately trying not to drown. I'm searching for Amy, but the waves are too high and every time I see her, the tide sweeps me away and the agony is too much to bear. I can't save my only child. *You had one job, Kat.*

And now I'm on a boat in the middle of a huge ocean, just bobbing up and down, nothing for miles, and I'm calling Amy's name but she's not answering me.

I'm suddenly aware of a sound. Something under the boat is knocking – there's something under the boat and I can't get to it. Is Amy under the boat? In my panic, I open my eyes to help her – but I'm still on Zoe's floor. Someone's knocking on the front door, a really heavy, persistent knock. I think it might be the police with bad news. But then hasn't Zoe already told me the bad news? I don't know.

She leaves the kitchen to answer the door, and I try to call her, but no sound emerges. In the distance, I hear a voice, it's familiar, but I don't know who it is, my brain can't assimilate any information. Zoe's talking, she's trying to sound bright and breezy, I know her so well. Even in this state, I can imagine her face, what I now know to be the fake smile, the endearments. 'Sweetie,' I hear and then another voice – Jodie, screaming.

I am weak, but try to reach for one of the wooden chairs engraved with hearts. If I can drag myself to my feet I might be able to get to the door, escape. But as I reach for it, my weight is too much and it comes crashing down on top of me. I hear myself give a yelp of pain as I crash heavily back down onto the tiled floor.

# CHAPTER THIRTY-TWO

'Kat, Kat… it's me Josh.' I'm suddenly aware of someone grabbing me. 'Wake up, wake up.'

'She just fell, she was holding a milk bottle, she dropped it. She just fell, she'll be fine,' Zoe's saying, as I try to tell the truth, but struggling to speak past the pain in my head.

'She won't be fine, Mum. I heard you shouting. What happened?'

'What happened? I might ask you the same question! Can't you do anything on your own? Why did you have to call your bloody boyfriend?'

'Because you locked my bedroom door and I couldn't get out,' Jodie hisses.

Then I hear Josh, I think he's on the phone, and Zoe's yelling at him. 'We don't need an ambulance, just leave it, Josh, she's coming round. Look, she'll be fine. Will everyone stop being so dramatic, a good night's sleep is all she needs.'

But the very thought of being asleep in Zoe's home now fills me with horror. I'm trying to tell Josh things aren't right, but I can't compose a sentence.

'Amy,' I mumble. 'Ask… where… Amy is…'

'She wants to know where Amy is, why is she asking that?' Josh is saying. 'I don't understand.'

'It was an accident.' Jodie's crying and Zoe's telling her to shut up.

'Take… me… in the car,' I'm saying to Jodie now. 'We have to… get out.'

'No, she'll be fine, I'll bathe her head,' Zoe snaps, trying to manhandle me across the floor.

'Come on, Kat,' Jodie suddenly says, leaning down, putting her hands under my arms, and for the first time in her life she goes against her mother's wishes. 'Grab her, Josh, let's get her to the car.'

As Zoe yells her protests, with their help I am lifted to my feet and they virtually carry me through the front door and throw me in the back of the car.

I'm vaguely aware of my arm dangling, it bangs against the car door as the kids try to squeeze me into Jodie's tiny Fiat, but I'm so terrified I feel no pain.

'Drive, drive,' Josh yells, and I see Zoe running towards the car to try and stop us, but Jodie sets off and the car screeches away down the country roads.

'What the fuck?' Josh is saying.

'She's mad, she's mad,' Jodie says. 'If you hadn't come when I called you, she'd have smashed Kat's head in and I'd still be locked in my room.'

'But why? I don't understand,' he says.

I hear this, and I'm nodding, but unable to contribute to the conversation. I'm lying in a foetal position on the back seat, holding my head and groaning in pain.

'I'll tell you everything, but first, let's get Kat to hospital.'

As Jodie drives, I see early-morning sky whizzing by above me, still starry, still dark, but with the promise of morning. But not for Amy. And even in this state, with a headache from hell and blood everywhere, I know that Zoe is right. If Amy isn't here anymore, then I don't want to be here either.

# CHAPTER THIRTY-THREE

Despite an awful lot of blood, a mild concussion and six stitches, I'm awake, though still confused later that morning in hospital. Richard's here, sitting by my bed; and I've never been so pleased to see him – I can't believe I ever doubted him.

'What happened?' I ask.

I suddenly remember what Zoe told me about Amy and start to cry. 'Amy?' I say.

He shakes his head. I hear a noise coming from my own throat, an animal sound I don't recognise as me.

'She killed her… Jodie killed her,' I wail.

After all the care, the friendship, someone I thought of as a daughter has killed my child. And her mother, my friend, covered it up.

'Where is she?' I ask, knowing I'm talking about her body.

'They haven't found her yet,' Richard says. 'Just know she's in peace.'

As the effects from the injury wear off, the realisation of what we're now facing becomes clear. I almost wish that I'd got to the hospital too late, and they'd let me die, I just want to be with Amy.

Over the next couple of hours, I cry and sleep, aware of Heather leaving and returning, of Detective Mather appearing at my bedside – or is that just a dream? I drift between waking and sleeping, and nothing makes sense, I'm traumatised by the shock of grief.

Eventually, by early evening, I'm able to sit up, and Richard holds my hand and we talk about how we want Amy to be remembered.

Heather comes back to see us.

'Where is she?' I ask.

'We're out there looking,' she says gently. 'Zoe's told us where she left her...'

'Where?' I ask.

'In the Cambrians, about thirty miles outside Aberystwyth on the road back to Worcester – she hid her in a ravine.'

I groan at the thought of Amy lying somewhere in the mountains. Amy whose favourite colour was lavender, who loved dancing to Lana Del Ray and eating Cadbury's flake, had been left in the cold and rain.

'Did she leave her there to die?' I ask, knowing I can never forgive either of them for what they've done.

'From the information we've been given it seems she was already gone – she died on the beach, so her suffering wasn't extended beyond that.'

I nod. I know she has to be honest, it's part of her job to tell me straight – but to hear it is brutal. She'd been through so much and was starting her life, with so much to live for.

'How did they take her from the beach without being seen?' Richard asks.

'No one was around because the weather was so bad. Zoe then drove away with Amy in the boot.'

'I can't believe it,' Richard says.

'We've had a full confession from both,' Heather confirms.

'They had no choice – if something had happened to Kat they might have got away with it,' he says.

'Jodie finally rebelled,' I say, 'and in doing so she sacrificed herself.'

I know she was just a pawn in Zoe's plan to keep her out of prison, but Jodie has some kind of a moral compass. She may have taken my daughter's life – but she gave me mine. I wish it had been the other way round, but this is how it is, and we will both have to live with Amy's loss.

'It seems that they used their position as your friends, always watching and listening, to direct the narrative away from themselves. They tried to convince Kat that Amy had been unhappy, that she'd run away, but when Kat didn't buy it they changed strategy. Then someone commented on Facebook that the stepfather was responsible for Amy's disappearance, and it was a gift to them. They started a campaign for you to be in the picture, Richard,' she says, looking at him, 'and with a fake account they posted the same message on your Facebook wall, Kat.'

'I remember it well. *Ask your husband, Kat – he knows exactly where she is!*'

'By then they'd begun a 360 campaign, throwing Richard in as the main suspect, but still keeping the running-away story going.'

'Sandra Wilson. The woman who said she saw Amy at the station.'

'Fake account… as was most of the trolling. This was a full-time job,' she adds.

Richard just shakes his head. 'I knew they were doing something with the Facebook page, using it for their own agenda – but I honestly thought it was Jodie and Josh just playing with fire… it never occurred to me that Jodie was involved.'

'She knew everything,' Heather says, 'and your suspicions were right, Richard – Jodie was using the page to point a finger at whomever she could to detract from her and her mother. Directed by Zoe, Jodie was feeding false information to us from the Facebook page too.' Heather then says, 'It did occur to me that you were rarely left alone. If it wasn't Zoe it was Jodie – they were a tag team.'

'You're right, when the Facebook page was closed down, I finally had an hour or so to myself – it felt weird.'

'You were becoming dependent on them, and if Zoe couldn't be there, Jodie was immediately dispatched by her to stick by you and keep an eye on developments. If they heard or saw anything, they'd immediately adjust the story, try and influence you one way or another.'

'Like they did with Richard?' I say, looking at him and feeling terrible.

'Jodie's admitted none of the allegations she made against Richard were true.'

'Were the flatmates in on it too? They said they saw Richard leaving Amy's room.'

'Yeah, that wasn't a lead – and it *wasn't* Richard. Looks like there was a late-night visitor, but Ahmed admitted he hadn't actually "seen" him. Amy had told him it was her stepfather.'

'Why?' Richard asks.

'We're not sure – she might have been joking, and Ahmed just believed her.'

'We'll never know because she can't tell us,' I say, overcome at the realisation that she's dead.

'And Tony Russo, he was hanging around the uni trying to coerce the flatmates into saying I'd been there too?' asks Richard.

'Yes, Tony Russo went to the uni and asked around. Someone repeated the misinformation to him, that the stepfather had been seen in Amy's room. He took it and ran with it – those were whispers he was only too delighted to hear,' she adds.

'I wouldn't put anything past him,' I say. 'But it's all meaningless now. Amy isn't here and I invited her killer in, I encouraged them to play together, the sister she never had, my second daughter – and I failed to protect her. I never saw it. I was so busy trying to save her from Tony and the big wide world, I couldn't see what was right in front of me – I brought the danger in.'

'Stop this,' Richard's saying in a soothing voice, rubbing my back. 'Please don't ever blame yourself, you're a wonderful mother.'

'Not anymore,' I say.

Heather reaches out her hand and holds mine. 'You'll always be Amy's mum,' she says gently. 'And we're going to find her and bring her home.'

I'm allowed home later that day, and I can't stop crying because it isn't home without Amy and it devastates me to think she'll never, ever be here again. This is the home we made, and even though she'd gone away, she still lived here – the third piece in our family jigsaw. Amy completed us. There have always been three of everything, from sets of mugs, to bars of chocolate, to the three high stools tucked under the kitchen counter – one for each member of our family. And then I remember Harry, our cat, another part of our family who came to us that Christmas as a kitten – he'll miss her rushing in and scooping him up, pushing her face into his soft, fluffy neck. She'll never do that again, and she'll never dance in the kitchen or sing along to the radio in the car with me, or eat chocolate flake and get the crumbs all over the sofa. This makes me cry harder, because I used to tell her off about eating chocolate on the sofa, it made me really cross – and I hate that I was ever angry with her and I hope she knows I didn't mean it and how much I loved her… and always will.

Richard and I don't even try to sleep. We don't know what the next few days will bring, and it's hard to imagine. But I know they'll be worse than the last few, and I didn't think that was possible. This time we have no hope, and that was all that kept us going, so I'll just keep walking through the hell that awaits me.

'I'm so sorry for not believing you,' I say, finally. 'My mind was all over the place and people kept presenting me with evidence, and what seemed like facts, and in the end I just went along with it.'

'Don't apologise. You have been through the worst thing anyone can go through, and it isn't even over yet. You were just looking for something tangible. You were presented with information that pointed directly to me, and I don't blame you for being suspicious.'

'It's been hard for both of us. I just hope you can forgive me for not standing by you. I can't get through this without you.'

He folds me in his arms and I weep silently into his chest.

'Our job now is to keep Amy's memory alive,' Richard says. 'No one knows her like we do… like we did, and together we have a shared history – let's talk about her every chance we get, let's look at her photos, remember the Christmases, the holidays, birthdays. Between us we can keep her here.'

I take the pile of photograph albums from the cupboard, spread them on the floor and we sit up all night with Amy. And at 7 a.m. we finally go to bed for a few hours, hoping against hope to find sleep, so we can forget that she's gone.

We wake about noon, not that we really slept, and both wander aimlessly through rooms, trying to find some purpose. Richard goes into the garden and I follow him out there, I need to be near him.

Then at about 1 p.m., there's a knock on the door.

Richard's washing his hands in the sink, and I'm nervous, so call him to be with me. I know what this is, it's the news I've been dreading since last Sunday, when I first realised something wasn't right.

Richard joins me at the door and we open it together, Heather is standing there flanked by two police officers.

'Kat,' she says, 'we've found Amy.'

# CHAPTER THIRTY-FOUR

Driving to Aberystwyth with Richard is bittersweet, and I'm crying as we pass through the mountain roads.

Such a lot has happened in just a few hours, even the sun has come out – a low, wintery sun that warms the grey landscape, and it makes me dare to hope. I still can't quite believe what's happened – Heather came to our door with the news, but it wasn't the news we were expecting.

'We've found Amy,' she said. 'Just off the mountain road, between here and Aberystwyth.' She took a breath. 'Kat… I'm not supposed to tell you this, because she hasn't yet been formally identified, but the girl we've found – she's alive.'

At this, I crumpled. Everything inside me had been ready for the worst news I would ever hear – with this news, my body shut down, unable to take any more.

Apparently Richard caught me and carried me through into the living room, followed by Heather and the two officers, and all they could tell us was that when they found her she was still breathing. Just.

Zoe had given a vague description of where she'd abandoned what she thought was Amy's body. The rescue helicopter was immediately sent to that area, had been circling all morning, and suddenly spotted Amy's bright-purple jacket on the ground; it helped to save her life. They managed to get her into the air ambulance, and she's now in Aberystwyth hospital, where she's receiving fluids, being kept warm and doctors are confident she'll wake soon. At the moment, that's all we know.

In between signal loss I'm receiving text and call updates as we drive there. I'm told she's weak, but she's doing okay, and the glorious phrase they used was, 'We're optimistic for a full recovery.'

I'm cautiously hopeful. There have been so many ups and downs I won't believe she's okay until I'm with her and can check for myself. Words aren't adequate enough to express my fragile, exhausted undercurrent of joy that she's still with us. I'm dying to hug her, and tell her that Mum's here now – it's all going to be fine.

'Imagine being in the dark all alone on the side of a mountain?' Richard's saying as we drive along.

'I know, and the irony is I've spent her life telling her to keep warm and put a coat on. I've collected her from nightclubs at two in the morning and fed her vitamins and organic vegetables and… her best friend does… this to her… But Zoe and Jodie? I just can't believe it, they were there for me, all the time holding my hand, telling me how much they cared.'

'I blame Zoe,' Richard says, and for once I agree with him. 'She's always been so manipulative; a horrible, controlling woman who's only out for herself.'

'Yes, she's a good liar too. When I think of the performance she put on as soon as Amy went missing – it's frightening.'

'I did think at one point Amy's lecturer might be involved, but she'd never mentioned him to you, had she?'

'No. Anyone who knows Amy knows she wouldn't be interested in an older man,' I say.

'Did you ever, for a moment, think that Zoe or Jodie might be keeping something from you?' he asks.

'I wish I could say I did, but I had no idea. And if I did think they were hiding anything, I thought it was to save my feelings!'

We both give a little laugh at this to release some of the tension.

'I keep going over stuff from the past, the way Zoe overreacted when I told her Amy was in the top class for English. She hugged me and screamed – I thought she was pleased for me.'

'Try not to think of it now, it'll spoil your good memories,' he says. 'This has been the worst time and such an ordeal for Amy, but if it's taught us anything, I think it's definitely proved that our girl is as strong as an ox.'

'Yes, over a week on a mountain in November with no food, just spring water – I need to stop with the worrying.' I smile, knowing, as a mother, that will never stop. From the minute they are born, a child holds a little bit of their mother's heart in their hand, they carry it with them wherever they go, and we go with them.

'It could have been so much worse,' Richard says.

'Absolutely, she could be in another country with Tony, never to be seen again… or worse.'

'I didn't say anything, but I thought he'd kidnapped her,' he says. 'I kept telling myself and you that she'd run away because I couldn't face the alternative…'

'No,' I say, and touch his hand.

For years my hatred of Tony and my need to keep him away from Amy has dominated my existence. But now I know there are worse things that could happen than Tony spending time with our daughter… and if it's what she wants, then she's old enough now to make her own decisions, I won't interfere. Well, not too much!

'The thing that scared me most – if it had been Tony – was that we know what violence he's capable of,' Richard's saying. 'I'll never forget the first time you came to my office asking for representation, your black eye… the smashed cheek. God, and the hand – your hand was so badly injured.'

'It still hurts in the cold,' I say, stretching my left hand, and remember…

*I had to close my eyes because I didn't want to see the hammer coming towards me, crushing my cheekbone, blackening my eye. I cried out in agony – but it wasn't enough, there was more to be endured. My hand was jammed in the car door, blood oozing from my nails. And later my head banging against the brick wall of our house, as I stood in the back garden trying not to cry out. I wasn't allowed to make a noise in case someone heard. No one heard, no one saw, but I knew.*

'He was so out of control, so vicious, I honestly believe he'd have hurt her,' Richard says.

'Perhaps he would.'

I'm looking down at my hand, remembering the pain, but that was nothing to the injuries Tony inflicted. But back then, no one wanted to know about psychological violence, coercive control, manipulation – injuries had to be visible. And in truth, Tony never laid a finger on me. That's why he's still so aggrieved, so resentful – because he knows he didn't cause the black eye, the damaged hand, the bruising – it was me.

Now things are different, people can be convicted for psychological damage, the laws have changed. But then I had no choice. It was the only way I could get him out of our lives and keep Amy safe from his mental manipulation, as bad as any black eye.

After he'd left us, Tony scared me with so many threats of taking Amy off me. So one night when he came to my flat drunk, I antagonised him and he became verbally abusive, and loud. This ensured that the neighbours knew he was there in case I needed any witnesses – and after he'd gone, I put my hand in the car door, and slammed it shut. I then called the police and had him arrested. Several weeks later, while out on parole, he came round to scream at me because I'd lied to the police and blamed him for my injuries. So when he finally left, I used my unbroken hand to hit my face with a hammer. Then I crept outside and smashed my head against the bricks, before calling the police and an ambulance – my estranged husband had physically abused me again.

I hurt myself so that when I walked into the office of Richard Ellis, the solicitor, he would see my injuries and take the case. The endgame was that Tony would never get custody of Amy – not even weekend visitation. Photos of the smashed cheek, the black eye and the damaged hand all helped me to keep her. I did it only for her, and I hope, one day, she will understand and forgive me. Tony was selfish, and a bully – but he never physically hurt me, and I should never have done what I did. But I'd do it again if I had to, because she's everything to me.

I glance over at Richard as he drives, so relieved, one hand on my knee as we go over the mountain road to Aberystwyth. He thought the injuries were genuine, because that's what I told him, and he unknowingly put his career on the line fighting for me, and I love him for it. But now isn't the time to reveal secrets and lies and dwell on the past, now is the time to celebrate Amy's safe return and look to the future. Because now she has a future again, and I'm excited for her to embrace it, to continue where she left off – this was merely a pause.

I remember talking to another mother in the hospital when I was there with Amy; she also had a child with cancer, but sadly her little one lost the fight. I saw her a few years later, in the supermarket, and asked her how she was.

'Invincible,' she said, which I thought was rather an odd word to use, but she went on to say, 'When you lose a child, you go through the very worst you can imagine. But on the upside, there's nothing else the universe can throw at you – you are invincible.'

I've lived with the shadow of this loss twice in my life now, and it's agony. But having children is agony. From the minute they're born we hold them to us knowing life will never be the same again. The worry never leaves us, but one day the children will – and we are left with our empty nests, and full desks, and we tell ourselves we now have time for ourselves. But what we don't realise is that we are never ourselves again after having children, they shape us as much as we shape them.

We arrive at the hospital; Heather's waiting in reception for us. I immediately flinch, and brace myself for bad news.

'Is she… is she?'

'She's out of the coma,' she says, 'and she's asking for you.'

I grab Richard's hand and we rush through the hospital corridors to her. My world is back on its axis.

# EPILOGUE

## *Amy*

Wow! What a week I've had. It all started last Friday night. Without any warning, Jodie Walton turns up on my doorstep. No text, no message, no Snapchat to say she's invited herself to Aberystwyth, to announce her arrival. Just sneaky old Jodie trying to take me by surprise. 'I feel so bad, I'm sorry, Amy,' she was saying, pretending she felt bad, but really she just wanted to talk about how she was all loved up with Josh, my ex, and rub my nose in it. I'd been really hurt when I first found out – I mean, my best friend and my boyfriend were hooking up. Really? So I tried to get over it by working hard, going out a lot and I met someone else.

It was pitch-black, raining and bloody freezing, but Jodie decides she's come to the seaside, so wants to walk on the beach. I go along with it to get her out of the flat. I didn't want to be rude. I mean, she is – was – my best friend, really, so I agreed we'd do a quick walk. My plan was to let her waffle on, feed into her drama for twenty minutes then put her on the train home. I'd made the mistake of telling her I was going home for the weekend and she suggested she stay the night, and we could travel back to Worcester together Saturday. But no way was that happening, so I told her I was going on a date and he might end up staying. I couldn't tell her anything else about him because I'd promised I wouldn't tell anyone about us.

I was meeting him later – he never turned up at mine until late, but I wanted to shave my legs and put on my new underwear, and Jodie was holding me up. I kept talking about this date with a hot new guy, but classic Jodie, she didn't get the hint, and as we walked along the beach she kept banging on about how upset I must be about her and Josh. It was like she *wanted* me to be hurt! I told her I was totally fine about it. But what she *really* wanted was for me to still want him, she's always been like that – only wants what I have.

I was really frustrated, I was *dying* to tell her my new boyfriend was much older and really gorgeous, but she'd think I was just saying that to pretend I was over Josh and ask to see his photo. I couldn't show her my phone and the selfie of him lying on my bed with no clothes on. Even though he's old, he's still pretty fit, and I knew she'd be SO jealous, but she'd also be straight on the phone to mad Zoe, who'd wet herself over the fact I was having an affair with my lecturer. She'd be all scandalised and rush to tell Mum, saying how sorry she was for her, while having bloody orgasms over it, because for once it wasn't *her* daughter in the shit.

I knew Mum would be cool. I mean, for a start, Dave and I looked so cute together, and Mum's always said I need someone kind and mature who loves me. Josh was kind and he loved me, but he was not mature like Dave, who understood different kinds of wine, and he'd sometimes bring a bottle from his cellar and we'd drink from these glasses my mum bought for me to take to uni. I didn't want them – I had a fishbowl, you see – but Mum insisted. 'You'll be glad of those,' she'd said and sneaked them into my suitcase. It felt so sophisticated drinking wine from a glass while we talked about books and Dave read his favourite passages to me – Hemingway, Nabokov and Dostoyevsky. We discussed stuff like 'post-modern interpretation' and 'the human condition' and it was like having a one-on-one tutorial – with sex and alcohol. Awesome!

He'd play me old nineties songs on his phone all the time. I can't remember them all, but one song was about this guy losing his religion and Dave said it wasn't about religion at all. He knew what it meant – how awesome is that? Of course the tragedy of all this last Friday night, when Jodie turned up, was that I couldn't tell her anything about Dave and our amazing relationship. So she thought I was still pining for bloody Josh – and she was being such a smug bitch.

'I just don't want to hurt you,' she said, *still* going on… and on as we walked along the freezing cold bloody beach. 'You've always been the pretty one, boys always fancy you – but someone really likes me now, and I can't help that it's your boyfriend, I'm sorry.'

I'd told her loads of times it was okay, but she just kept going and after half an hour of this, I lost it.

'I don't fucking CARE Jodie,' I yelled. 'You can have Josh, you've always wanted what I have. And you stole my green Urban Decay eyeshadow last year. And don't try to deny it, I saw it in your bedroom.' She had looked so shocked, like she had no idea I knew. 'Anyway, it looks shit on you,' I added. 'And I'm glad I live so far away now, because you can't follow me round like a lost puppy. I let you hang around because I felt sorry for you – and Mum told me I had to – and my friends all hated you, by the way, in fact everyone at school hated you because you're such a sad cow. But I told them you were okay, harmless. But you aren't okay, Jodie, and you aren't harmless. You've always copied me – my hair, my clothes, everything I have you want and try to take it, from my fucking best eyeshadow to my boyfriend, who B-T-W will soon realise how boring you are when I'm not around and will dump you. And, babe, stop saying you're sorry about it, I think we both know, if I *wanted* him back, I could have him back.'

Okay, I'll admit that was mean of me, but she's mean, she just hides it well – and she knows it's true, that Josh was only with her because he was missing me and she was second best. She's not happy with grabbing my boyfriend, she wishes she was Mum's daughter too – always hanging round Mum and creeping, 'Hey, Kat, let me make you a cup of coffee', 'Hey, Kat, watch me do a handstand.' And Mum's just nice and mumsy and goes along with it. But me and Richard can't stand her – or Zoe, we see the way she used to look at Mum, dead jealous. When I was home, we were always bitching about them when Mum wasn't around, and Richard's impersonation of bossy old Zoe is hilarious. She's controlling, and Jodie's needy, and pretends to be shy and sweet but always loves a drama that puts her in the middle of the frame. Ugh.

So I know I should probably have stopped there, but I was really pissed off with Jodie's whining. 'Just fuck off, Jodie,' I said, and turned away from her to walk back up the beach. I knew she'd be pretend-crying, trying to play the victim, and so I kept walking. Then suddenly, from nowhere, I heard this screaming and she was lunging at me, and I couldn't get my breath. She was pulling at my hair and my jacket, and I tried to push her away, but she'd taken me by surprise and she was proper fighting me. I was so surprised I couldn't fight back.

Even though the tide was out, the ground was wet and we were sliding about on these huge pebbles and I just felt myself fall. And then I hit my head, really hard. I can't remember much about what happened just after that, I think I must have been semi-conscious because I heard her crying. Then she was sobbing on the phone to her mother and I must have been out for hours because next I heard was Zoe's bossy voice hissing at Jodie, 'Do you realise you've ruined your life?' And Jodie was saying, 'Mum, let's call the police,' and Zoe said, 'Okay, call the police, and you can explain to them why you're here and your best friend *isn't*.' Next thing, I'm been put into a sleeping bag, they're dragging me along the beach and I'm being dumped like a sack of potatoes in the back of the car.

'Are you sure no one's seen you? Does anyone know you were here with her today?' Zoe said, all panicky – you could tell by her voice she was shit-scared. 'Okay, so, as always, I'll clear up your mess. I'll have to dump the body off the mountain road.'

I was *really* scared then, and I thought I was crying, but my body wasn't doing anything – and I could feel all these things, but I couldn't move.

Then Zoe told Jodie to take my phone, my room key and my cards out of my bag, and to go back to my flat. 'She lost her flat key, her room's unlocked,' she said, still really freaked out. 'Good. That should make it easier to get in, even *you* can't cock that up,' her Mum said in a really pissed off voice. 'In the morning, put some of Amy's clothes on,' she said, and now I could hear Jodie retching. It was horrible, and Zoe was yelling. 'STOP. THIS. NOW!' Then it all went quiet for a few seconds and Zoe just carried on with her instructions like a bloody robot. 'You have to make sure none of her flatmates see you, but go out, lock the door, go into Aberystwyth, and take cash from her account – do you know her pin number?' She said she might be able to work it out. Thing is, me and Jodie always knew the passwords to each other's phones. I never changed mine because I could always remember it – my birthday. And my bank account PIN is the same – that would've been her first guess, and she was right.

Zoe was still talking quite loudly, she sounded mean, and I could just see her in my head, holding Jodie by the shoulders like she used to when she wanted her to listen. 'Then after you've got the money, text Kat to say, "Hi Mum I'm having lunch with the girls," or whatever Amy would say, because you know what Kat's like, if she doesn't hear from her every five minutes she calls the bloody police. ARE YOU LISTENING?' I heard a whimper, and Zoe started on again. 'Then when you've texted, walk up and down the area near the pier. There are shops and hotels there and who are bound to have CCTV cameras, you have to convince anyone looking at those cameras that you are Amy – bouncy walk, happy smile. Okay?'

I don't know what happened then, because I felt myself drifting off, but the car was moving. I felt this bumping sensation, and the next thing I know, I'm being dragged from the car by my feet. Even with the noise of the wind I could hear her heavy breathing as Zoe hauled me out, pulled me along the ground. Everything inside me was still locked up, and I couldn't *move*. Then I felt the force of her boot in my back and the sensation of falling and rolling. I thought I was dead.

When I woke up, all I could see was this big grey mountain and the odd sheep. Honest to God, I felt like I was in a film and someone was going to shout, 'It's a wrap,' any minute. But no one did, and though I tried to walk, I couldn't, my leg was bending in the wrong direction and I was in agony.

I must have lay on the ground for days, drifting in and out of sleep. My phone had gone, so I couldn't call for help and I was all over the place in my head. I was thirsty and I missed my cat, Harry… and my mum. Thinking about Mum and home made me cry.

The *Daily Mail* said my survival was a fluke, pure luck. Where I landed after being thrown (yeah, cheers, Zoe – not!) I was near a tiny trickling stream of fresh water, and I was able to put my hand out to reach it to drink. Apparently that's why I'm still here.

It was such a weird time being on my own for so long, it really messed with my head. I kept hearing that old guy from the nineties singing about losing his religion and I wondered if Dave was looking for me. I thought about him a lot when I was dying, alone in the cold on the side of a mountain. I thought about how he used to turn up really late, and we'd have awesome sex and then he'd have to leave SO early in the morning. I was like, 'Why don't you just stay in bed, who cares if my flatmates see you?' But he didn't want them to know.

It was so funny watching him leave, creeping down the corridor at dawn, scared someone might see him. Once, one of my flatmates did see him – it was Ahmed, I think. He asked me who the old man was and I panicked because Dave said if I told anyone he'd been in my room he'd lose his job and his wife would freak – so I said it was my stepdad just dropping something off.

So, now I'm back home, I'm dying to see Dave again. I called him yesterday, and he said he'd been really worried about me. He said he wanted to call but his wife is giving him a really hard time – she found a present he'd bought for me. He'd signed it, 'To My Lolita,' and when she found it in his desk drawer, his wife Laura basically lost her shit. She's a lecturer at Aber too, but apparently she's been on long-term sick leave because she's suffering from depression or something. Shame really, I feel bad for her, but one of my flatmates told me Dr Laura McKenzie is a bit of a psycho and so possessive. She's called me a few times this week, says it won't end well and I'm not the only first year he's slept with, he does it all the time – but I don't believe her because Dave says he loves me, and he wouldn't say it if he didn't mean it.

I've been home a week now and I've been in all the newspapers, on TV, and people recognise me wherever I am. I'm like a celebrity – I've got 20k Instagram followers since I got off that mountain. And when Zoe and Jodie's court case comes up next year and they make the TV drama all about me almost dying on the side of a mountain, my fucking Instagram will explode.

This morning I was in Sainsbury's and a cute-looking boy shouted, 'You go, Amy!' And in Costa with Mum yesterday these girls came over and wanted to take a selfie with me. Mum was like no way, but I said, 'Mum, I've just had my eyebrows done, and my contouring is on point today, so why the hell *wouldn't* I be photographed?'

And she laughed and said, 'Yeah, why the hell not? Do it. Arguing with you is like arguing with myself, you're pretty formidable, Amy – nothing and no one gets in *your* way.'

'Because I'm just like my mum,' I said. Nothing and no one got in her way when I was missing. She just kept on fighting for the truth, and God help anyone who tried to stop her. Mum saw my rucksack in Jodie's room, found the scarf and then just went for it, Zoe even tried to kill her, but Mum was well fierce.

Oh yeah, and my dad got in touch again last week. Mum said it was up to me if I wanted to see him. I wasn't sure, he'd been really mean about Richard when he'd first messaged me – and that was before I even met him. He said Richard had him put in jail, and he split up my mum and dad because mum ran off with him. Talking to my dad made me annoyed with Richard, but when I met Dad he was vile about Mum too. After talking to Richard I realised Dad's just mean about them because he's jealous of what they've got. Anyway, I asked Mum if she thought I should meet him again. I was hoping she'd just say no so I could tell him I wasn't allowed to, but she suggested I agree to meet him on condition she and Richard weren't discussed. So I met him in London, where he's living now, and he took me to this cool wine bar and I tried to tell him about my life, and my course at uni and how I'm going back next September and starting all over again because I need time to heal (and do interviews with magazines!). But he wasn't really listening, he was staring at this girl in a mini-skirt, and when he wasn't looking at her he was talking about himself. He's in some band and he's really buzzing about it – said they're going to be huge, but I doubt it – they're all fifty and bald, too old to do anything really.

I got bored and said I had to be somewhere, and then he said, 'I might be able to get us a TV interview – all about you on the mountain, and if you'll do it as the main guest, they'll let my band play on the programme.' I realised then what he's like and that was before he started begging, saying, 'Please Amy, it'll be a father-and-daughter special.'

And I said, 'In that case I'd better make sure Richard is on with me,' and repeated that I had to be somewhere. I won't be seeing him again. Richard's my dad – I don't need another. In his own straight Dad-like way Richard sees things clearly, he understands me sometimes in a way even Mum doesn't. The other evening, she was making plans for us all way into the future, and he just said, 'Kat, she left home once, she hasn't come back, she never will – Amy's only ever going to be here for a little while.' Of course Mum dismissed this and told him I wasn't going anywhere soon, which made me smile.

It's pretty awesome being home, with Mum and Richard buying me stuff and letting me do pretty much anything I want to. Josh was one of the first of my friends to come and see me, he told me that him and Jodie were never a thing, she made it all up so she could break us up. Josh got better-looking and he's more mature these days. Mum keeps inviting him over and he stays for tea and then we go up to my room, but Mum's constantly knocking on my bedroom door with hot chocolate and cookies. She thinks me and Josh are still six years old, but trust me, we're not playing Snakes and Ladders in my room – and one of these days she's going to breeze in with a tray of cookies and get quite a surprise.

'Oh, it's lovely having chicks back in the nest again,' she said the other day, as she wandered in, and I'm like, 'Mum, WTF, please knock before you come into my room – and stop being weird!' But she just laughed, she's happy, and making a fuss of me, which I used to find annoying, but after everything, I'm okay with it – after all it was Mum's fussing that saved my life. She never gave up on me, and I owe her big time.

Christmas is just around the corner and I'm excited to be home, but not as excited as Mum! She makes all my favourite foods, we chat, watch TV together, go shopping for presents and we're singing in the car again just like before I went away to uni. And when she isn't hugging or feeding me, Mum's crying happy tears and saying stuff like, 'Amy, you've no idea how happy I am that you're back home, you're safe here where no one can hurt you. I can finally sleep at night now.'

I haven't told her about my plans to go travelling yet. Thailand I reckon. Or Cambodia. Perhaps with Josh, or even with Dave – he called me this morning, says he wants us to run away together. Richard's right – once you leave home, you never go back, and I'll soon be bored here – can't wait to see the world. But I know Mum's looking forward to a family Christmas – so I won't tell her just yet, don't want to upset her. I'll save it for the New Year.

# A LETTER FROM SUE

Hello!

Thank you so much for reading *The Empty Nest*. If you would like to know when my next book is released, you can sign up by following the link at the bottom of this page. I promise I won't share your email address with anyone, and I'll only send you an email when I have a new book out.

*www.suewatsonbooks.com/email*

I hope you've enjoyed reading *The Empty Nest*. The idea came to me recently when my daughter, Eve, left home to go to university, and I thought, 'how crazy is this?' We've nurtured and protected her all her life, and at the tender age of eighteen we drive her to another city, move her into a house full of strangers, and leave her there. I remember driving home and, to quote Kat, 'I felt like I'd left one of my limbs behind.' Just like that first day at school, the sense of loss and the shock at how quickly our children grow and leave us hit me hard.

Thankfully, my daughter loves university life and is fine (and eventually so was I!) but it made me think about the empty nest our children leave behind – how is it filled? And what if there is potential for real danger, both inside and outside that nest?

I've loved writing this one, even though writing it has made me worry even more about my daughter than usual! I'd love to know what you think – so do get in touch.

Meanwhile, I'd love to see you on Facebook, become a friend, like my page and please join me for a chat on Twitter.

 www.suewatsonbooks.com

suewatsonbooks

@suewatsonwriter

# ACKNOWLEDGEMENTS

As always, my huge thanks to the wonderful team at Bookouture, who all contribute so much to each and every book. With special thanks to Lauren Finger and Jade Craddock for picking up on my mistakes, and to Kim Nash and Noelle Holten for getting my books out there for readers to discover.

As always, I'm indebted to my editor Isobel Akenhead, who gracefully accepts my incoherent forty-thousand-word synopses, ideas written on Post-it notes, and novels with more than one ending. Thank you for going along with the madness, and for helping me to turn it all into a book.

Thanks to Sarah Hardy for reading this at an early stage, and giving me the benefit of her thriller-reading wisdom, and razor-sharp eye for detail.

Thanks to my family and friends for their continued love and support. And last but never least – to my daughter Eve, for always calling to let me know she's safe – and saving the sanity of this helicopter mother!

CPSIA information can be obtained
at www.ICGtesting.com
Printed in the USA
BVHW070859271019
562039BV00001BA/8/P